# BULL'S EYE

SHANNON BAKER

Severn River Publishing
www.SevernRiverBooks.com

ISBN: 978-1-64875-419-7 (Paperback)

# ALSO BY SHANNON BAKER

**The Kate Fox Mysteries**

Stripped Bare

Dark Signal

Bitter Rain

Easy Mark

Broken Ties

Exit Wounds

Double Back

Bull's Eye

Close Range

**Michaela Sanchez Southwest Crime Thrillers**

Echoes in the Sand

The Desert's Share

**The Nora Abbott Mystery Series**

Height of Deception

Skies of Fire

Canyon of Lies

**Standalone Thrillers**

The Desert Behind Me

To find out more about Shannon Baker and her books, visit

severnriverbooks.com

*To Janet Fogg*
*The road will be lonely without you.*

# 1

You know how you feel on a cold night when you're cuddled under your blankets, cozy and secure in your warm spot, and everything is as it should be? Then you're forced to get up for a drink or let the dog out. When you get back into bed, the sheets are cold, and nothing feels right.

My life felt like that, one big cold spot where nothing fit right.

That was a whole lot of philosophical hoo-ha for a sheriff on a mission.

The sun beat down on the rodeo grounds. A slight breeze kicked up, just enough to rain dust on the pickups and horse trailers lining the fence around the arena and circling in wider arcs across the pasture. The hills stretching across miles of prairie still appeared thick with green, juicy grass, but summer had just gotten serious and the prayers for rain had already begun.

The covered bleachers held about two hundred or so hardy souls out for the Grand County July 4th Rodeo. Only it was July 3rd. We traditionally held our rodeo early so contestants could compete and get on down the road to the next one. This weekend was the Mardi Gras of rodeo, and cowboys, cowgirls, bulls, and broncs wanted to hit as many as they could to rake up points. All those points counted at year-end to qualify for the National Finals in Las Vegas. And that, dear friends, meant big money.

I marched toward the stock trailer parked behind the bucking chutes, where it had no business loitering. But Dwayne Weber, being a wheeler-dealer and believing rules didn't apply to him, probably stopped there to flash his logo on the side panels where everyone could see. He and his wife, Kasey, were making a splash on the rodeo scene with their bucking bulls.

It might be Tuesday, but it counted as a holiday, so the stands and rodeo grounds were full. I'd spent most of the day out here, making myself visible in my brown sheriff's uniform. I even smashed an official ball cap over my wild curls to make me look more sheriff-like. I hated that I needed to prove myself to the five thousand good citizens of Grand County, but my sister, Louise, had some bug up her bonnet that made her file a recall election against me.

Dwayne leaned toward a guy I didn't recognize, just short of invading the poor man's personal space. The guy wasn't a Sandhiller, obvious from his skin's pallor and khaki chinos, a long-sleeved Oxford shirt, and loafers. I imagined so much sand had sifted into his shoes he felt like he stood on a dune, unless he tended to sweat, and then it'd be mud. In his late fifties, maybe, his hair was cut short and neatly combed, like that of a lawyer or accountant.

Dwayne wasn't as handsome as I figured he considered himself. Over six feet, blond, heavier than his doctor probably thought healthy, he had a permanently sly look in his small eyes, too big of grin, and over-eager manner.

His face held exaggerated friendliness, and even from here, words like *pedigree*, *futurity*, and *payout* filtered to me. I figured Dwayne was pitching shares of one of his bucking bulls to this clueless city dweller. There was a lot of money to be made in bucking bulls; I'd heard of one earning a hundred thousand in one year. But it was risky business, the same as black-jack or sports betting. This guy should be cautious because Dwayne was slick enough to sell wool to a sheep.

Even though Dwayne's eyes flicked to me, he continued his spiel.

I didn't wait for a break. "You got a bull in there?" A snout the size of a football sniffed at the slats of the trailer. Through the narrow opening, his black head loomed above me, and the trailer rattled when he shifted his two thousand or so pounds.

Dwayne lifted his chin in an arrogant way. "That's Alameda Slim. I just saying how—"

I didn't let him slide into his pitch. "We've got mutton bustin' coming up, and we don't need a wild bull scaring the sheep."

Dwayne winked at the guy. "Slim won't scare anyone. He's bred to buck in the arena, but other'n that, he's a pussycat."

I gave him my serious sheriff-taking-no-guff face. "You need to move your trailer. You're blocking the entrance."

Dwayne raised a hand as if in dismissal but didn't turn to me. "Gotcha."

The man he spoke to gave me an unsure smile and interrupted Dwayne, who had continued on about the virtues of a bull's maternal breeding. "Go ahead and move your trailer."

Maybe it took an outsider to respect my authority without a threat. I tipped my chin toward him in appreciation and then gave Dwayne an expectant raise of eyebrows.

A squeal and scratch sounded from the loudspeaker in the crow's nest. "Testing, testing. Well, that's an A plus right there." Bill Hardy ranched up north and had been the rodeo announcer so long even the 'yotes in the surrounding hills recognized his jokes. "Calling Sheriff Fox. You're wanted in the arena."

Toad farts. As my ex-husband, sheriff before I took his job, told me: "You're always campaigning." For now, that meant standing in front of the crowd.

Dwayne sneered at me.

Before I spun away, I said, "Get that trailer moved."

Bill's voice echoed through the grounds. "Did you hear about the snowman who got upset when the sun came out? He had a total meltdown." Only Bill laughed. Maybe because no one was listening, but probably because it wasn't funny. "We're getting the barrels set up, folks. But in the meantime, Sheriff Fox is gonna give the results of the cake auction, and the little tykes will go at the mutton bustin'."

I tried for a jaunty pace to the middle of the arena, sweaty not only because of the temperatures in the nineties, but because I hated being in front of a crowd and, even worse, having to speak.

The sun felt like a spotlight, and I did my best to appear relaxed and capable. With no mic handy, I shouted, but only those sitting near the fence of the arena would be able to hear. "First of all, a big thank-you to everyone who bid in the auction and those who won a cake. Your contributions will help fund the 4-H clubs in Grand County for the next year." I said some more rousing things about how 4-H benefits the county, but most of the crowd focused on the cute three-foot-high cowboys and cowgirls entering the arena by the bucking chutes.

While I listed the top five money-makers and their cakes, heading for Jade McPherson's winning contribution of her famous rum cake, a dozen sheep were herded into the arena by a few parents.

Beyond the chutes I caught sight of my nine-year-old twin nephews and their newest compatriot. From the mischievous grins on their faces, I figured trouble was brewing. After this presentation, I'd track them down.

The outsider with Dwayne had wandered off, but Dwayne hadn't moved that trailer. I'd given that yahoo all the slack I intended to today, and as soon as I rounded up my nephews, I'd slap a citation on Dwayne.

I focused back on the stands and shouted louder. "Special thanks goes to Aileen Carson, who coughed up the winning bid f—" A clank and shout interrupted me. I whipped my attention to the gate and the kids, sheep, and stock trailer.

Holy... The back of Dwayne's trailer gaped open and banged closed again. With the gate unlatched, the behemoth of a bull could escape out the back. Before I finished the thought, a big, black, snorting mass of muscle and mad banged the gate open and leaped into the dust at the mouth of the arena. Forget about a bull in a china shop—this guy was big enough to take out a tractor dealership. With all the finesse of an elephant on ice skates, he whacked the rattling gate with his butt, which seemed to fire him up even more.

Someone must have unhitched the trailer gate. I had a suspicion of three someones.

Slim, who was anything but, flew away from the trailer and pounded onto the sand with a clatter of hooves and a crash of rippling mass like a fire-breathing, leather-coated dragon.

About eight kids, ages three to six, milled around in the arena, most of them standing along a fence waiting for their turn to climb on a woolly sheep and hang on while the docile critter ambled a few paces, maybe turned around, and, in a wild move, shook. A safe form of bull riding for the tykes.

Most of the sheep were in a pen, but the one meant for the first rider, four-year-old Tyler Kirshenbaum, had somehow escaped his wrangler before Tyler could be mounted on his back. That must have upset the little guy, because he was chasing down the sheep, who seemed intent on running to the bull for protection.

Not aware of anything except his chance at winning a ribbon skittering across the dirt, Tyler pumped his short legs as fast as he could. Directly into the path of the snorting bull.

Slim swung his head to the right and left, sending a string of snot into the sunshine. He hopped one way, then spun the next, more graceful than that deadly bulk had a right to be. He was probably used to crashing out of a loading chute, not jumping out of the back of the trailer, but once in the arena, he must have figured his job was to buck.

Running through the loose dirt of a freshly groomed rodeo arena is like slogging through molasses, but I was moving before the trailer gate slapped open again.

The bull jumped and twisted, tail flying. He planted his front feet in the dirt and kicked with his back. When they walloped into the sand of the arena, he lowered his head and bowed his back and levitated, then planted his front feet just long enough to whip from his shoulders and fling his back feet around. He spun as if he had no backbone, threw his head up, showing off deadly horns, and then did the whole thing again.

Tyler's eyes were on the sheep headed toward the open gate and freedom.

All of this came at me in slow motion as I prayed for wings on my feet to make it to Tyler before he stepped in front of the bull's sledgehammer hooves.

Tyler slipped in the dirt, his face a flare of red-hot rage. The bull jumped and twisted, bearing down on the little boy that he probably didn't see or care about.

Tyler pushed himself to his feet, tears streaming, mouth open to scream at the world for this unfairness. My boots sank in the dirt as I struggled to run, feeling like you do in a nightmare when the monster's hot breath hits the back of your neck.

Slim probably wasn't targeting the little boy; in fact, he might be having a good time, doing the job he was bred and trained for. But each jump and twist brought him a few feet farther into the arena, and Tyler seemed to be on a collision course.

The bull landed on his front legs and kicked his back legs out again, his hips swiveling like liquid steel, hooves like spears. He landed close enough to Tyler that the ground shook and the little boy finally noticed.

Tyler froze, mouth open, eyes so wide the whites could probably be seen from the top row of the bleachers.

By some miracle, I reached Tyler before the bull made another move. I scooped him into my arms, not pausing, and kept on my slogging run toward the wooden fence.

A huff from the bull, and hot air and snot hit my neck. He'd hook me on those horns and toss me like so much hay. In two steps, with one arm circling Tyler's waist and the other outstretched, I launched us to the second plank of the fence, grabbed hold with my free hand, and lunged to the top, somehow flinging Tyler over and into the arms of a cowboy, who was immediately assaulted by Tyler's mother. She wrenched the boy away and fell to the sand with him in her grasp.

The bull smacked into the plank below my boot, pounding the fence and sending vibrations through me. He spun away, tail flipping, head high in triumph. He trotted into the arena, already calming down. If he were a dog, he'd be waiting for his cookie after doing his tricks.

Before I caught my breath, a wrangler was in the arena, and Dwayne followed on foot. I wanted to at least glare at Dwayne, but he didn't look at me. They managed to get the bull turned toward the trailer they'd backed to the fence. Its gate swung open like a friendly welcome. The bull seemed to recognize sanctuary and happily hopped inside, making the whole thing sway and rattle. Someone else clanged the gate closed and latched it.

Bill Hardy's voice clamored over the roar of the crowd. "Welcome to the rodeo, folks. That's some excitement, and let's hear a cheer for our own Sheriff Fox. She's darned sure Tyler Kirshenbaum's hero today."

I sat up on top of the fence and waved to the stands, feeling a little better about life in general. But experience had taught me that just because there's a silver lining doesn't mean that cloud's not full of hail.

# 2

Take that, Louise. Saving Tyler Kirshenbaum in front of a crowd of voters might put a crimp in Louise's plans to oust me as sheriff.

Louise's real reason for filing was illogical and murky. It had something to do with her messed-up thinking that I was responsible for our mother fleeing to Canada with her former lover to avoid a felony charge. I think she just wanted someone to blame for a pain with no cure.

By law, she had sixty words to use to explain why I should be recalled. She did it in fourteen: *Kate Fox has been derelict in her duties and should be removed as sheriff.*

This left the person gathering petitions wide margin for interpretation. Dahlia, for instance, my ex-mother-in-law and a woman who'd drawn a target on my back from day one, probably told people I gave my family preferential treatment by not prosecuting my youngest brother when he got caught up with a drug cartel. But that wasn't my call.

Another person might say I spent too much time helping my various brothers and sisters with their ranches and projects instead of patrolling the county. But I was on call pretty much 24/7, and being sheriff took priority. The truth was, the duties didn't usually take a whole day.

I wound through the crowd, feeling more comfortable in my skin than I had in weeks. Maybe it was my imagination, but it felt like people were friendlier, and most had a favorable comment about the incident. I turned from accepting accolades from Aileen and Jack Carson and thought to get a cold drink at the concession stand to wash down all the heat, dust, and my ego.

"Kay-Kay!" A shrill voice rang out, and two-year-old Beau raced toward me on his little legs.

Beau was a pretty good buddy of mine since I'd taken care of him when he was only weeks old. I whisked Beau up and into my arms, quickly scanning to see if he wandered the grounds alone.

Unfortunately, he was with his mother, not my particular favorite, since she was married to my ex, Ted...after having an affair with him while we were still married. The Nebraska Sandhills covers more than twenty thousand square miles, but with a cow-to-people ratio of more than sixty to one, it's a small place. You were bound to run into every resident more frequently than was ideal. So, like a family—but maybe not the Foxes currently—we did our best to get along.

Roxy, tall and buxom to the point where it made a person question her boobs' authenticity, wore a short, fringed skirt and an embroidered Western shirt, along with the knee-high...moccasins? She'd performed the national anthem before the Grand Entry, which would account for her getup. Even if it looked like she wore a Halloween costume for sexy Pocahontas, I envied anyone not wearing my suffocating brown polyester uniform. What I wouldn't give to feel air moving across any bare skin.

Roxy hadn't noticed Beau's escape because she was gabbing at Mach speed with her best friend—if rivals can also be friends—Kasey Weber.

Roxy glanced our way and saw me and Beau hand in hand walking toward her. Maybe she hadn't known he wandered off, because she seemed surprised, but then took on that Roxy sparkle and loped a few paces to meet us. She threw her arms open to me. "Kate. Oh my God. It's so great to see you."

As if we were long-separated lovers, when actually, I'd seen her the night before at the Long Branch. And also, we weren't friends. Too bad I hadn't made an escape plan.

She wrapped me in a perfumed embrace that nearly had me gagging. Beau hugged my legs.

These days, being enveloped in love was unusual for me, but smothering can kill you, and I struggled for air.

When Roxy backed up, she grabbed my hand and dragged me over to Kasey, and Beau toddled on my heels. "I was just saying how amazing you're taking this whole recall thing. I mean, having your own sister file against you and the entire county signing the petition. And here you are, hanging out at the rodeo as if nothing is even happening."

Static popped and crackled, and Bill Hardy's cheerful voice blared out. "What do you call a belt made of watches? A waste of time." He paused for the nonexistent laughter. "But there's no wasted time here in Grand County this afternoon. Looks like we're back in business, friends. We've got some of the finest steer wrestlers in Nebraska to compete for your enjoyment this afternoon. Let 'em know you're here for them."

A smattering of cheers rose, not nearly as loud or enthusiastic as Bill's introduction.

At close to six feet tall, Kasey towered over my five foot three and earned her nickname High Pockets. Usually, she wore her thick blond hair in a braid down her back, but today she'd blown it out to cascade like a golden waterfall. She was completely made up, way more tasteful than Roxy's false eyelashes and dark eyeliner. She gave me a cynical tilt of her mouth that didn't quite resemble a smile. "What's your plan for after the election?" She paused. "If you get recalled, I mean."

I grumbled, "They haven't gathered enough signatures yet." At least as far as I knew.

Roxy slapped Kasey's arm. "You shouldn't say that."

I bent over and lifted Beau up and bounced him, making conversation with the small man to avoid the two tall women.

Kasey raised an eyebrow at Roxy. "Come on. If she gets recalled, you know they'll appoint Ted and you'll be back at Frog Creek the next week."

Roxy's lips puffed in a pout. "It doesn't seem fair."

Forced to stand there and listen to Roxy and Kasey dissect the situation added insult to injury. Beau patted my cheeks and repeated, "Kay-Kay." I made faces for his pleasure.

The crowd gave a sympathetic "Oh."

Bill Hardy boomed over the grounds. "That's tough luck for the cowboy from Bassett. Put your hands together and send him home with some Grand County love, folks."

"Look." Roxy pointed behind the chutes. "There's Gidget Bartels. I'll bet they're here to check out the bulls."

A woman, maybe even shorter than me, marched through a crowd at the far end of the stands. From here, I couldn't see her expression, but she seemed set on a mission.

Roxy twisted to look through the crowd. "Is Wrangler here? I haven't seen him." She settled on me for a minute. "Wrangler is like the cutest. Well, besides Ted, of course. I hear he's got an older brother in Rapid City who isn't married. I'll introduce you and be your wingman."

Maybe I could throw myself in front of a speeding steer and end this all now. I set Beau down, and he slipped his sticky hand into mine. I gave it a squeeze, and he blessed me with a sweet grin.

Kasey whipped her head around, and when she located Gidget, she tensed.

Roxy didn't notice since she'd latched onto her idea. "I'll have everyone over for grilled steaks."

Before Roxy could continue, Kasey strode away in the opposite direction of Gidget.

Roxy raised her eyebrows at me. "Well. Guess Kasey's done talking to us." She leaned closer to me as if sharing a confidence. "Kasey's not having a good day. She and Dwayne had another fight. Frankly, I'm worried about their marriage."

I swung my arm up a bit so Beau could twirl underneath and didn't engage with Roxy's gossip.

Undeterred, she said, "Normally, I'd be super supportive of Kasey, because girls have to back each other. But Kasey is not an easy person. I feel like in the last year—well, since I got pregnant, really—she's gotten harder and more hateful. I think she's jealous because Dwayne doesn't want kids."

I sent up a silent prayer for some excuse to flee from Roxy. But what happened wasn't what I'd hoped for.

From somewhere behind the bucking chutes, a shriek rocketed through the air. Louder than Bill Hardy's prattle and definitely not a playful scream of a girl being teased. This howl snaked up my spine and twisted through me like a live wire.

Paralyzed for a split second, I was on the run before I knew it.

# 3

Another wail erupted, then sobbing coming from a stock trailer parked toward the back of the other rigs. A few people ran with me, and more stood like rock slabs, heads turned toward the awful sounds.

I drew close enough to see the wide dips and swirls of Kasey and Dwayne Weber's logo for their bucking bull business on the side of the trailer. Something terrible had happened in there. Hiccupping and gasping slithered out when I approached the back, as if whoever was in there couldn't catch a breath, and every sound she made was laced with panic.

The door to the stock trailer was opened a few inches, and I grabbed hold to pull it and squint inside. The trailer walls were solid metal until about chest high. Then slats continued up the side to let in only the barest light and air. A scatter of hay lined the floor of the two-stall trailer. The back stall was open, but the gate to the front was closed.

When my eyes adjusted, I focused on the gagging and gasping. Gidget Bartels. She was propped against the side of the trailer, her feet splayed in front of her. She held her hands over her mouth, and when she saw me, she started bawling at top volume. "He's there." She devolved into supersized sobs with garbled words that made no sense.

Behind the gate, a massive animal with a little brain and an inbred propensity to fight snorted and stamped, flicking his tail like a whip and

causing the whole trailer to tilt and sway like a boat in a hurricane. Whatever she'd seen to scare the bejesus out of her was only identifiable as a
lump in the darkest corner.

From the size and shape, it might have been a few sacks of grain. It
might have been a stack of horse blankets trampled by the bull. Maybe
Dwayne had stashed a couple of saddles and tack in the stall. But Gidget
wouldn't be hysterical over gear. And no matter how my mind tried to skirt
the evidence, my eyes understood.

Dread twisted through my gut, but the first thing to do was help Gidget
to her feet while trying to look past the gate to the dark front of the trailer.

Though she was no taller than me and slender as a wood nymph, wrangling Gidget took balance and strength. I succeeded in getting her to the
back of the trailer and stepping down into the dirt. By then, a crowd had
gathered.

I spotted Aileen Carson, who I knew had a kind and gentle manner, and
I motioned her over. While draping Gidget onto her, with Gidget contin-
uing to sob and gasp, I said, "Can you find a place where she can sit down?
Maybe a pickup?"

Aileen helped Gidget limp away, and I scanned the crowd again,
picking out Tuff Hendricks. "Get Eunice. Tell her to bring the
ambulance."

Eunice Fleenor, the driving force behind the Grand County EMTs,
would be like water in a firestorm. She always kept the ambulance on
standby at rodeos, football games, and sometimes the Cowboy Shootout
just for good measure. You never knew when one of those numbskulls
competing to see who could shoot the most pheasant in one morning
might mistake their drinking buddy for a feathered friend.

To the rest, I raised my voice. "Stay back." I sounded so authoritative I
almost impressed myself. But I wasn't all that excited to step back into the
trailer with the unmoving heap on the floor that was obviously a body and,
above it, two thousand pounds of hooves and muscles that would do more
than leave a bruise. It could crush and kill.

I'd barely made it to the interior steel gate when the trailer shook.
Someone landed on the platform and hurried toward me.

"What's happened? Where's Dwayne?" Kasey thundered toward me with such force my raised hands on her shoulders hardly slowed her down. She made it to the gate and squinted into the stall.

And now another blood-chilling scream ratcheted into the trailer, echoing off the metal walls and making me squeeze my eyes shut.

"Dwayne!" Kasey reached for the gate latch intent on going into the stall with the riled bull.

I grabbed her hand and pulled it back. "No. We need to get the bull out of there first."

She stared at me as if she would've liked to put a fist through my face, hesitated, and glanced at the bull. "Yeah." She ran out of the back of the trailer, shouting instructions and demands, and within seconds, onlookers sprang to action. I kept my eyes on the figure in the corner. The one Kasey had claimed was her husband. I tried to figure out a way to get to him, but with the snorting, pawing two thousand pounds of rank and menace, I couldn't squeeze into the stall. Dwayne didn't move.

While plenty of people gawked, ranchers are no strangers to emergencies. In the middle of a pasture or on an isolated homestead, they rely on themselves to figure out how to solve crises. Someone shouted to bring a trailer and back it up to Weber's. Someone else managed the crowd while others stood at the ready to guide the driver backing up to arrange the open trailer gates to form an alley between the two.

This incident would fuel conversation for weeks, but for right now, the Sandhillers got down to business.

The bull watched with mild consternation. He'd probably been hauled to enough rodeos and events the ruckus didn't panic him. What he felt about a man puddled into the corner of his stall was hard to tell. He stepped back and forth, rocking the trailer, but he wasn't bucking or kicking. My guess was that he wanted out of the confined space.

I headed in to unlatch the gate and shoo the bull out, something I'd done hundreds of times with tamed horses or relatively docile cows, but an animal with this much potential for harm rightfully made me hesitate.

Kasey put a hand on my arm to stop me. "Slim knows me. He won't hurt me."

Slim, the gargantuan black bull, probably knew Dwayne, too. But that hadn't stopped him from doing damage. I stepped out of the trailer and slipped behind one of the gates, leaving an open alley for the bull to go from one trailer to the next.

Kasey stepped into the trailer and spoke in a low voice. "Hey there, big Slim. We gotta get you away from here." She made her way to the gate.

The ambulance pulled up without flashing lights or siren, for which I was grateful. Eunice Fleenor, in her fifties with a gray buzz cut, legs as long and lean as Kasey's, and the manner of a drill sergeant, hurried to me. "What's going on?"

"I think Dwayne Weber got stomped by a bull."

Eunice frowned at me, then leaned forward to peer inside the trailer. The sun beat down, but with the trailer roof and only eight inches between the side slats, the interior was in shadow.

Surprisingly, the colossal bull had stopped swaying and rocking the trailer. He snorted, his sides heaving, his head facing Kasey through the gate.

Kasey spoke low and melodic. "Gonna open this up, and you're gonna move on out." Knowing how she probably wanted to reach her husband, it seemed impressive the serene way she dealt with the bull.

She released the latch and swung the gate open. The bull took a tentative step toward the back of the trailer. Kasey reached up and patted his shoulder like you'd pet a dog. "Get on up there, Slim. That's right."

I don't know what her heart was doing, but mine had thudded out of my chest and into my throat. Moments ago, this bull had spun and stomped like it was his job. Which it was, since he was bred to buck. And Kasey treated him like a beloved pet. It was some kind of magic.

She walked alongside Slim, the animal who'd probably just killed her husband, directing him down the ledge of her trailer, into the dirt. It took a little urging to convince him he wanted into the other trailer, but Kasey showed no sign of impatience. She poked him and slapped his butt. "Get up, Slim. Come on." She brought to mind a lion tamer at the circus, urging a dangerous beast with only words and soft nudges.

As soon as he took that hop into the trailer, she grabbed the gate and swung it closed.

I was already in the trailer running to Dwayne, Eunice hot on my heels. We both skidded to a stop when we got to his body crumpled in the corner.

By the scant light allowed in from the slats, it was plain from the twisted angle of his neck that Dwayne wasn't coming out of the trailer alive.

Kasey stomped up behind us with her arms folded across her chest, staring at Dwayne like she wanted to kill him for being dead.

After checking for his pulse, Eunice stood and faced Kasey. "I'm sorry. He's gone."

Kasey glared at her. "No shit." Then she gave Dwayne one more venomous stare, her eyes narrow and glistening. "Goddamn it, Dwayne." She spun around, slammed a palm into the side of the trailer, and stomped out.

# 4

By the time Eunice and Harold Graham, another EMT, had Dwayne loaded into the ambulance and on the way to Ogallala, news of the tragedy had spread through the fairgrounds. I'd called the Grand County coroner, Ben Wolford, an aging attorney who lived in Broken Butte. He hated the hour-long drive to Hodgekiss, so, as usual, he gave me authority to process the death. The rodeo committee canceled the remaining events, and Bill Hardy wrapped it all up without so much as a knock-knock joke.

Pockets of people gathered here and there over the grounds to have one last beer and talk about the unexpected death, but most people had driven off, leaving a haze of dust on the bone-dry afternoon air.

It was so danged hot I considered bumming a cold beer off someone. But knocking one back while wearing my sticky, airless sheriff uniform wouldn't be good optics, as my sister Susan would say. Even if we were on the edge of the known universe, someone was bound to have a camera.

Dwayne Weber wasn't one of my favorite people, but that didn't keep me from that black, tarry feeling of injustice at someone so young being taken away so violently. I didn't know if he was even forty. Slim hadn't trampled on Dwayne's face, but he'd planted a hoof squarely on Dwayne's heart, crushing the ribs. Looked like he'd stamped on Dwayne's legs and twisted them up too. I'd seen a fair amount of death in my time as sheriff, but I doubted I'd ever get used to it. Dwayne's face, the color of spoiled hamburger, his eyes slitted open in a way that no live person could hold, his legs bent unnaturally at his hips and knees. I hated the scene seared into my brain.

I had no idea where Kasey had fled. I couldn't judge her reaction to seeing her husband turned to a heap of flesh and bone. Shock can do funny things to a person. It wasn't unheard of for anger to wash in ahead of grief. I also didn't know what had become of the hysterical Gidget Bartels.

The rancher who owned the trailer that Slim was loaded into said he'd drive the bull to the Webers' place and unload him in the pens. I figured Dwayne and Kasey were showing off three or four bulls here at the rodeo—but not their best bulls. Those they saved for the Professional Rodeo Cowboys Association or Professional Bull Riders (PRCA and PBR) events, where the real money was. They'd bring a couple of their less impressive bulls to this local performance, just to get the word out and make a little money. Stock breeders did more business at rodeos, ropings, and other events than they did in their offices. Even small county fairs could be a chance to turn a buck.

The rear gate of the trailer squealed as I swung it closed and latched it just in time to see my ex-husband, Ted, drive up. After three years of divorce, his tall, lean good looks didn't thrill me anymore. There was something about lies and betrayal that washed the attraction right out of a man.

"Roxy took Kasey home," he said.

"That's probably for the best." Roxy would know if Kasey had family to call.

"Michael is going to help me load the rest of Weber's bulls and get them home." Michael was one of my younger brothers.

Since most folks didn't bother taking the keys from their vehicles in Grand County, Ted wouldn't need to track down Dwayne's keys. He started for the cab, then stopped. "Kate?"

Uh-oh. If Ted was thinking about bringing up a topic long enough to walk away and then reconsider, it wouldn't be something I wanted to discuss.

He turned to me with one of his sympathetic faces. Hard to say if it was sincere. "I heard about the recall."

Who hadn't? "I'll bet your mother is happy as a badger in a henhouse. A recall is top on her wish list."

He tilted his head as if in apology. "I loved being sheriff here, and it hurt when you stole it away from me."

As much as his cheating hurt me? As much as me having to leave my home and find a new life? But, you know, I wasn't bitter. Also, suddenly unemployed by his mother, I'd needed a job. And now she was trying to make me unemployed again.

Ted leaned toward me as if to emphasize his sorrow. "But getting it back this way isn't what I intended."

He was looking for absolution. Not my job anymore. "You wouldn't turn it down if it came your way, though."

His eyebrows lowered over those killer brown peepers. "I'm not the one who messed up the job enough that someone could file a recall against me."

"You know as well as I do, I didn't mess it up. Dahlia has been angling for a way to get rid of me since we announced our engagement. She probably thought she'd succeeded when we got divorced. But me being sheriff is too much for her to stand."

He raised his head with an amused glint in his eyes. "My mother didn't file the recall."

He might as well have punched me in the gut. I wouldn't let him know he'd hit his mark. "Maybe not. But she's enjoying it more than anyone."

He chuckled as if throwing a flaming torch onto the straw roof of my life was a joke. "She is that." He climbed in and started up the diesel dually pickup and drove off, covering me in another layer of dust.

Intending to find my cruiser and head home to shower, I started walking toward where I'd parked south of the concession stand. A hoarse voice stopped me.

"Kate. Hold up."

Gidget Bartels scurried toward me. Her poofed and sprayed platinum blond hair had lost its shape and now looked like a helmet with one spike sticking straight back. Her pink shirt was half untucked, and dirt smeared her jeans. Mascara smudged under her eyes, and distinct tear tracks cut through her foundation, which was probably a shade or two darker than her natural skin. She kind of looked like Tammy Faye on crusade.

I waited for her to catch up. I was paid to deal with gruesome scenes, but Gidget could be traumatized by it. "I'm sorry you had to see something so awful."

I waited while her eyes filled with tears again and she blinked and swallowed several times to gain control. She did, which I found admirable. "Wh-what did you find out?"

That seemed like an odd question, and I tried to come up with a civilized way to tell her what she must already know. "It looks like Slim got spooked and knocked Dwayne over. He probably reared and came down on Dwayne's chest."

Gidget studied me as if she couldn't make out what I'd said. Finally, she answered. "Slim was as gentle as a bunny rabbit."

I'd seen him hopping around the arena, and Slim looked nothing like a sweet bunny, even if you stuck a cottontail on him.

Gidget continued. "They brought him to the fair to see if they could get someone to buy him for a commercial herd because he wouldn't buck."

Good luck with that. Most ranchers chose bulls from breeders based on their lineage and proven ability to provide good calves. I didn't know many who'd pick up a failed bucking bull. But Dwayne wasn't always on the up and up. Who knows how he planned to pitch Slim to some unsuspecting rancher.

Gidget seemed like she genuinely liked Dwayne—something I found hard to fathom—so I tried to be gentle. "Bulls aren't predictable, and they're big. I'm sure Slim wouldn't intentionally hurt anyone." Instead of saying, *Bulls are like Dwayne. Dumb, testosterone-driven beasts who couldn't care less about stomping a person.*

She shook her head, a fire lighting her face. "Not Slim. That stupid Kasey gentled down all the bulls. I'm telling you, someone killed Dwayne."

How did she come up with that? "That doesn't make any sense. He was in the stall with an agitated bull. His chest was crushed. Pretty clearly a livestock fatality." Livestock fatality? Was that a searchable term, or did I just coin it?

Gidget scanned the fairgrounds. Ted and Michael and a couple of others were loading bulls near the pens behind the bucking chutes about a hundred yards away. Everyone else had wrapped up their business and left. The sun inched toward the hills to the west, and this year's July 4th rodeo would go down in history. More for the death of a local bucking bull breeder than for Jade McPherson's rum cake.

Gidget focused on me with intensity, her vivid blue eyes sharp. "It's Kasey. I heard her and Dwayne fighting an hour or so before I found him in the trailer."

"Husbands and wives fight sometimes." If you were like me and Ted, more than sometimes. "It still seems unlikely someone killed Dwayne." I pictured his legs, bruised skin, those dead, half-open eyes. Stuff of nightmares.

She stomped her little bitty foot, raising a puff of dust under her boot. "You don't understand. He was going to leave her."

Several things struck me. If Dwayne was indeed going to leave Kasey, how did Gidget know, and what did she care? And would Dwayne leaving her drive Kasey to murder? Because I'd think it'd be more likely for Kasey to murder Dwayne if he stayed; his leaving—at least if it were me—might be cause for a party.

I watched Gidget closely when I asked, "So you think she somehow dragged him into the bull's pen and kept him there until Slim tromped him?"

She planted her hands on her hips. "She would have knocked him out, dragged him into the trailer, and then put the Hot Shot on Slim."

I played that out in my head. Six-foot-tall, 150-pound Kasey knocking out Dwayne, who had about as much muscle as Slim, and dragging him into the stall while no one at a rodeo grounds full of people witnessed it. I shook my head. "That seems unlikely."

She raised her eyebrows. "Really? How likely do you think it is that Dwayne, a man who raises bulls and is around them all the time, would climb into a tight stall like that with a bull as big as Slim? The gate was shut and latched. He wouldn't do that."

"You just said Slim wouldn't hurt Dwayne. Maybe he thought the same thing and both of you are wrong."

Gidget came at me then, her child-sized fist raised and finger pointed at my chest. "Why won't you listen to me? Kasey threatened him. She said she'd kill him, and she did. Arrest her."

I backed up to keep her shiny fingernail from impaling me. The brown uniform ought to give me a bit more authority, but she was worked up. "There's no proof his death was intentional. From what I saw, it looked like an accident. It's a tragedy."

She stood in front of me, breath puffing in and out like a miniature toy train, her makeup smeared, and her face red with rage. "No wonder you're being recalled." She stomped away like a whirlwind on the prairie. Too tiny to be a real twister.

I trudged to my cruiser, now the only vehicle at the fairgrounds, feeling nearly as mad at Dwayne as Kasey had seemed to be.

# 5

The sun was dangling close to the western hills, and I drove to my bungalow north of Hodgekiss. I planned to grill a burger and sit on my front porch, enjoying the sunset and watching the ducks float on Stryker Lake. The puddle of a lake spread out in front of my house, making up for any shortcomings of my century-old, thousand-square-foot house, including the unfinished basement.

When I'd been bullied into buying the house, I'd believed it was more of a consolation prize for my failed marriage and loss of my home and job on the three-thousand-acre Frog Creek Ranch than a cozy new home all my own. It'd taken nine months of living at my parents' house, in my old bedroom, for me to finally concede it was time to be an adult and live solo. But now this cottage felt like home, and I relished my solitude except for the company of the coyotes, deer, birds, and occasional skunk. Not to mention my silly standard poodle, Poupon.

He wouldn't be in the yard like other dogs, waiting with excitement to welcome me home. There would be no body-wriggling tail-wagging. No whining or piddling with sheer joy. Poupon would be draped on my couch, where he was strictly forbidden. But the fool loved me. I knew it, even if he didn't.

I was glad to see Dad's old Dodge pickup parked outside my house when I made it home. Smells of meat grilling hit me as soon as I climbed from my cruiser, and smoke rose from the back where the grill sat by the kitchen door. That was a good sign. It meant Dad had been back from his job as conductor on the BNSF railroad long enough to nap and plan supper. For once, I'd stocked my fridge and cabinets with food, some of it even perishable, and my garden was in full tilt. Tomatoes, of course, but also green beans, beets, and carrots. No zucchini or summer squash because, for the same reason you neutered and spayed feral cats, it was irresponsible to bring more unwanted produce into the world.

Dad had even mowed my yard. I might not love that my father, now divorced and recovering from a heart that wasn't so much broken as disintegrated, was living with me, but it had some perks. He still worked on the railroad, even though he was eligible for retirement, so he was gone thirty-six to forty-eight hours a couple of times a week. When he was home, he slept, did a few chores, took care of the necessities of life, and then was gone again. Aside from taking up a shelf in my bathroom and leaving crumbs in the kitchen, he wasn't a bother.

I admired my garden from afar as my boots clacked up my broken cement walkway to the front porch. The screen door squeaked as I opened it and bumped softly behind me when I walked to the open front door.

Voices floated from the kitchen. Specifically, a woman's voice. There hadn't been any other vehicles out front except Dad's pickup. And Elvis, of course, but my 1973 Ranchero was parked in a rudimentary carport I'd built across the yard from my house.

Poupon was as expected, and I tugged on his collar to make him ever-so-reluctantly place his front paws on the floor. "No dogs on the furniture."

"No! You leave those where they're at. They need to cook longer." The woman's voice sounded teasing.

Dad responded, in a lighter tone than I'd heard for a long time. "You're going to cook all the goody out of them."

They bantered back and forth, seemingly unaware that a car had pulled up and someone was now in the house with them. That's absorption.

Having rousted Poupon from the couch, I directed him out the door and into the yard, then made my way back through the front room with an arch that acted as demarcation between living room and dining room. Well, I called it a dining room, but it was only large enough for a four-foot round oak table and four chairs. The doorway to the kitchen was beyond that. My bedroom was opposite the front room, then Dad's bedroom sided the dining room. The one bathroom was off the kitchen.

The kitchen took up about a third of the house. Not a lot of counter space but big enough to contain a table and my crowning glory, a refrigerator with ice and water in the door. I realized normal people wouldn't think twice about that, but for me, it meant success.

Since dusk had cast shadows, the overhead fixture of the kitchen brought everything to stage brightness. Dad stood at the stove, close—really close—to Deenie Hayward, who was sautéing something that smelled of garlic and onions. If I hadn't been mildly shocked and—trying to deny—disturbed to see my father flirting so openly with a younger woman, my mouth might have watered at the smell.

Having come this far unnoticed, there was no way to make a smooth entrance. So, I cleared my throat and said, "Uh. Hi. What's cooking?"

Deenie squealed and spun around, a wide grin on her face showing crooked front teeth. She seemed delighted to be so surprised. Dad's face reflected her good mood, and his eyes twinkled in a way I'd worried wasn't possible for him now.

He stepped back, not seeming the least bit embarrassed to be caught nearly cuddling with a strange woman in my kitchen. Okay, well, I knew Deenie Hayward, of course. So, she wasn't a stranger, although I might stick with her being strange. Deenie, short for Gardenia, was about the same age as my oldest sister, Glenda, and had grown up in Chester County. I couldn't give her bio beat for beat, but she'd been married and divorced—maybe twice—and moved away, moved back, moved away again, and now was back. I thought she waitressed at the café in Edgewood.

"Katie. I didn't expect you home this early. The rodeo usually goes on longer. Bull riding after dark, and that." Did his hand stray to Deenie's waist and then drop? Yes. I was sure it did, despite my trying not to see it.

That Dad hadn't already known about Dwayne's death when it had happened hours ago was true testament to his distraction. Dad had a preternatural connection to all news in Grand County. He didn't often bring up what he knew, and if pressed would only cough up the barest information, but he was aware of it all.

Deenie motioned me toward the stove. "Now that you're here, you can back me up. The mushrooms need to cook down a lot more, don't they?"

She was one of those women who had a "reputation," as Grandma Ardith would say. I had no beef with Deenie, though Louise seemed mortified Dad had anything to do with her.

Tonight, she wore cutoffs, tight across a plump rear and squeezing out a muffin top. The ruffled sleeveless shirt plunged but not enough to be called risqué. She stood barefoot at the stove, but flip-flops were tumbled by the back door. Her light brown hair was scraped into a messy bun, and she wore little makeup. In short, she looked comfortable and at home.

I gave the frying pan a look and a big inhale. "I side with Deenie. But, holy macaroni, it smells heavenly."

Dad snapped his fingers in defeat. "Who am I to argue? I only have two steaks, but there's plenty for three people. We'll divide them up."

I held up my hand, panicked at being a third wheel on a bicycle built for two. "Oh no. I'll change and go to the Long Branch."

Deenie grabbed my arm. "You'll do no such thing. I told Hank, I said, 'Those steaks are way too big. I could never eat that much.' And he said, 'We'll keep the leftovers, and Katie can have them tomorrow.' So, you'll get it tonight when it's freshly cooked."

Dad shooed me out of the kitchen. "Go take a shower and change. I set up a table outside, and I think the mosquitos are thinned out because I lit a citronella torch. Come on out when you're ready."

A citronella torch? Table in the backyard? Dad was the guy who ate fried baloney sandwiches with ketchup. He owned two pairs of Dickies for work and one good pair of jeans for dress-up. No-frills Hank had set up a picnic with torches.

I went to let Poupon in, feeling like the time I visited The Cosmos in the Black Hills and never could figure out how they made tennis balls roll uphill. The world had twisted, and nothing felt on an even keel. Who was this man in the Dad disguise? He'd shaved and combed his hair. He wore a button-up shirt, for cheese sake, and was also barefoot.

Wait.

Barefoot. Both of them. I didn't want to think why.

Thankfully, the kitchen was empty when I walked through on my way to the shower. I took an extra-long time cleaning up to let my mind shuffle back into place. It was coming up to two years since Mom had left us. Dad was due for some fun. It was me who needed the attitude adjustment.

When I joined them out back, the sun was a memory. I didn't know where Dad had found a few strings of Christmas lights or when he'd strung them from the peak above the kitchen window to a stake he'd planted in the yard, but he'd created a cheery spot for the table. Since I didn't own a picnic table, he'd also acquired that somewhere. In other words, this wasn't a spontaneous dinner. And I'd ruined it.

Poupon traipsed after me, pretending he didn't want to be with me but keeping close. He plopped down in the grass and rested his head on his paws.

Deenie and Dad sat next to each other at the table, a bottle of wine planted between them, glasses half-full. Wine. Of all things. She laughed at something he said, the crooked front teeth looking kind of cute.

I stopped halfway to the table. "I think I'll go into town, make sure there's no trouble after the rodeo. You know, sometimes people keep the party going and it can get out of hand."

Dad leaned back. "They'll call you if they need you."

Deenie patted the place across from her that they'd set for me. "Sit yer butt down. The food is all ready, so let's dig in."

This would be the most uncomfortable evening of my life, if you didn't count the night in the hospital when I discovered my husband was having an affair and his mistress and my mother-in-law witnessed my humiliation. But seeing no way out, I sat.

Dad brought the steaks from the grill and divided both in half, making healthy portions for each with meat left over. Deenie brought out the mushrooms, baked potatoes, and a fresh garden salad. It was a meal fit for royalty. Since a good deal of my meals at home were taken standing at my sink or wandering around my yard, this felt like fine dining, though I declined sharing their wine and opted for a cold beer.

Poupon's eyes were on level with the table when he came round to inspect it. "You'll have to wait for leftovers," I said to him. He sat next to Deenie and plied her with hopeful eyes.

She pouted her lips at him, then said to me, "Can I give him a bit of gristle?"

"Sorry. He's got enough bad habits." I pointed at him and gave a stern order. "Go lie down."

He lifted his nose and turned his face away from me. But when I started to rise, he must have decided I was serious, and he got to his feet and wandered a few steps away to drop, sighing in despair.

Deenie cut into her steak with gusto. "I'm impressed with your discipline."

Deenie didn't seem the least annoyed to include me. She told a story about waiting on two retired couples from New York who had rented an RV and were touring the West together. They'd spent two nights at a KOA in Deadwood and were disappointed they couldn't find Swearengen's Gem Theater or any bars or restaurants that offered canned peaches. They were peeved Timothy Olyphant wasn't wandering around Main Street, as I suppose you would be if you got your history from HBO. They were bored by the Badlands and irritated there wasn't a visitors' center with interactive exhibits, or refreshments at Wounded Knee.

We told stories and laughed while we ate until Dad asked about why the rodeo ended so early.

I hated to bring down the mood, but I gave them the news about Dwayne being trampled in the trailer.

Deenie teared up. "Oh, how awful. Poor Kasey. She must be wrecked. And you, having to take care of all the details. This is terrible."

Dad's hand slid across the table, and he squeezed Deenie's fingers. He said to me, "It seems strange Dwayne would get into a tight place with a bucking bull."

"Gidget Bartels told me that bull is gentle, and Dwayne trusted him."

Dad and Deenie took that in, gave each other a look, then Deenie said, "Why would Gidget Bartels know?"

Her question about Gidget seemed on point. "Gidget thinks Kasey killed Dwayne." It seemed like a safe place to drop that.

Instead of dismissing it outright, Dad furrowed his brow. Of course, he wouldn't comment, because that was his way.

Deenie elbowed him. "Right? That makes so much sense."

Wait. Had he spoken?

No. His lips hadn't moved. That was weird.

Dad gave a tilt to his head as if saying, "Sure does, if you think about it like that." Though he didn't say anything.

Deenie tapped her hand on the table. "I should have known. I mean, Dwayne was in the café last week, like middle of the morning. Said he was killing time, and I didn't think anything about it. Gave him the last piece of cherry pie and went about my day."

Dad was nodding, as if she were answering the riddle of the Sphinx.

"And then Gidget comes in right before noon, so before the lunch folks. She says she has a craving for cherry pie, but since we were out, she'll take apple."

That seemed to seal it all for the two of them, but I kept looking at Deenie, waiting for the punch line.

She turned to me, saw my questioning face, and said, "Don't you see? I never said boo about cherry pie. But she knew there was no cherry pie. And how would she know that unless she'd talked to Dwayne, who had the last piece? And she'd a said she'd heard it from Dwayne, except it was a secret she'd seen him. So obviously, Gidget and Dwayne are having an affair."

That was a leap. But it did seem reasonable.

Deenie leaned across the table. "I wouldn't have said anything about it to anyone, except you're the sheriff, so you might need to know." She beamed at Dad. "And Hank probably knew anyway, but even so, I know he won't tell tales." Back to me, she said, "I'd sure appreciate it if you'd keep it to yourself, though. I hate gossip."

"Of course." We sat in silence for a moment, me thinking about Dwayne's death.

Gidget said she'd heard Kasey and Dwayne fighting. And I'd seen Kasey give Gidget the evil eye and take off like a dog after a rabbit. It seemed Kasey might have been more of a danger to fun-sized Gidget than to full-grown Dwayne.

Deenie tapped the table again. "And that's why she thinks Kasey killed him, because Gidget's filled with guilt. If she can make Kasey into a murderer, she doesn't have to feel bad about sleeping with her husband."

Dad and I both stared at Deenie for a couple of seconds.

She threw her head back and let out a childlike bark of laughter. "I'm a true-crime junkie. I can solve a murder even when there isn't one."

We all laughed, and then Deenie sobered and zeroed in on me. "Are you sure Dwayne's death wasn't murder?"

I didn't like the way that sent a chill through me.

# 6

July Fourth dawned like a jalapeño with the promise of habanero by midmorning and ghost pepper by noon. This hot streak was predicted to last several more days, with winds expected to pick up in another day or two. I figured this kind of weather could lead people to bad behavior, kind of like full moons and the Santa Ana winds. I didn't necessarily want to mangle and maim, but I was not in the mood to wear my stifling uniform and toss candy from my cruiser at the July Fourth parade.

I didn't know how late Deenie stayed. Despite sleeping with my window open, I never heard Dad drive her home. He was gone when I woke up, and it wasn't my business if he'd already gone back to work or had stayed with Deenie.

Poupon and I went about our morning routine and found Hodgekiss already hopping and Main Street lined with families waiting for the parade to begin. Almost everyone watching had a kid or grandkid participating, and most of those kids would be marching with one group, racing back to the beginning of the route, and joining the next. Maybe two or three times if they were on the football team, in marching band, and in one 4-H club or another. Since the route was short enough to jog it in a minute or two, it made sense to rinse and repeat.

I eased the cruiser to the assigned place at the beginning of the parade, right behind Eunice and Harold in the ambulance. Last year a passel of nieces and nephews had ridden with me and threw candy to their envious friends along the route. But since they were Louise's and Michael's kids, the brother and sister behind the recall, I didn't have anyone to ride shotgun this year. Poupon napped in back and wasn't much help.

I couldn't blame it all on the heat or my scratchy uniform. Not even on the sadness of a death at the rodeo yesterday. The recall stuck in my craw, for sure. But I felt unsettled and awkward. As the middle child, I was used to being overlooked and invisible. I liked it that way. But these days, I felt seen, and not in a good way.

All of my life I'd been part of the Fox family. Brothers and sisters insulating me, even though I didn't always like it or recognize it. Today, Louise would host the family cookout in the backyard of my childhood home. I supposed everyone would be there, except me. Instead of making baked beans or brownies, I'd be on my own.

I tried not to focus on my woes as I bipped the siren and flashed the lights and flung handfuls of candy to everyone along the two-block route. Then I parked the cruiser behind the courthouse, and Poupon and I meandered out to greet our constituents and take in the cheerleaders, the extension clubs, and the preschoolers in their decorated wagons.

We found a spot in front of the post office that provided a sliver of shade. Sarah, my best friend since kindergarten and now my favorite sister-in-law, lumbered up to me. Six months pregnant, she appeared ready to pop now, or maybe she carried twins, or from the looks of it, a baby Beluga. Her thick chestnut hair shimmered down her back. No ponytail meant today was a good day, though she still looked pale. Her eyes focused on the curb, where two-year-old Brie, decked out in cowboy boots, hat, and shirt all in a vibrant red, was toddling after Tootsie Rolls and Jolly Ranchers.

Satisfied Brie wasn't getting into anything other than a lot of dirt, Sarah elbowed me. "I just ran into Brian Talbot at the Long Branch."

Poupon slid down next to the post office wall and rested his head on his paws, clearly exhausted by riding in the parade.

I deadened my eyes and shot Sarah a crusty look.

"What?" She wouldn't make eye contact. "He's divorced, has his own ranch, only two kids, who will be out of the house in ten years. And he's not bad-looking."

"If you don't count the beer belly and the fact Minnie left him because he was lazy."

A twinkle lit her face, letting me know she'd been teasing. "There's got to be someone that interests you. How about giving Heath Stratton another whirl?"

The new vet—"new" because he'd only been here three years—and I had struck up a friendship, but there wasn't spark enough to light an ant's campfire. "Stop trying to hook me up. I'm happy in my singlehood." Mostly. When I wasn't thinking about Glenn Baxter and how I'd screwed up what could have been the love of my life.

"Someone's got to take over mating you up now that you and Louise are on the outs." She cocked her mouth in a taunting way.

Too bad I couldn't take that with light-hearted humor. Sarah assumed this rift between me and Louise would blow over in time, but I wasn't sure I had that much forgiveness in me, and I was fairly certain whatever grievous deed Louise thought I'd done wouldn't be easy for her to throw off. "No one can be as annoying as Louise, so don't even try. Stick to your role as sidekick and loyal friend."

"Sidekick, huh." She punched my arm as she'd done since we were five. Usually done with affection, but never with gentleness.

Jade McPherson joined us. In her forties, Jade had inherited one of the largest ranches around from her uncle who'd had no children. She'd grown up in Connecticut and attended an Ivy League school but had moved to Grand County a couple of years ago to try her hand at ranching. She wore a floppy black sunhat, tight jeans tucked into fashion boots, and a flowing long-sleeved white shirt. She pulled her sunglasses down to study Poupon. "Is that your dog?"

I nodded, not feeling too self-conscious at his scraggly appearance. I'd let his carefully clipped poodle style go all natural, so his apricot curls were unruly.

"Not much of a cow dog, is he?"

I got that a lot. "It's okay. I don't have any cows."

She considered that, then let it go. "They tell me you saved the day at the rodeo."

It was nice to know "they" were talking me up. "Things escalated pretty fast."

She seemed to consider that, then changed the subject. "I also heard Dwayne Weber died. That's awful."

Where Roxy appeared from, I didn't know. Like someone's silent fart, she arrived unexpectedly and with the same welcome. "I know, isn't it awful?" She tapped Jade on the upper arm. "I heard your rum cake earned the most at the auction."

Jade lit up, then turned back to me with a more sober expression. "He was a real creep. I wouldn't be surprised if Kasey didn't finally have enough of his BS and killed him herself."

Roxy gave a fake gasp as if shocked.

May Keller walked past. She was so old she probably witnessed the disappearance of the settlers on Roanoke Island, but she was so contrary she'd never say what happened. She interjected before moving along. "Amen. Wouldn't blame her if she did." Of course, three-quarters of the county thought May Keller had offed *her* husband sometime after the Second World War.

Jade lunged after May, who had stopped to pet Poupon. She gave us a distracted wave as she caught up to May. Probably going to ask advice on haying or something.

The 4-H Dog Club, all six of them, stopped in the street and performed a sit and stay to varying degrees of success. Poupon closed his eyes, plainly disdainful of his more domesticated kin.

On the other side of the street, Dahlia Conner stood decked out to kill in her tight Bedazzled Wranglers tucked into high-heeled cowboy boots and clingy T-shirt I might call a bit low-cut for a woman in her mid-sixties. But then, I probably wouldn't have thought twice about it if it hadn't been Dahlia, my ex-mother-in-law, wearing it, and there wasn't anything I wouldn't judge her about. She handed a clipboard to Aileen Carson.

I didn't need to be a lip-reader to know what Dahlia said. It would go something like this: "I'm not trying to influence how you vote. We just want to give Grand County citizens a chance to weigh in."

Only, the good people of Grand County had weighed in three years ago when they voted me sheriff. There was really no reason for a recall. I'd done my job well. Really. I'd solved three murders—four, if you count my mother shooting an intruder. I'd found a missing girl and stopped a drug cartel from getting a toehold in the Sandhills.

Across the street, Aileen managed a polite, if uncomfortable, smile. With reluctance, she took the clipboard and pen and signed the recall petition.

As if she felt me behind her, Dahlia slowly swiveled her head in my direction, *Exorcist*-style. Her skin wasn't green, but that didn't make her less scary.

A bubble of sulfur popped inside me.

Sarah and Roxy both followed my gaze to see what caught my attention.

Roxy grabbed my upper arm before I could make a clean getaway. "I really hope you win the recall."

I kept my tone light even though I fumed inside. "They need to gather enough signatures to force an election." Maybe enough friends and family would rally behind me and refuse to even sign the darned thing. Especially after my heroics yesterday.

She waved her hand. "Oh, sure. But they'll get the signatures today, probably. Look at this crowd."

Yeah. A girl could hope.

In a nod to the heat, Roxy wore a short denim skirt and a tight T-shirt with sparkling words that read, *It's not easy being a cowgirl, but if the boot fits.* "I feel so sorry for Kasey. I mean, losing Dwayne is bad, but he's part of her business, and they were doing so good. Did you notice all the people there yesterday just for the bulls?"

Sarah located Brie, saw she was fine, then said, "Oh yeah?"

Roxy's glossed lips smacked. "TJ Simonson. He doesn't usually come to Grand County, but he was there. I think he's getting into breeding. And then the doctor from Denver. I know he was part owner in Lucky Luke."

Sarah and I made eye contact and had a silent conversation about how we wished Roxy would disappear.

Roxy lowered her voice to indicate tragedy. "Lucky Luke died a few weeks ago, though. He got struck by lightning. Really broke Kasey up."

Sarah pretended to be interested. "That doctor had to have invested thousands. He can't be happy about that."

Roxy was matter-of-fact. "That's the nature of the beast. Bulls aren't guaranteed. Like the stock market. You take your chances. You can win big, but you can lose big too."

Sarah and I hit our Roxy limit at the same time. Sarah spoke first. "I've got to get Brie out of the heat." Off she went, scooped up her daughter, and hurried away.

Giving Sarah a silent point for leaving first, I backed up.

Roxy stepped with me. "Are you going to Kasey's later?"

Um. I hadn't planned on it. But now that she mentioned it, I should make a condolence call. "Sure."

She seemed pleased. "I'll be there most of the day, of course. But I'll need to leave to be at Louise's for fireworks."

Yeah. Even my ex was going to spend the holiday with my family.

I called to Poupon, and we wandered through the crowd, responding to people commenting on little Tyler's narrow escape, more than a few bringing up Dwayne's accident. I smiled and teased or commiserated with people I'd known my whole life.

But Dahlia shoving a recall petition under everyone's nose gnawed at me. Everything felt a little off.

Being sheriff had given me a lifeline after leaving Ted. More than a livelihood, the job gave me focus, and I believed I helped people. I could go back to ranching. In fact, my niece Carly had offered me her ranch's foreman job.

But now that there was a recall, I didn't want to lose. I'd rarely been accused of being competitive, but I'd been universally labeled stubborn. I felt dragged to the line and my heels were plowing sand.

The parade had about petered out, with only a few more kids on bikes left. A group of younger folks gathered at the top of Main Street. I recognized the lanky frame of my youngest brother, Jeremy. He had his back to me and his head bent, facing a cluster of about a half dozen people. Happy to see family that hadn't filed a petition against me, I sidled over and slapped a hand on his shoulder. "How's it going?"

He jumped, clearly startled to see me. His handsome face crashed from amused to irritated in a split second, and my heart plummeted to my stomach to splash in the bubbling sulfur pit. Without a word to me, he snapped his chin up to his buddy. "Gonna get a Coke at Dutch's." He marched away, grinding my heart in the dust.

Tuff Hendricks, Jeremy's friend since they were mutton bustin', gave me a sympathetic frown. "Sorry about that. He's got a flea up his butt about your mom."

Louise and Michael must have gotten to Jeremy. Maybe I didn't need every one of my brothers and sisters in my cheering section, but it felt like the bleachers on my side of the field were thinning.

Four other people stood in the group, all of them looking like they'd like to bust out and stampede away from me. It took a second to understand why. Dahlia's sister Rose stood on the other side of Tuff, holding a clipboard and pen.

She carried about thirty more pounds than Dahlia and wore a Grand County Consolidated High School Longhorns T-shirt over baggy jeans. Rose clicked her tongue and twisted her mouth in a sheepish way. "Caught me."

Two other men, friends of Jeremy's and Tuff's from high school years ago, found fascinating things to study on the ground. Tuff shrugged. "I signed it, don't be mad. It don't mean anything yet. I promise I'm gonna vote for you when it's real."

After a few mumbled syllables that might have been "hi" and "goodbye," Rose and I watched the guys beat a retreat. Rose sighed. "You know I've always liked you, Kate. You're a damned sight better sheriff than Ted ever was. But you know Dahlia. She's really hard to say no to. It's family."

Yeah, family sticks together. Except when they don't.

# 7

On our way back to the courthouse and the cruiser, I thought about how to spend the rest of the Fourth of July. No family picnic for the first time in my life. I'd take some time to visit Kasey, but after that, I'd be on my own.

A state trooper car had pulled up in front of the courthouse. If we had a trooper stopping by on a holiday, it couldn't be good news. I paused as the trooper pushed himself from behind the wheel.

I couldn't help my grin to see Trey Ridnour straighten and greet me with a jaunty salute. Trey was stationed in Ogallala. We'd worked a couple of cases together and had developed a friendship. At one point, we'd hoped it might be more, but Trey didn't like the idea of being involved with a sheriff, and I didn't like having someone feel they had to protect me—especially after he'd taken a bullet trying to keep me safe.

Tall and broad-shouldered, with blond hair now covered by his Smokey Bear gray hat, he had a wide face prone to blushing. He was a handsome man, especially if you were one of those women who fell for a guy in uniform. Which I wasn't.

I didn't have a type, unless you called pining for one particular man a type. Since that door had slammed shut for me, I really needed to branch out. Trouble was, I didn't really want to.

I hurried to Trey, Poupon in tow. "What are you doing up here?"

Trey's face was teasing. "I drove up here to see you, of course."

We stood in the blazing sun. "That's nice, but you wouldn't drive eighty miles just to wish me happy Fourth of July."

He hedged. "Well, and to ask you if you know Kasey Weber."

Now I was curious. "Of course. It's Grand County. Does this have something to do with Dwayne's death?"

Trey tilted his head toward the courthouse. "Mind if we talk inside where it's cooler?"

That didn't sound good. "Sure. The AC is turned down, but the commissioners' room will be fine." We walked to the building, and I unlocked the front door, letting us in.

I followed him to the commissioners' room, and we sat at the long, scuffed conference table. He took off his hat and placed it upside down on a chair next to him.

I sat across from him, not bothering to turn on the lights because it would make the stuffy room seem hotter. "You've got me curious," I said.

He folded his hands in front of him on the tabletop, his hair damp and darkened where he'd worn his hat. "We got a call last night from a woman named Gidget Bartels."

That was interesting. Why would Gidget call the state patrol?

"She said she'd talked to you about Dwayne Weber's death, but you shut her down." He watched me, giving me a chance to answer.

"Well, yeah. She found Dwayne's body smashed by a bull. She was pretty upset."

"She was still upset when she called us. I didn't talk to her, but Pete, the guy who took the call, said she was nearly hysterical."

I understood being upset by what she'd seen. And if she and Dwayne were having an affair, that would make it worse. "Why was she calling you?"

He looked uncomfortable. "She insists Dwayne's death wasn't an accident. She thinks his wife killed him. And she said when she told you that, you wouldn't listen."

And he came all the way up here to tell me that I hadn't been sensitive enough? "Gidget might have been having a relationship with Dwayne. It's possible she's overreacting because he's gone, and she can't publicly mourn him as she'd like. If she loved him, it would be awful not to be able to plan the funeral or all of that stuff."

His cheeks reddened, making me wonder what was coming next. "That could be. We assumed there was something going on with her and Dwayne for her to be so worked up over his death, and for her to be the one who found him. But the thing is, when she called, we got a hold of the funeral home and had them remand the body to the ME."

Because a distraught mourner threw out an unlikely accusation, they called in the medical examiner? "Okay. What did she find? That he'd been stomped on by a two-thousand-pound bull and his neck had been broken?"

Trey squirmed a little. For a seasoned officer, he seemed unsure of himself. I'd seen him act with confidence at other crime scenes, so I assumed he was nervous for what he was about to tell me. "Well, yeah, his neck was broken, and he'd been stomped on. But the thing is, his neck was broken first, and it looks like there were bruises that are consistent with a struggle and someone wrenching his neck."

Whoa. He might as well have slapped me with a two-by-four. I sat back. "She's sure?"

Trey nodded, not enjoying himself.

Chicken in a biscuit. I'd really screwed up this time. "How did I miss that?"

Trey shook his head. "We all make mistakes, especially when the scene seems obvious. I mean, a guy in a stall with a bull. But this is coming at a bad time, with the recall and everything."

"You know about that?" Of course he did. The law enforcement community in western Nebraska wouldn't fill the home bleachers for an eight-man football team. And they gossiped more than a magpie convention.

I was the only officer in Grand County, an area as big as Rhode Island. Ted had the next county over, and two others made up our co-op. That was a lot of ground for four officers to cover, even though we had a population way less than Memorial Stadium during spring scrimmage. (Go Big Red.)

The state patrol was on hand to help out. They had the resources and labs to process what we couldn't. And the expertise and manpower to lend.

Trey ran a hand through his hair, making it stand up. "I know you're a good officer. This recall is bogus. I don't know what happened with your mother, but I know you weren't trying to help her escape. And as far as your brother, the law was on his side. He hadn't actually committed any crimes."

My stomach lurched at the thought of being the center of so much gossip. Before I even ran for sheriff, I'd solved the murder of Carly's granddad. I'd brought down two corrupt county sheriffs and had exposed a railroad theft ring. Maybe it was wrong to be so proud of my record, but damn it, I'd done some good for Grand County. And now, because Louise thought I was somehow destroying our family, all of it had been called into question and I had to defend myself, not only to the people of Grand County, but to my law enforcement peers.

No doubt Mom's past catching up to her had hit our family like a tsunami and torn it from its foundation. Louise wanted someone to blame. But I was getting pretty damned tired of being the Fox family scapegoat.

I tried to drive that dump truck of garbage aside to concentrate on what Trey was telling me. "So, Dwayne was murdered. I'll go with you to tell Kasey."

Trey tapped his fingers on the table. "I can handle it solo."

"I don't mind, and Kasey knows me." I thought about how she'd been acting yesterday. No signs of grief. Angry and cold. It made sense to me, but what would Trey make of it?

He looked aside. "Yeah." He hesitated and slowly turned back and held my gaze, looking as if he had to force himself to stay focused. "You're not really part of this investigation."

His manner and words warned me of what I didn't quite believe. "But it's my county."

Again, Trey looked away before settling back on me with the kind of compassion a doctor might show giving a bad diagnosis. "But you didn't take any action, and now it's with us."

The state patrol normally handled the bigger, more complicated cases for rural counties in Nebraska. But Trey knew I would hate handing over the reins.

I let out an incredulous chuckle. "I know this county and the people in it better than anyone. You don't think I'd be helpful in this?"

"What I know is that you're friends with Kasey Weber, and she's our prime suspect."

My mouth dropped open. "She's your prime suspect? Based on what? Without even investigating?" I thought for a moment. "And we're not what I'd call friends."

He held up a hand. "We're only beginning. But the point is, I think maybe you'd have a conflict of interest. Especially now, when your whole career is dangling on accusations of favoritism."

I slapped the table. "That's such a pile of worms. You know—"

He pushed back. "Yeah. I know. But I'm trying to protect you."

I stood and put my weight on my palms to lean over the table. "I thought we were clear on you never trying to protect me again."

Crimson snaked up his neck and joined his rosy cheeks. "I'm not taking another bullet, for God's sake. It's my job to investigate murders. So let me do my job. You take care of the county business and try to salvage your job."

He stood and picked up his hat.

I kept lockstep with him as he walked out of the commissioners' room and headed to the front door.

He stopped and fitted his hat on his head. "I know you hate this, but do it my way and you'll come out looking better."

I folded my arms. "For the record, I don't think Kasey did it."

He laughed. "Of course you don't. I've never seen you take the easiest route." He abruptly stopped.

I stated what he'd obviously realized. "Except yesterday, when I didn't even examine the body."

He sighed. "It was an honest mistake. Any of us might have done it. It's just really bad timing." Sure. He'd said that before. Probably rehearsed it on his drive from Ogallala.

I watched him stride down the sidewalk.

# 8

Sarah and I arranged to meet and go to Kasey's later that afternoon. With no pressing sheriff business and not even a salad to make for a family cook-out, Poupon and I went home for lunch, and I repaired the fence surrounding my property.

While I pounded nails, I muttered. "Not my investigation." "Huh." "Kasey killed him." "Lazy investigation."

Then my stomach flipped and twisted like Slim in the arena yesterday. I'd missed the signs that Dwayne had been murdered. It didn't matter how much of a knight I'd looked like at the rodeo. I'd botched an investigation. And now I was on the outside.

Several times I pulled my phone from my pocket, intending to call any one of my siblings. I wanted someone to tell me they loved me.

They wouldn't in so many words, of course. But Diane might straighten me out on what to wear, Susan would probably tell me about a guy she met that might be right for me, Douglas would have a book suggestion, Michael would tell me something one of his daughters did, Robert would try to get me to cut hay for him tomorrow, and Jeremy would ask my opinion about a horse he wanted to buy.

But all of that was my imagination. Some of them were on my side, some of them thought Louise was right. All of them were busy and wouldn't appreciate a random call in the middle of the day. So, I shoved my phone back in my pocket and kept working.

Showered and in civilian clothes, jeans and a short-sleeved shirt, I left Poupon to guard the house and drove Elvis to meet Sarah.

We met at the high school, and I climbed into Sarah's pickup and left my car. I was surprised not to see little Brie in her car seat.

Sarah flicked her thick, smooth hair behind her shoulders. She'd lost most of her baby weight after Brie's birth, but with the bulge of her belly, she'd added roundness to her cheeks and a thin layer on her neck. She was still prettier than I'd ever been. "Robert's turn."

I wriggled jazz hands. "Two wild women out on our own."

I loved her throaty laugh. "Fifteen years ago, when we were skipping classes and starting our weekends at Thursday Night Three-fers, you'd have never convinced me a wild time would be making a condolence call on a new widow."

Her laugh died as we both considered it. "I wonder what Kasey will do now?" I said.

Sarah pulled onto the highway, looking serious. "I always wondered what kind of marriage they had. Dwayne came on to me more than once, and Robert said Kasey got drunk and tried to kiss him a couple of years ago after the fair."

"Maybe they were grooming you for swinging."

"Ew. But even if they weren't that close, I can't imagine losing your husband and business partner so suddenly. Not that I thought Dwayne was all that great in either department."

I kept Deenie's theory about Dwayne's faithfulness to myself. "I wonder how many bulls they have. Will Kasey be able to handle it all alone?"

I didn't tell Sarah that Kasey would also have to deal with an investigation.

We pulled into the yard, and my stomach dropped. I wasn't surprised there were other visitors, just disappointed one of the vehicles out front was Roxy and Ted's fancy pickup. May Keller's rusty blue Toyota pickup was also there, and I liked May, so maybe they'd cancel each other out.

Kasey and Dwayne, now just Kasey, lived a few miles east of town. They had several acres, big enough for bull pens and two pastures out back.

Their house was visible from the highway, a manufactured home with a lean-to garage and a redwood deck.

Sarah reached behind the seat and pulled out a covered casserole dish. She caught my eye and raised one side of her mouth in a "whatever" motion. "Chicken pot pie. It's what I had in the freezer. What'd you bring?"

I held up the brown bag she must not have noticed. "Bulleit I bought in Broken Butte a while back and haven't had a reason to crack open."

Sarah's mouth puckered in irritation. "Witch. Death and bourbon are a natural pairing. You'll make the rest of us look bad."

Kasey might need to knock back the bottle after Trey had talked to her.

Another change from our youth. "Witch" wasn't Sarah's first choice for me, I knew. But she had a toddler now and was cleaning up her vocabulary. The circle of life. Since I'd grown up with Dad, who hated cursing, I'd always kept it clean.

Sarah motioned with her head to a new silver Ford F-150 Super Cab with Arizona plates. She tilted her mouth down and raised her eyebrows in a what-have-we-here expression. She shoved the dish at me, and I barely had hold of it before she peeled off to check it out. She cupped her hands and looked in the passenger-side window, then whistled. "Computerized display panel, the whole nine yards. This thing could finance Brie's college career."

I glanced at the logo on the side. Steffen Rough Stock, and a brand that looked like a circle with a slash above and under it. Probably a friend of the Webers' from their rodeo connections.

I kept walking toward the deck. "Only if you send her to a state school. It'd never be enough to send Brie to the Ivy League."

Sarah rejoined me and took back the casserole dish. "Not everyone can be Glenn Baxter, you know."

Hearing his name felt like a taser and pepper spray at the same time. I know, because I'd experienced both at sheriff training. I didn't utter a sound, though my breath hitched. I'd have thought that after two years the wound of Baxter leaving me wouldn't still bleed. My voice sounded as normal as ever, so at least I could now hide my devastation. "I wonder who it is. Does Kasey have a rich uncle or something?"

Sarah popped up the stairs, her steps light despite carrying the extra baby weight. She seemed to be handling this pregnancy in better health than her first, though I knew she tired easily. "No clue. Kasey and I aren't any closer than you are." Balancing the dish in her palm, she pulled the screen open and knocked on the hollow front door. My bungalow might be old, but I did like the solid feel of the doors.

Through the door, and probably the windows and thin exterior walls of the manufactured home, we heard low voices and felt people moving around. When no one opened for us, Sarah flicked her head at me and turned the knob.

Before we stepped inside, I heard a pickup on the driveway and turned as my brother Michael drove past the house on his way to the barn. "Just a sec," I said to Sarah.

She bobbed her chin at me and continued inside.

I bounded down the steps to intercept Michael. It wasn't that I had something in particular to say. I hoped maybe we could mend a fence or two if I acted like he hadn't sided with Louise in the recall.

He'd had to slow to skirt the vehicles near the house, so I was able to step into his path and force him to stop. He kept his eyes ahead and didn't roll down his window.

Michael and Douglas barely looked like brothers, let alone twins. Where Douglas was big, not necessarily fat but with a softness and welcoming way about him, Michael was like four hundred pounds of burning energy compacted into one-forty and a five-nine frame. His hair, as dark as mine and probably as wavy, hadn't grown longer than a quarter inch since he'd been ten years old. He didn't have the time to mess with it. Everything about Michael was quick.

My stomach knotted at his rejection. But we'd butted heads before, and we could fix this. At least, I hoped so. I knocked on the passenger window and waited while he reluctantly rolled it down. With a cheery smile, I said, "Happy Fourth of July. Whatcha doin'?"

Though he sat still with his face placid, his eyes darted around, clearly impatient. "Not that it's your business, but I'm checking on the bulls."

That was nice. Michael might snub me, but he did the right thing by helping out Kasey. "Guess you'll be going to Louise's later."

He didn't look at me. "I gotta go." He gave me the back of his head as if he couldn't stand to breathe the same air and looked at the parked vehicles as he reached for the window toggle. He jerked and drew in a startled breath. As if hit with a cattle prod, he glanced at me, his face pale, and he hit the window button.

"Hey!" The window slid up. "What's the matter?" He was younger than me, but maybe he was having a heart attack. Or maybe a sharp stab of indigestion. Except his eyes had a flash of fear.

With one glance over his shoulder, he gunned his pickup toward the barn. I thought it was weird that he didn't stop out front but pulled to the side away from the house, parking out of sight. I surveyed the place, saw only the few visitors' vehicles parked in front of the modular home, and shrugged.

One thing was clear, he wasn't ready to make amends. I clumped up the steps and into the house.

I slipped into the five-by-five vinyl-covered entryway. Beige carpeting took over from there, marking where the living room began. The beige theme continued with fabric couch and love seat. Two leather recliners kept vigil in front of a large-screen TV mounted to the wall. Three windows covered most of the far wall with blinds fully opened but no drapes or other coverings. They showed the view of bull pens and the barn, but not Michael's pickup. A hall opened off the living room that must lead to two or three bedrooms.

To the other side of the entryway, a dining room table and chairs filled the space in front of the breakfast bar and behind that, the kitchen. Oak cabinets lined the kitchen and narrowed the opening above the breakfast bar, and though I couldn't see it from where we stood, I knew the same vinyl flooring found in the entryway also covered the kitchen floor. Not a big kitchen, but nevertheless, all of the visitors had congregated either in the space between the sink and breakfast bar or were seated on two barstools.

The smell of coffee filled the air, even though it had to be in the nineties outside. The counters were lined with pans and casserole dishes, evidence of the good folks of Grand County doing what they always did, feeding grief.

Looked like only women were making the call this afternoon. Dwayne's friends would probably stop in later. It wasn't a rule, of course, just seemed men preferred to wait until they'd finished working for the day before cleaning up and heading to town, no matter what the reason. Which didn't make sense on a holiday. But maybe men were downright scared of Kasey.

May Keller poked her head from the kitchen. "Unless you got cookies or coffee cake in that bag, you can turn around and go home."

Roxy pushed around May. "Kasey is grateful for everything." She held Sarah's casserole and peeled the foil back to peek at it. "Okay to put it right in the freezer?"

From the corner of the kitchen, Sarah flicked her fingers in a go-ahead motion. She'd have already put her name on the bottom with a Sharpie. She might not get the dish back for a year or two, depending on Kasey's habits, but she had others.

Roxy disappeared through a door off the kitchen that no doubt led to a mud room and stairs to a basement.

Aileen Carson and Myrna Hardy stood up from the breakfast bar like students suddenly dismissed for recess. Aileen, wearing a crisp pair of jeans and flowered shirt, hair curled and makeup on, obviously had fixed up for her trip to town, as she normally did. "Guess I'd better get going." She eased past us on the way to the door. "Good seeing you both."

Myrna was hot on her heels. "Yeah. I need to cut up a fruit salad for tonight."

Roxy returned to the kitchen. "Thank you both for stopping by. I'll be sure to tell Kasey you were here."

Aileen opened the front door. "Let me know when the funeral is and where, and I'll get the food lined up." She was president of the United Church of Christ Ladies' Club (yes, they still called it that), and it was her duty to apportion which church women's group would bring desserts, salads, or furnish the meat for the funeral dinner. It all depended on the church Kasey would use.

Roxy picked up their abandoned coffee cups and replied that she sure would, before setting the mugs in the sink.

Aileen and Myrna disappeared in a rush. My guess was that they'd only been waiting for someone else to show up so they could escape. They wouldn't want it to look like no one cared about Dwayne's passing. But many, and I'd assume Aileen and Myrna were in that group, didn't approve of Kasey and Dwayne and would feel uncomfortable here. That didn't mean they'd snub Kasey in her time of need.

Aileen and Myrna's departure left Roxy, May Keller, and the mystery driver of the fancy Steffen Rough Stock F-150 with Arizona plates.

May grumbled as she made her way around the counter to plop down at the stool Aileen had vacated. She wore her everyday look, whether to a July Fourth parade, a condolence call, or the hayfield: work clothes of dusty Levi's cinched at her waist in a way that suggested she'd evaporated quite a bit from when she'd bought them two decades ago, and a plaid Western shirt with snap buttons and fabric so thin it threatened to disintegrate at any moment. Her cigarette pack was in danger of falling from the fraying front pocket, which would be a tragedy for May. "Can't understand why nobody brought sweets. Casseroles and coffee. Jade McPherson even brought a cold cut tray. I ask you, does anybody want cold cuts?"

Sarah cocked an eyebrow. "Not when they could have her fabulous rum cake."

I pulled the Bulleit from the bag and set it on the counter.

May raised her eyebrows at me and gave me a wicked grin. "Girlie, you're invited to all the funerals from now on."

Roxy clapped her hand on her chest, bare as usual from her scooped-neck, blinged-up T-shirt. "Kate. I can't believe you did that."

The mystery woman stepped from the far corner of the kitchen where she'd been half-hidden in shadow. Not much older than Roxy, so maybe early forties. Even if we hadn't seen her expensive rig out front, she gave off the whiff of money. She wore Wranglers, like most good Sandhillers. But unlike May's jeans, these didn't sag or bunch. They looked tailored specially for her. She wore a simple T-shirt, the kind I'd pick up at Target, but hers somehow looked like it cost a hundred bucks and—unlike the style of someone else we knew—wasn't cut low to show off her cleavage. A delicate gold chain circled her neck, and a charm I couldn't make out rested on her chest. Her hair hit just below her shoulder blades, and the blend of blonds suggested the benefit of a skilled colorist.

She smiled in approval and nodded at the bottle. "Wise woman."

I tipped my head to her. "Thank you."

Roxy clapped her hands. "Oh, Kate. This is Maureen Steffen. Maureen, this is Kate Fox."

Maureen thrust her hand through the opening above the breakfast bar, beside where May sat with her fingers fondling her cigarette pack. "Glad to meet you. Any friend of bourbon is a friend of mine."

Roxy pointed to Sarah. "And Sarah Fox. Sarah and I had babies only two weeks apart. My son, Beau, and her daughter, Brie. They're besties. So cute together. You should—"

Maureen grasped Sarah's hand, cutting off Roxy and making me like her immediately. "Hi, Sarah."

I glanced around the house. "Where's Kasey?"

Roxy blinked her eyes to emphasize her point. "She should be resting. I got here right after the parade, and heaven knows I've tried to get her to take it easy."

Roxy must have missed Trey's visit. I wondered how Kasey was taking it.

Roxy blathered on. "I'm hostessing because she wouldn't have her mother here, of course. And I don't blame her. That woman is a mess. You need someone sensitive who really understands grief and loss. I'm more than happy to do this."

Roxy didn't seem to realize she was babbling. But then, self-awareness wasn't her strong suit. "Kasey just won't stop. Right now, she's looking through paperwork. Maureen asked her some questions about the bulls, and away she went."

May Keller shoved her coffee cup across the counter toward Roxy. "If you'll spare us all your twaddle, I'd take another cup of joe."

Sarah eyed the coffee cup as if weighing whether she ought to join May. She let her gaze drift to the bourbon, then seemed to give it all up and said, "What about the bulls?"

Maureen placed her hands on the edge of the counter, displaying a perfect French manicure. "I wondered who they were registered to. If they're part of the corporation, it'll be much easier for Kasey going forward than if he put them in his own name."

Curious, I wondered how to ask Maureen's relation to Kasey without being rude.

I shouldn't have worried. Because May Keller was in the room.

May watched Roxy as if making sure she poured the coffee correctly but said to Maureen, "Who are you? You got them Arizona plates and the fancy rig. Are you a sorority sister or cousin or something?"

Roxy gasped. "She's Maureen Steffen." The way Roxy said it, she might have been announcing Maureen as the Queen of England.

May, Sarah, and I kept our focus on Roxy, waiting for the rest.

Finally, Maureen's deep-throated laugh rang out. "Not much for PRCA or PBR circuit, are you?"

"Oh my God." Roxy sounded supremely apologetic. She slid the full cup toward May. "You guys, this is Maureen Steffen. Steffen Rough Stock? As in the National Finals championship bull five years in a row? Torn-A-Tious? You know, like tornado."

We all shook our heads.

Maureen said, "I always thought that was a stupid name. Fred thought being named after a tornado was obvious, but no one ever gets it."

Roxy tried again. "Hellfire?"

"Nope," Sarah said, speaking for all of us.

Roxy flapped her hands on her thighs in defeat. "Bell Ringer? Night Storm? Emasculator?"

Maureen held up a finger. "That last name was mine."

May rolled her eyes and sipped her coffee. "Don't suppose there's any cookies in that jar over there." She pointed to a crock on the counter next to the sink, but Roxy wasn't paying attention.

Sarah laid it out for anyone who might doubt. "You know Kasey from the bucking bull business."

Rapid footfalls made us turn. Kasey strode in, wearing gym shorts and a T-shirt and in stocking feet. Her blond braid swayed as she came toward us and slapped a few manila file folders on the dining room table. "Actually, Maureen and I haven't met before."

Kasey's eyes weren't swollen. Her skin wasn't red and splotchy. She must not be an ugly crier like I was—and almost everyone I knew. Or maybe it hadn't struck her yet. Grief was a personal thing, but folks around here would get all snippy at Kasey's apparent chill. I didn't think she needed to put on a wailing display, but maybe a tear or two would keep people from gossiping. Kasey surveyed the dining room and kitchen. "Myrna and Aileen gone?"

Roxy nodded. "Myrna brought a small ham. I put it in the freezer. Aileen brought a five-pound can of coffee."

Kasey frowned. "The ham I can use. But a can of coffee? Really? It's probably the cheapest shit she could find."

Sarah, who could be as caustic as they come, looked taken aback by Kasey's ungraciousness. "You can always donate it to the food pantry in Broken Butte and no one would know."

Kasey flicked her eyebrows as if that would be too much bother.

I'd never thought of Roxy as particularly considerate, so it surprised me when she said, "I've been keeping a list of who brought what. The funeral home will give you a bunch of thank-you notes. I'll help you write them."

I must have given her a curious look, because she said to me, "When Brian died, there were so many things to do. It would have been nice to have some help." Brian was Roxy's first husband. He'd married her after his wife, my sister Glenda, died of cancer. Then he'd died in a small plane wreck.

Sarah shot a look to me that might have been guilt or embarrassment that we'd never volunteered to help Roxy. But either emotion would be a stretch for Sarah, who didn't have any more love for Roxy than I did. At least, she didn't used to.

Kasey's dry eyes and gruff manner wouldn't have helped her with Trey. What had he said? How had she responded? Damn it, I should be part of the investigation. But my career as sheriff, my reputation, and my status in my family might rest on me steering clear.

Maureen watched Kasey with sympathy in her intelligent eyes. "I always meant to introduce myself. We never had the opportunity."

"But you're here now?" I hoped it didn't sound rude to question her.

Maureen watched Kasey as if protecting her. "I was in Greeley when I heard about Dwayne's accident."

Greeley, about sixty miles north of Denver, hosted one of the biggest July Fourth rodeos. Important stock breeders would be drawn there.

Maureen continued. "I knew Dwayne, of course. He made it to a lot of the events. But I just had to come even though Kasey and I had never met. I lost my husband five years ago, and I know how hard it can be."

Kasey dropped into a dining chair and pulled a folder toward her. Her voice carried a hard edge. "We should have met before. Not many women in this business."

Maureen opened a cabinet, closed it. Opened another and pulled out two juice glasses. She set them on the breakfast bar and repeated the motion to bring six glasses. She snatched the bottle from the counter and walked over to the table, peeling the seal off the top.

Sarah didn't hesitate. She scooped three glasses into her hands and placed them on the table. May brought her coffee over. I grabbed the other three glasses, and we ringed the table with Kasey.

Maureen splashed bourbon into the glasses and slid them to us. When we all held ours, she raised hers and said, "To women taking over the world."

Sarah caught my eye before I tipped my bourbon back. She seemed as curious about the toast as I felt. Shouldn't a toast be something more relevant to a new widow? I might have toasted Dwayne. Or maybe to Kasey and healing. Maybe those toasts would have been lame, too.

Kasey threw her shot back and winced. May Keller swallowed hers whole and set the glass down as if she'd taken a swig of water.

Roxy had a small bit and wagged her head. "Oh. I'm not used to this anymore." If I cared enough to question her, I might be skeptical about that.

Sarah had enough to wet her lips and pushed the glass toward Kasey. "I just wanted a taste. Can't have it because of the baby. You can use it more than I can."

Kasey closed her fist around it. "Sure can. Thanks." And down it went. She sucked on her teeth.

Since I wasn't in my highly attractive uniform, I figured I was off duty. An afternoon snort wouldn't hurt. I took a nip, enjoying the heat.

I figured if one of the top bucking bull breeders liked bourbon, she was probably used to a higher-quality hooch than I'd provided. But Maureen drank with apparent pleasure. She set her glass down and focused on Kasey. "What did you find out?"

Kasey paged through papers in one of the files. "I wasn't worried about the bulls. I made sure they were part of the corporation."

Maureen nodded approval. I couldn't get a handle on her age. At first, I'd thought in her forties. But she seemed so sure of herself, I wondered if she was older and having money gave her the resources to look younger. "That's really smart."

Kasey peered up at Maureen. "Dwayne was married before. He told me he'd bought some nice things, like jewelry, a pickup, some other stuff, and put it in his name. So, he got to keep it all in the divorce. Like, she didn't even know he had it. Then he sold it all. I mean, I didn't think Dwayne would ever screw me over." She sucked in a giant breath. "But I'm not stupid."

Roxy blinked and flicked her head. "I can't believe you'd be that cynical. When you get married, you should trust your spouse with everything. That's what being married means."

Hominy and hot sauce. Sarah and I exchanged another look, this one clearly saying, "Are you hearing this?"

May Keller to the rescue again. She slurped her coffee and said, "Kasey's got it right. Men can't be trusted." She plopped her cup on the table and pointed a finger at Kasey and Roxy. "You two twits should know better. You got men who cheated *with* you. What makes you think they wouldn't cheat *on* you?"

Kasey wrinkled her mouth in agreement. "Assholes."

Roxy gasped in offense. "Ted and I were destined to be together. His first marriage was a mistake."

Boy, was it ever.

Sarah's eyes twinkled with either suppressed laughter or outrage on my behalf.

Maureen tipped her head to the file Kasey had in front of her. "So, what are you checking?"

Kasey spread out the pages. "A few months ago, I upped Dwayne's life insurance. We had a big fight over it. He pays the bills." She froze, and the skin seemed to tighten around her eyes. Then she let out an irritated puff of air. "Paid the bills. I wanted to make sure he'd paid it. It would be like him to lie to me about it."

Huh. What do you say to that? Apparently, not much, since no one spoke for a moment. It seemed like a good opportunity to take another sample of the bourbon.

Maureen must have felt the same way. When she'd had a drink, she set the glass down, a bit of amber still at the bottom. "And did he?"

Kasey reached for the bottle. "I can't find the damned policy." Kasey sloshed bourbon in her glass. "Where did this come from?"

Roxy clamped her mouth shut, probably hating to give me credit.

Sarah answered. "Kate brought it."

Kasey held up her glass in a toast. "You're my new best friend." Everything about her felt like a glinting shard of glass. Maybe she feared a single crack would lead to her shattering. She flipped open another file.

Maureen reached for the bottle, and May shoved her glass down the table. "Good idea, dearie."

Kasey's face screwed up, and she spewed, "I'll be go to hell."

We all stared at her, and Maureen glanced at the file Kasey stared at. "What is that?"

Kasey slammed the file closed. "Nothing."

# 9

What I wouldn't have given to lurch across the table and grab that file. Whatever was in it surprised Kasey, but I couldn't tell if she was happy about it or furious. All emotions seemed the same on her, as if her seams would split at any moment and she'd be nothing but dangerous shrapnel. It was best to stay cautious.

The sound of *Monty Python's Flying Circus* theme sounded in the dining room, and Sarah flinched. She pushed her chair back. "Sorry." The song erupted again as she stood and pulled her phone from her back pocket.

Maureen watched her with curiosity.

I shrugged. "She discovered *Monty Python* when we were in high school. She thinks it's hilarious." I took a breath to ask Kasey about the file or Trey's visit or why she didn't seem to feel sad about Dwayne, basically none of it my business, when Kasey spoke and rescued me.

"I guess I ought to have the funeral at the Episcopal church. Dwayne's brother and his father will be here. But I damned sure do not want Cara Duncan to sing. God, her voice sounds like a strangled elephant. And you know what, she's fatter than an elephant, too."

Okay, that was unnecessary. Cara, who had a powerful voice and some natural talent, sang at her share of funerals and weddings. She'd never had training and hit as many sour notes as sweet. Still, she was a kind and generous woman and didn't deserve that.

Roxy patted Kasey's hand. "I agree. I'll sing and play my guitar. I don't have to do one of those churchy songs. We can pick out something Dwayne liked."

Kasey pulled her hand away. "We'll pick out something I like."

Sarah walked back in. "That was Robert. I've got to go. The pivot broke down, and he needs me to pick up a part in Broken Butte."

Maureen acted surprised. "It's a holiday."

Sarah was already on the move. "But the alfalfa needs water. Robert called the irrigation place, and they're going to leave the part by the gate."

I stood up, feeling a pleasant tingle from the bourbon. "I should get going, too." Not that I had anywhere to go.

Roxy slid back from the table. "Ted's had Beau all afternoon, so he'll need a break. And I probably need to give Beau a bath before we go to Louise's because Ted always lets him play in the dirt." She fluttered her eyes at Kasey. "That is, if you think you'll be okay here without me. I mean, I can stay if you need me to."

Kasey fixed Roxy with a spiteful stare. "Isn't Beau a handful every day? And he's Ted's kid, too, so why can't he give Beau a bath?"

I wanted to defend Beau, but I was too busy with my snit that Ted and Roxy were going to Louise's but I wasn't.

Maureen piped up. "I can stay. I hear the only lodging in town is the Long Branch, and there's no point in my hanging out in one of those rooms."

Roxy gave Maureen an overly sympathetic look. "Oh dear. I'm so sorry. I used to have a super-nice house on the Bar J, only about ten miles north of Hodgekiss. I would have loved to have you. But now we're in a little rental in Bryant. We just don't have the room."

And The Roxy Show began again.

"But we're thinking we'll be moving back to my husband's family ranch very soon. The house isn't that much bigger, but at least it's ours and we'll be able to remodel."

Again, Sarah's expressive brown eyes let loose with what I'm sure was, "She has no clue what she's saying. Wait for it..."

May Keller was watching Roxy with so much disdain dripping from her face it might stain her shirt.

It suddenly dawned on Roxy that if they made that expected move back to the ranch, it would be because I lost the recall election and Ted was the new sheriff. She closed her mouth with a pop and stared at me. Then began the backpedaling. "Well, that's not a done deal, of course. It's just a possibility." She turned to Kasey and started a new tack. "Well, then, I guess I'll take off. Ted gets frustrated when Beau gets overtired."

I leaned on the back of my chair. "I never worried too much about Ted getting frustrated."

Roxy pinched her lips together in a prim line. "I know."

That was too much for Sarah. She finally released a belly laugh, so much deeper when she was pregnant. "That's right. If you'd only greeted him with a martini at six o'clock every night so he could relax, you'd still be married."

Maureen watched all of this with curiosity. "You've lost me."

May knocked her on the arm. "Listen up." She pointed to me. "She used to be married to that namby-pamby sheriff, Ted Conner." She pointed to Roxy. "She used to be married to the widower of her oldest sister." She pointed back at me.

As an aside to the room at large: "Who was probably the best of the whole lot of Foxes. Rest her soul."

I didn't disagree with that.

May pointed back to Roxy. "But then her husband, the widower, died. And she's one of them that can't be alone, so she ups and gets this one's no-good husband." Finger back at me.

I had to admire the way Maureen seemed to grasp the narrative.

May kept her spotlight on me. "So's this one, she decides to get her own revenge, and she runs for sheriff. And because she's related to three-quarters of the county, she gets elected and," May waved her hand at Roxy, probably to encompass Roxy and Ted, "these two yay-hoos end up moving to the next county when the two-timer finagles an appointment to sheriff."

Maureen gave me a curious look. "So, you're the sheriff?"

May slapped her on the arm again. "Wait up. I ain't finished." She settled herself back in the chair. "She's sheriff for the time being. Because there's a recall election and that," May popped up again as if remembering she had to go, "is another story for a different day when I don't have so much to do."

May carried her coffee cup to the kitchen. "I better get. Not because I got some man I gotta do for, mind you." She scowled at Sarah and Roxy. "I got a mess of green beans from the garden that needs to be put up."

Kasey didn't bother thanking May, Sarah, or me for stopping by. That didn't hurt my feelings. As I kept reminding myself, people aren't always on their best behavior when death knocks them upside the head. But I did feel a little bad for Roxy, who was obviously trying to be a good friend. And feeling sorry for Roxy put me in a foul temper.

# 10

It hadn't been a terrific night for me. I'd left Kasey's with Sarah and, after she dropped me off at the high school to retrieve Elvis, drove through Hodgekiss on my way home. I saw most of my siblings' vehicles parked around Louise's house, not counting Susan, who lived in Lincoln, and Diane, who hadn't been back to the Sandhills for months. It wasn't something I was proud of, but I punched my steering wheel at the sight of Ted and Roxy's pickup out front.

I headed home for a meal of earthworms and pity all served in a bitter sauce. I'd kind of hoped Dad would be home, though I hadn't expected him. If he'd gone back to work last night, it would be another twenty-four hours before he made it home from his trip. But seeing the empty parking space in front of my house made me feel even more lonely. On a whim, I called my older sister Diane in Denver. She wasn't known for her comforting personality, but at least she was on my side. I hoped so, anyway.

She picked up on the third ring. "I've got about four minutes before I get home so...go."

I climbed from Elvis and walked through the gate of my white vinyl fence. "It's a holiday. Did you go into the office?" As an executive at a national bank, she worked long hours. I suspected she ran the world, not simply her piece of it. She was somehow involved with a covert group that had drawn Carly in. All I knew was that it was founded by students at the military school Carly's grandfather and father had attended, and they had extracted people from dangerous situations in foreign countries. I presumed there was more.

I didn't ask questions, not that Diane or Carly would give any answers.

Diane spouted, "Ever thought of using a blinker, asshole?" Obviously, she was driving. To me, she said, "It's not a holiday in the rest of the world. But I'm done now and have to pick up Kimmy and Karl to go see fireworks downtown. They were supposed to work on their math lab assignments, but I'll bet the babysitter let them play video games all afternoon." Diane didn't believe in letting her kids' education slide over the summer, so she had them enrolled in extra programs. "I swear, that kid would let them eat chips and atrophy in front of the monitor all day if I didn't threaten to dock his wages if they don't get As."

It seemed impossible Diane and I had been raised by the same parents. We'd found out we might not share as much DNA as we grew up believing, but it seemed clear we'd both reacted to our unconventional upbringing in different ways. Diane strove for control of the universe, while I wanted to live a quiet life of integrity. "You don't do that, do you?"

There was a rumble like a garage door going up. "I should. But his mother is our head legal counsel, and I think she'd sue me." The car door dinged on her end. "What's up, Katie? Jeremy having another love child? Susan quitting her job and joining the circus?"

I trudged up the stairs and onto the front porch. "Why would you say that?"

"Because you're always out to save one brother or sister. So, tell me, who is it this time?" Rustling and a door squeaking told me she made her way from the garage to the modern monstrosity of a house in an upscale Denver suburb she called home.

"It's Louise and this stupid recall." On the couch, Poupon opened his eyes with what looked like supreme effort. I nearly fainted when he thumped his stump of a tail in greeting. It might be the most blatant affection I'd ever received from him.

"For fuck's sake, Kate. Why would you let that bother you?" Something banged, and she shouted, "Kimmy. Karl. I'm home. You'd better have finished your assignments."

I gave Poupon's collar a gentle tug, and he stood up. "It bothers me because it's my *job*. And because, well, what the heck? She's my sister. Why would she go after me like this?"

Kimmy, now eleven and in a stage so awkward all we could do was hope and wait, spoke in a squeaky voice in the background. She was joined by Karl. Diane must have lowered the phone, and they had a conversation. I could wait for them since Diane was a single mother and their time mattered.

I directed Poupon to the porch and held the screen door for him to descend to the yard. I plopped on the steps.

Diane came back on. "Listen, I've got to go. We need to meet my date in an hour, and my fabulousness doesn't happen by itself."

"You have a date?"

"Not the subject. Here's the deal: You're getting worked up over a nowhere job in a nowhere town. Why would you want to stay in Hodgekiss? There's no future. No career. No culture. There's nothing for you there except being taken advantage of by everyone and their sister. And yeah, I mean Louise and that brood of goody-goodies she's raising."

Speaking of goody-goodies, I thought maybe I'd tell her about Mose and Zeke and my sinking suspicion they had something to do with Slim getting loose yesterday. "But I—"

"Call me this weekend. Better yet, come see me. I need to set you straight." She hung up without saying goodbye. As usual.

The evening didn't improve, but I felt a little better after a good night's sleep and watching the sun rise over Stryker Lake.

I made myself eggs and toast, showered, and dressed in my uniform, wondering if I'd get to keep wearing it, even though it was hot and unflattering. It was possible friends and family would hold out against the crazy scheme and Louise would *not* get the required signatures.

The blackbirds created their own racket. Most mornings it seemed like they welcomed me to the day, happy I'd share the sun glistening on the lake's ripples, the breeze stirring up smells of the prairie and fresh beginnings. Today, though, I caught a ripe scent of something rotten by the lake, a dead fish or other animal. And the birds' racket sounded like they were blaming me for all the ills of the world. Maybe they were yelling at me to go back to bed and forget the whole day. Even though I knew it was my bad mood talking and I tried to tell myself to quit being so dramatic, I couldn't seem to lift my spirits.

Not even the garden cheered me as it usually did. Something was eating my tomatoes, and a closer inspection revealed the horror of potato bugs. I might be down on all things Mom these days, but some of her upbringing stuck with me. The part about being connected to the Earth and all living creatures ran deeply in me. However, there was a limit to my tolerance, and potato bugs pushed that line. I felt certain the name wasn't technical, and it might not be the same insect people called potato bug in other parts of the country. These were slimy abominations with pinchers. As far as I knew, the only way to rid yourself of potato bugs was to pick them off by hand. And man, you'd have to go a long way to find an uglier bug.

I swiped at sweat on my forehead. Heading into another day of scorching weather. Maybe Poupon and I could slip off to a lake and spend the day on a blow-up raft. It would beat the heck out of sweltering in this uniform.

It was a relief when the sound of a vehicle roaring over the hill brought me to the front yard.

The road ended in my yard, so anyone coming this far was on their way to see me. Maybe it was Dad coming home from work. Or Louise apologizing and saying she'd stop the recall.

When Carly's black pickup emerged through the dust, I broke into a grin. She was exactly the cure for my blues. Now twenty-one, Carly had been my ward for a few years, and she'd always be my favorite niece.

In true Carly fashion, she drove about fifteen miles an hour faster than I thought prudent and braked on the other side of my fence, raising a cloud of dust. She bounded out of the pickup and through the gate, stopping to ruffle Poupon's ears as he stood in the yard to greet her.

"What are you doing here so early? Want some coffee?" I half turned to the house.

She caught up to me. "Naw. I'm taking off for Lincoln. I promised Susan to be there to move our stuff to the new place."

Carly was a year younger than my little sister, Susan. That was how it sometimes worked out when your parents decided to have nine children. Susan had graduated last year from the University of Nebraska (Go Big Red), and Carly was about to start her junior year. Susan had her first real job in Lincoln, and she and Carly were living together, along with Susan's best friend and longtime roommate, Saskatchewan, or Sask, as he was affectionately known.

Having Carly home for the summer had been wonderful. Since cancer had robbed us of Glenda nine years ago, I'd been Carly's surrogate mother. I wasn't a great substitute for my amazing sister, but I loved Carly with all my heart. She'd gone missing for almost two years, and it had shredded me. Now, I wanted to keep her in my sights 24/7, but I knew enough to let her go, even if it tore me up. I tried not to let her see how much I hated sending her off again when summer ended. I might not be her real mother, but I suspected this wrenching sense of loss was what was meant by the empty-nest syndrome.

"I'm glad you came to say goodbye. When do you think you'll be coming back?" Keeping it light. Upbeat. My heart was not breaking because she'd been at Louise's last night and hadn't stopped by or called.

In the morning sunlight, Carly's light dusting of freckles looked like gold flecks. Her blond hair, still wet from the shower, hung halfway down her back, and she wore gym shorts, flip-flops, and a Husker T-shirt I thought might have been her father's. Poupon inched to position his head under her dangling hand, and she absently ran her fingers through his apricot curls.

"It'll probably be a week or more before I can get back. We're on track to start haying the big meadow this week. Rope thinks we'll have enough hay to get us through the winter." She'd inherited her grandfather's sizable ranch and planned to return to run it after she finished school.

"With all the spring rain and your herd reduced, I'm sure it'll work out fine." I tried to sound casual but was afraid where she was heading with this.

She shifted from one foot and tapped her flip-flop on the heel of her other foot. "Rope's getting old. Tired." Her intense focus urged me to understand her meaning and say yes.

I hooked my thumbs in my utility belt. I didn't have it fully loaded with my gun and flashlight, though cuffs dangled from the loop in back. "I can't commit to the job. You know that."

She thrust her hip out, a sure sign she was not happy with my response. "That's the thing. You *can* commit. I saw Dahlia at the rodeo and the parade. She had a ton of signatures. Louise is sure it's going to happen."

This was a stinging slap of betrayal. "You talked to Louise about me?"

She tossed her head back, her blue eyes bright. "Oh, come on. She's family. Am I supposed to shun her because you're mad at her?"

*Yes. That's exactly what you should do.* I mentally slapped myself. "No, she's your aunt the same as I am."

She grinned in that mischievous Carly way she'd had since she was in diapers. "I wouldn't say the same, exactly. But yeah, my aunt. Anyway, you don't need to wait for the recall. You could resign. Save us some time."

Indignation rolled in the bottom of my gut, gaining girth as it gathered speed. "You think I'll lose a recall? People know Ted will be appointed, and that'll leave Chester County in a pickle." Unless Chester County appointed me. Would that be irony? Coincidence? Or about the stupidest thing I could do.

Carly gave an uncommitted eyebrow waggle. "Why take a chance when you can take charge and resign now?"

"Or Louise could drop this whole ridiculous process and let me keep my job."

Carly widened her eyes in exasperation. "Okay, sure. But then in a year you'll need to run for reelection. And every four years after that. But, if you walk away now, you can take the foreman job at the Bar J. Never have to campaign again."

While never campaigning again and having a certain security sounded nice, the idea of quitting made me queasy. If I resigned, allowed them to appoint Ted as sheriff, I'd lose. Everything.

It wasn't so much Ted would get away with cheating on me and creating a family with Roxy and even getting his job back, though that didn't thrill me. It was that quitting would be like admitting I'd done something wrong. And I hadn't. "I know you don't understand, but I like being sheriff. I'm good at it. I don't want to be run out of the job because Louise is butt hurt."

"Have you talked to Granddad about this? He's going to tell you not to cut your nose off to spite your face."

I grimaced at her.

"And Grandma—"

I spun away from her before she could go any further. I hadn't healed enough yet to talk about my mother.

She grabbed my arm. "You may not want to hear it, but Grandma would tell you to meditate on it and you'd find the answer. Well, I don't need to meditate. I can tell you right now, you don't belong as sheriff. You are meant to be on a ranch. And I need someone. Not next year or the year after. Right now."

It rankled me that another family member tugged at me to do what they wanted me to do and tried to make it sound like they had my best interests at heart. "So, you want me to quit my job and run your ranch for two years, and then you'll come back and then what? We'll run it together until we have a falling-out and ruin our relationship?"

She bristled up, sparks in her eyes. "I don't know why you're being so stubborn. We'd make a great team."

The last thing I wanted to do was fight with Carly. Yet, my dander was up, and I raised my voice. "Family shouldn't be in business together."

She matched my volume. "I need you, and with the recall, it's like it's meant to be. If you don't take this job, I'm going to have to quit school and do it myself."

That rattled me. "You can't quit school. This—" The roar of a diesel engine stopped me, and Carly and I spun around to stare at the hill, waiting to see what disaster would strike next.

# 11

I was surprised when Maureen's silver Ford F-150 popped over the ridge and drove up. Even more surprising, the back doors on either side opened, and Roxy and Sarah both slid out.

Roxy reached into the back seat and, after a second, pulled Beau out and set him on the ground. Sarah leaned in, I assumed to unbuckle her own toddler.

Poupon gave a welcoming woof to his hands-down favorite living thing on the planet, Beau.

Carly turned curious eyes to me. "What the hell is this about?"

I shrugged and waited for the triumvirate to make their way through the gate.

Roxy wore capris in a blue and pink floral pattern, not at all in her usual Western flair. Her hair was fluffed in a way that probably cost her a half hour at minimum, and she wore a full complement of makeup. She chatted and waved her hands at Sarah in an animated way, probably continuing a story she'd started in the pickup.

Sarah's face had a stoic quality, as if she'd been subjected to Roxy long enough. She wore cutoffs with one of Robert's plaid Western shirts buttoned over her baby bump, old tennis shoes, and her hair in a ponytail, which told me she hadn't intended to come to town today. Brie rode on her hip, and Sarah deposited her in the grass next to Beau as soon as they came through the gate.

Maureen looked as put together as she had yesterday. Her jeans remained crisp and clung to all the right places. Her blond hair bouncing with her stride along my cracked walk, Maureen looked like President of the Planet.

Brie clapped her hands in glee at Poupon, who had hurried over to the kids, nose down, tail wagging. He'd developed a fast affection for Beau when Roxy and Ted had a meltdown weeks after they'd had the baby and Poupon and I ended up caring for the little peanut. Frankly, I'd bonded with Beau, too, and not surprisingly liked him far more than I did either of his parents.

Maureen ignored the two kids, the dog, and Roxy's incessant blabber. She made her way to me and Carly. "Good morning, Kate."

I nodded, curious and amused to see the circus arrive at my house. I introduced Maureen and Carly. "She's here to help Kasey Weber." That seemed like the most accurate way to explain Maureen.

I hadn't told Carly about Dwayne, but she'd have heard about it by now. She dipped her head in Maureen's direction, no formal handshaking here, and said, "Man, that really sucks. He wasn't very old."

"And not too bright, apparently, or he wouldn't have been in a trailer with a buckin' bull." Maureen made a clicking noise in a what-can-you-say kind of way.

Naturally I didn't volunteer that Dwayne had probably been dead before he'd ended up in the trailer and so had no hand in being in the tight space with a dumb bull.

Carly looked taken aback by Maureen's dismissive statement. "Well, it's still a sad thing."

By then, Roxy and Sarah had joined us.

Roxy clapped her hands in almost the same way Brie had earlier. It was way cuter when a two-year-old did it. "Carly! It's a bonus getting to see you. You need to come over to dinner some night before you go back to school. I know Ted misses you, and I don't feel like we've seen my sweet step-daughter at all this summer."

Maybe Roxy thought calling Carly her stepdaughter was a special form of affection, but Carly's jaw jumped like she bit down on something sour. Her smile was less than sincere. "Too late. I'm on my way to Lincoln now."

Roxy fake pouted. "Oh, pooh."

Carly's gaze flicked to me, then quickly to Sarah, and all three of us did an internal eye roll.

Sarah said, "How's Rope getting along? I saw him at Dutch's last week, and he didn't look great."

*Thanks, Sarah.*

Carly shot me a meaningful look and answered Sarah. "He's hanging on but really wants to retire. I'm trying to convince Kate to take over."

Maureen watched this with interest. "Take over what?"

Carly summed it up quickly. "I inherited a ranch, and I need a manager."

Maureen assessed me. "And Kate can manage a ranch?"

Carly laughed. "I guess so. She kept Frog Creek in the black for a long time, and that place isn't half as good as the Bar J."

Maureen turned to me. "So why are you sheriff if you're such a good rancher?"

Roxy piped up, "Oh, Beau. No, no." She ran over to where the kids were petting Poupon. I couldn't see that any of them needed an intervention.

Sarah laughed at Roxy's obvious ploy to avoid dealing with why I lost my job.

Carly answered Maureen, "She ran for sheriff because when she got divorced, Ted's family kicked her off the ranch. But she doesn't need the job anymore, so I don't see why she doesn't manage the Bar J."

Sarah raised her eyebrows at me as if asking the same question.

I held up my hands. "Because I like being sheriff. Okay?" For emphasis, I repeated, "I actually like it."

Carly flicked her hand at me. "Whatever." She started across the yard, flip-flops smacking on her heels.

"Where are you going?" God, I hated her leaving in a huff, and I was embarrassed by the hurt in my voice.

She didn't turn back. "Gotta get on the road."

The rusty knife twisted in my heart when she didn't say goodbye, love ya, or promise to call me later.

Sarah watched Carly, then spun to me. One of the things I loved most about Sarah from the time we were knee-high to grasshoppers was her lack of sugar and hearts. Instead of giving me a hug with a gleam of sympathy in her eye, she smirked and said, "She's taking that well."

Sarah knew how bad I felt, so I tried to sound unconcerned. "She won't understand that it's not good for family to work together."

Sarah's face twisted in irritation. "Don't I know it."

I gave her a questioning look.

She waved her hand. "Oh, damn Garrett's being a jerk and really making a mess of things." She gave Maureen an aside. "Garrett is my older brother who ran off to make big bucks in Scottsdale as a lawyer and decided to come back with his son and take over." To me, she said, "He's decided he's in charge now and changing the way we've been doing things for years."

"Such as?" I asked.

Her mouth tightened, and her voice hardened. "You know we've been rotating pastures more often than Dad did. And Robert's balancing rations pretty often to compensate for the forage. It took us years of nudging and finagling to get Dad to go along with us. It's been working great. And all of the sudden, Garrett is questioning everything and wanting to go back to the way we used to do it."

"Are you sure he's against your plan? Maybe he just doesn't understand it."

Maureen let out a huff, and we both turned to her. She narrowed her eyes at me. "Do you hear yourself?"

*Hear myself, what?* I waited.

"Your knee-jerk reaction is to defend a man. You don't jump in to take sides with your friend, who obviously knows what she's talking about. No. You want her to rethink her position and accommodate the man."

"That's not—"

Sarah tapped her foot. "It's not? Why would you take Garrett's side? I haven't signed the recall against *you*. Where's your loyalty?"

They didn't give me a chance to think about what I'd said or why.

Maureen gave a sympathetic click of her tongue. "It's not just you, Kate. We've all been trained to do that. Look at Sarah, running to do her husband's bidding when he snaps his fingers. And Roxy having to hurry to her husband because he can't take care of his own baby."

Sarah drew her head back, clearly offended.

Before Sarah could deck Maureen, I stepped in. "Robert doesn't snap his fingers, and Sarah doesn't dance to his tune. There's a balance with her family, and Garrett is upsetting that."

Roxy rejoined us. "Did I hear you mention Garrett? Oh, Kate, he's just your type. Maybe we should plan a bowling night in Broken Butte or something. Me and Ted, Sarah and Robert, and you and Garrett."

Maureen stared at Roxy with the same expression I probably had looking at the potato bugs.

While we chattered about Garrett and family, the sun rose higher and dew evaporated from the grass. I wondered when they'd get to the point.

Sarah growled at Roxy. "Garrett isn't anybody's type, unless you like whining, entitled, spoiled brats."

"Oh." Roxy made big eyes at me like we were on the same side against Sarah. "Is someone not liking big brother staking a claim?"

Steam built behind Sarah's brown eyes, and I figured Roxy was about to get burned.

Maureen dismissed Roxy with a blink and said to me, "Recall and ranching aside, I'm glad you're still sheriff."

Now maybe they were getting to the point of their visit. I waited.

Animation flooded back to Roxy, and her chin started working like a bobblehead doll, making her curls bounce. "Can you believe what Trey did? I mean, I always liked him, but he's way out of line on this."

Sarah looked away from Roxy, that sour lemon pucker of tolerance on her face again. "I'm sure you know Gidget stirred up a hornet's nest and the state patrol's investigating Dwayne's death."

"Yeah?" I took them in, wondering where they were going with this.

Roxy blurted out, taking over from Sarah. "He's accusing Kasey of killing Dwayne. I mean, of all the things. He told her not to leave town."

I squinted at the ducks floating on the still surface of the lake. "The state patrol is taking lead on the investigation. I'm not involved." I didn't want to admit the reason I'd been cut out of the investigation was my own incompetence.

Maureen's voice sounded loaded with steel. "This is the way they do it. They put something out there and repeat it enough and eventually it seems normal. Next thing you know, Kasey's in custody and they've concocted a whole case against her. And they'll stack the jury and off she goes to prison."

Roxy nodded. Sarah watched me expectantly, intensity hitting me.

I held up my hand. "Who's 'they'?"

Irritation swept across Maureen's face, marring its smooth surface. "Men. This Trey Ridnour." She glanced at Roxy. "Her husband—all of them are probably in on it."

Roxy's Barbie doll face flushed in offense. "Hey!"

Maureen ignored her. "The good ol' boys will swoop in and solve this." She sneered on the word *solve*. "Because it will make them look good to have it wrapped up so fast." She zeroed in on Roxy. "They'll slap each other on the back, and your ex will be a hero." To me, she said, "You'll lose the election and end up out of a job again."

It sounded exaggerated to me, and I glanced at Sarah to share that split-second connection we had perfected in junior high. It meant we both noted whatever ridiculous thing that had happened, and we'd talk about it later, detailing our joint amusement or outrage. But Sarah was watching Maureen and gave an affirming dip of her strong chin.

I'd stand alone, I guessed. "If the only evidence they have is Gidget Bartels's claim, then it won't go far. I don't think there's cause for concern."

Roxy nudged my shoulder. "See? That's what I said. I mean, yeah, I can see how Trey might think Kasey has it in her to murder." She lowered her voice as if telling a secret. "I know Kasey can appear pretty and feminine, but she's tough, like a take-no-prisoners type personality."

"That can—"

She didn't need any input from me, apparently. "And with Dwayne having an affair with Gidget, Wrangler has motive, right? But, come on, they say someone wrenched Dwayne's neck."

"How did—"

I assumed Trey spilled the information on Dwayne's broken neck, since Roxy wasn't going to pause. "A woman couldn't strangle a man like that and then drag him under a bull. That's crazy."

It seemed Gidget and Dwayne's affair wasn't a well-kept secret.

Maureen's eyes closed for a second, as if an arrow pierced her forehead. "I'm strong enough to break a neck." The way she said it, it almost sounded like a threat to Roxy.

"How's Kasey handling all of this?" I asked.

Since reading the room—or in this case, the yard—had never been in Roxy's toolbox, she blathered on. "Well, frankly, she's not doing herself any favors. She told Trey to go…" She glanced behind her at the kids to make sure they couldn't hear her, then leaned closer to me and whispered, "Eff himself. I don't think she's taking it seriously at all. This morning when I got there—super early because I thought she'd need me—she was out feeding the bulls when she told me about it."

Maureen tucked a strand of honeyed hair behind her ear. "Apparently, Trey was there yesterday before we arrived. She never said a thing about it until this morning."

Roxy butted in again. "Maureen got to Kasey's after I'd been there awhile." She allowed a slight pause to make sure we registered her sacrifice to friendship outweighed Maureen's. "So Maureen and I decided we need a woman—you—to be on the inside. But I know how stubborn you can be, so I called Sarah to help us get you on board."

*Me, stubborn?* I tossed Sarah a questioning look. "You think I need to investigate this to clear Kasey?"

Sarah cocked her hip. "Look, I think this recall isn't a shoo-in and clearing Kasey will convince people you know what you're doing."

Wow. Way to sucker-punch me in the feels.

She tilted her head in a way I'd seen many times. It said I may not like the truth, but I'd best face it. "Aren't you tired of all this good-ol'-boys bullshit? We've put up with it long enough."

Oh, they wanted to slam a stick in the spoke of the social fabric of the Sandhills. That was an even bigger goal than investigating a murder. I didn't laugh. But I wanted to.

She probably knew that, because her voice hardened. "I've had it with this whole stupid system. I've got a business degree, was going to be a CPA. And then Dad begged Robert to come back and manage the ranch. Not me, his daughter. Robert. Who grew up in town, not on the ranch like I did."

She held up her hand. "Not that it means he's not a hell of a rancher, like you are, because he is. But damn it, it's my heritage."

I acknowledged her qualification.

"So, we change our life plans. And for the last ten years have been working our asses off. Paying tribute to King Alden, being patient."

Sarah's father, Alden Haney, ruled his family like a despot. Sarah had inherited his qualities of strength, smarts, and determination, and he probably took more pride in her beauty.

Sarah's eyes flashed. "It hasn't been easy. And it's not like we're rolling in the dough. We'd have been so much better off financially if we'd stuck to the original plan. If I'd gotten my CPA certification and Robert had finished his engineering degree, who knows where we'd be now. Instead of being hired help for my dad."

I knew all of this, but Sarah was on a tear, and I didn't dare stop her.

"But, you know, it was all okay because we really believed we were doing it for ourselves because we'd inherit the ranch someday." And now hard-headed and tough Sarah teared up. A function of pregnancy hormones, I assumed, since I'd seen her ride half a day with a broken arm and not utter a sigh. "Then the favored son returns home. Halo intact. And ten years of our hard work dribbles down the drain as Garrett gets Alden's blessing and plans on taking over the whole operation."

A storm built on Maureen's face. "That doesn't surprise me."

Roxy stomped her foot. "It's not fair. I didn't know you had a degree in accounting. You're so smart. You and Kate. But if you get a job, who will take care of Brie? I think a child should be raised at home, not some day care place where they neglect kids, or even worse."

No one bothered to respond to Roxy, who missed the point, as usual.

"Garrett won't really cut you out." As soon as I said it, I wanted to take it back.

Sarah and Maureen both glared at me.

Sarah folded her arms. "So, now you're an expert on that son of a bitch?"

Roxy snapped her head to the kids and seemed relieved they trundled toward the garden with Poupon in tow.

I held my hands up in surrender. "Sorry. I don't know Garrett that well."

I didn't, but my impression was of a guy who was trying to do the right thing. "It would be really crappy of him to take over. Have you talked to him about it?"

Maureen shifted in impatience. "Let's take them down one at a time. Right now, we need to clear Kasey. So, I'm going to send Trey Ridnour on a red herring in the bucking bull world."

Roxy gasped in her overly dramatic way. "What are you going to say?"

"There's a group of about a dozen cronies who are deciding what bulls make it to the bigger competitions. It's all payola and back-slapping. I've wanted to expose them for a while now, but I'm playing in their sandbox and can't really take a shit there. So, I'll suggest to Trooper Trey that Dwayne got sideways with them, and they took him out."

Sarah frowned at her. "You're going to frame someone?"

Maureen gave a mirthless chuckle. "Nothing will come of it. They protect their own. But it will buy us some time."

Roxy scrunched her face. "Time for what?"

Maureen's manner made me think of a snake slithering through tall grass, sneaky and deadly. "For Kate to find the real killer."

# 12

By the time Sarah, Maureen, and Roxy loaded up the toddlers and left, they had me fired up about the slow advance of Sandhillers to embrace equality. I shoved aside the facts that it was Louise, a woman, who'd filed the recall. It was my mother who'd thrown my family into a tailspin and devastated Dad. Not to mention Dahlia, who continued to thwart my life at every opportunity. I'd spent the last three years proving to Grand County that a woman could be a better sheriff than the men they'd elected in recent memory—namely, Ted. And I thought Maureen might be right, I was about to be elbowed out by the men, whether they deliberately did it, such as Ted, or were merely falling back into their comfort zone, as Trey might be doing.

Poupon and I zipped through Hodgekiss, back to full throttle after the holiday. Several pickups and cars lined Main Street in front of the post office, where, no doubt, word had already spread that Dwayne had been murdered.

We caught up with Kasey by the corrals, where she was tossing hay bales into the bed of her pickup. The sun pulled no punches this morning. It wanted the world to know who was boss and beat down with authority.

Kasey paused long enough to notice who drove up, then went back to chucking bales.

I walked to her. "You feed alfalfa in the middle of the summer? I'd think there'd be enough grass to keep the bulls happy."

She slipped me a side-eye and panted, "These aren't regular bulls that only need enough energy to screw. They have a job to do that requires lots of muscle."

Since she didn't act inclined to chat, I went straight at it. "I'd like to ask a few questions."

She spun around and pounded her gloved hands onto her hips. "I suppose you're here to accuse me of killing Dwayne, too."

Luckily, I wasn't easily frightened, because she looked ready to tear my head off. "Nope. I'm here because your friends asked me to help you out. They're afraid you're getting railroaded into a murder charge."

She snorted. "They'd be right. Which friends?"

I told her about the early meeting. "Why don't you tell me what Dwayne was up to and why someone might want to kill him."

She wiped at sweat on her forehead with her arm and glowered at the hills. "I wish I knew."

I waited, giving her an impatient scowl of my own.

A flash of irritated concession passed across her face, and she started talking. "When I married Dwayne, I thought I'd finally hit the lottery. You gotta know I came from nothing. Dad couldn't hold a job, was drunk more than he was sober. We were the kind of family that skipped out in the middle of the night owing three months' rent."

That would account for her rough exterior and that spiteful personality.

She sneered. "I know people don't like me."

I gave her a cocked head. "Can't see as you do much to improve it."

Dwayne had shown up in the Sandhills a while back married to Christopher Walsh's daughter, Helen. Christopher Walsh lived in Chester County and owned one of the oldest and biggest ranches in the West. Adored by her wealthy father, Helen never had to work. Like many in her situation, she'd drifted from one thing to another. Didn't finish college. Tried her luck at running the lumberyard but got bored. She excelled at hitting jackpots in Vegas (though no one knew how much she played before her much-touted payouts). On one of her trips to Vegas, she'd come home with the charming and handsome Dwayne Weber.

Their marriage had lasted about five years. Long enough for him to have squirreled away some money. That surprised no one. But what rankled respectable churchgoers like Aileen and Myrna was that Dwayne and Kasey's relationship predated the end of the marriage by a year or more.

Spoiled and entitled Helen might not have been anyone's favorite person, but having one of their own treated in such a way didn't sit well with the locals. When Dwayne and Kasey started raising bucking bulls and had surprising and early success in such a competitive business, well, that didn't make them the most popular Sandhillers, either. People out here applauded success, but not too much. In fact, they were happier if you were doing slightly worse than they were.

Her lip curled. "Why should I? Everything I have I've worked my ass off to get. Dwayne and I were starting to really hit it big. When Woody made it to the NFR three years ago, I thought we'd arrived, you know?" She showed a crack in her shell.

She referred to the National Finals Rodeo, the yearly Super Bowl of rodeos in Las Vegas with big payouts. Maybe I could get her talking and soften her up. "Woody. That always struck me as a weird name for a buckin' bull."

A hint of a smile tipped her lips. "Cartoon characters. Dwayne and I thought it would make us more memorable. A branding kind of thing. Woody was our first. Then Yosemite Sam, Lucky Luke, Alameda Slim." She swallowed hard. "Pecos Bill."

I hoped I sounded sincere. "That's impressive to be so successful in such a short time."

She drilled me with an icy stare. "You'd think, right? But Pecos died last winter, and that's when things started going south."

"But you have insurance, right?"

Fire ignited in her face. "Dwayne let it lapse. He was supposed to take care of all of that, but he's such a fuck-up." She banged a fist on the pickup and winced, maybe from pain in her hand or in her heart. "*Was.* So then, Dwayne quit entering bulls in events. And when we did, he was putting in the weaker bulls, and we quit winning. Which meant fewer qualifying performances, and the money just dried up."

I struggled to find a way to respond. "Man, that's rough."

She snorted again to let me know what a stupid thing I'd said. "And then it was Lucky Luke. When he got struck by lightning, I lost it. Really fell apart. Dwayne had to haul his body away so I couldn't see it. I don't know what's worse, to lose a business you've worked so hard for, or to lose someone you love so much."

She seemed more broken up over Lucky Luke's death than Dwayne's. "You're not helping me much. I'd like to find Dwayne's killer before they can pin it on you."

She pulled her lips back like a snarling wolf. "I'm not going to cry and snivel about Dwayne dying. The truth is, he was running this business into the ground. We weren't all that lovey-dovey for a while now. And I'll be a lot better off without having to drag his ass along with me."

So much for strong women and honesty. Can't say I didn't have sympathy for having a lying, cheating, dud of a husband, but her nastiness took the juice out of it.

I didn't think she killed Dwayne, or she'd be trying to cover her tracks instead of spouting out a motive for getting rid of him.

I wasn't getting anywhere with her. "Even if you won't do anything to help your cause, I'm going to keep looking. If you think of anyone who might want to kill Dwayne, give me a call."

She gave me that wolfish smile. "If I do, don't be surprised if they're related to you."

The way she said it made me feel like she'd released spiders across my back.

# 13

Poupon and I made it to the courthouse a few minutes past nine. Not before the County Assessor-Clerk Ethel Bender and the Treasurer Betty Paxton had punched in, of course.

After parking in my designated spot in back, we clambered up the stairs to the main floor to the smell of scorched coffee. Thursday was Betty's day to make coffee. That meant I could see the bottom of a full cup through the weak brew. Ethel liked it strong and bitter, so on Mondays and Wednesdays it might be standing at the top of the stairs ready to slap my face.

The two county offices faced off on the west side of the building, separated by a wide shiny corridor that reminded me of a fresh pan of Grandma Ardith's caramel. The county commissioners' room and general meeting room, which served as coffee station, took up a portion of the building next to Betty's office, with the wide corridor leading to the front doors opening alongside it.

My office was at the east end of the dark hall. Once a storage room, it had a few narrow windows toward the ceiling. With only enough room for a desk, a couple of old metal filing cabinets, and Poupon's luxurious and ridiculously expensive memory foam bed, we didn't spend much time there. The county's holding cell was behind a metal door off my office. Until I'd become sheriff, that cell hadn't seen much use.

All those citizens who thought I wasn't doing much law enforcing must not know I'd recently used that cell. Not that locking people up made me feel accomplished.

Today I needed to dig up Gidget and Wrangler's address before I took off to Broken Butte to talk to them. I knew they ranched somewhere in that area but didn't know what direction. I could do that on my phone, but it was good to check in to the office in case someone was keeping tabs on me. This recall had me paying too much attention to other people paying attention to me.

Poupon made for my desk chair before I lunged in front of him and plopped down. "Stretch out on that fancy bed. For what I spent on it, I could have had a weekend in Denver." If I stayed with my sister Diane and let her take me to dinner. But, you know, gas was expensive.

My old desktop, Bessy, might be wheezing her last, but she fired up and would live another day at least. I got the address and checked the time. If I took off now, I'd be back to town before noon, maybe with a suspect for Dwayne's murder to poke Trey with. After all, a man whose wife was having an affair might be mad enough to kill.

I coaxed Poupon off his bed and out the door when my phone rang. A wavery voice responded to my greeting. "They're back. This time I have proof."

He didn't need to identify himself or who he thought had returned. "Okay, Ralph. You stay inside, and I'll be right up."

Ralph Stumpf had to be ninety if he was a day. Since his "bride of seventy years," as he called her, passed away last year, Ralph called me every week or so for something. Last week, he'd been convinced "the hoodlums" had snuck into his house and stolen his wallet. I'd found it in the refrigerator next to the Miracle Whip.

Ralph lived one block west of Main Street in the last house at the top of the hill. It took only a couple of minutes for us to park out front under a cottonwood. Since Ralph liked Poupon, I let him out of the cruiser, and we tromped up the front porch. I knocked and opened the door. "It's Sheriff Fox."

Ralph tottered around the corner from the kitchen, a BB gun clutched in his arms. A smile lit his face. "And you brung your pup."

Ralph had spent a lifetime as a hired man on the Becketts' place in the southeast corner of the county. As a young man, he'd probably been tall and strong, but now he walked stooped over, a bulge between his shoulder blades; his glasses were so thick and heavy they seemed to drag down his head that was topped with a few wisps of white. A dusting of whiskers looked like snow on his face. "This time they left the door wide open. There's tracks in the mud."

I followed him through the kitchen, glad he had a house cleaner who came once a week to tidy up, so there were only a couple of dishes in the sink and not much mess otherwise.

Ralph picked up a candy dish from the counter. As he always did, he thrust it toward me. "Have one of these Werther's. Fern always loved 'em, and I keep 'em 'cause they remind me of her."

Who doesn't love a good hard candy? I unwrapped it and asked, "Is your gun loaded?"

He cackled. "Naw. I can't see to hit nothing, so what's the use?"

The door off the back of the kitchen still hung open. There were, indeed, mud tracks. But when I studied their path, I saw they ended across the kitchen, where Ralph's rubber-soled slippers rested on folded newspaper. My professional assessment was that Ralph had been out filling the bird feeder or watering his tomatoes and walked inside, leaving the door open. He'd come back in later to discover the open door and mud on the floor.

"I see what you mean," I said. I pulled out my phone and took a couple of pictures so he'd know I was taking it seriously. "Have you discovered anything missing?"

Ralph hmphed. "They musta been hungry 'cause I had a sandwich sittin' on the counter and they took it. Guess they needed it more than me."

Out of the corner of my eye, I noticed Poupon in the living room, slurping what looked like white bread off the coffee table.

"Whoever it is, they don't seem to mean you harm. I'll keep an eye out and drive by a couple of times a day. Be sure to give me a call if you have another problem. In the meantime, I'll spread the word around, and maybe someone knows something."

Ralph walked me to the front door. "You're a good one, Sheriff. I know

I'm an old codger and this ain't a big crime, but I sure appreciate you takin' the time to see me."

I patted his shoulder. "That's what I'm here for."

Before we headed out of town, my phone rang again. Betty Paxton, the treasurer, gave a friendly hello and then, "Leonard Bingham is here needing a pickup inspection for a Dodge he bought in Spearfish. Where are you?"

I told her about Ralph and that I'd be back to the courthouse right away. Got to keep those citizens happy.

Betty gushed. "You're so kind to help Ralph out that way. You know, when Ted was sheriff, he never took the time to help the old folks out like you do. I know you help Beverly every time a light bulb needs changing or her furnace filters go bad."

If everyone in the county had as high an opinion of me as Betty, even Louise and Dahlia wouldn't be able to push for a recall.

I made it back to the courthouse and chatted up Leonard while I did the perfunctory inspection and didn't once mention I thought he'd made a bad deal on a lemon. I stopped in my office to drop off the clipboard.

A weird thumping sounded on the outside wall of my office. The courthouse wasn't typically a place with lots of activity. Maybe two or three times a day a citizen pulled up out front, came in to pay taxes, get a driver's license, or register a vehicle. Occasionally someone needed a building permit or a vehicle inspection. Mostly, it was Ethel, her assistant, Brittany Ostrander, and Betty sending echoes in the quiet building. Once in a lunar cycle, Betty might turn her radio to a country station and twangy notes floated through the hall. But that was rare, and I hadn't figured out what precipitated her outbursts of music.

The tapping sounded again, loud enough for Poupon to open his eyes and maybe consider lifting his head.

Deciding he needed a little sunshine and exercise, I said, "Let's investigate. It's what they pay me for, and me getting paid is what keeps you in kibble, so you can be my deputy."

He closed his eyes but capitulated when I clapped my hands. Together we left my office, heading for the back stairs. Voices came from Ethel's office. It sounded like Ethel gave serious instructions to someone, and I felt bad for the poor citizen wanting to register a new double-wide or obtain a permit for a pole barn. They'd have to endure the recitation of statutes that I suspected Ethel carried verbatim in her head.

We burst through the downstairs door into dazzling summer sunshine and the smell of fresh-cut grass. The worst part of the sheriff job was being indoors on phenomenal days. That was if you didn't count having to issue tickets to friends and family and the occasional serious crime.

The good thing about it was that my schedule was flexible enough I didn't feel imprisoned often. The inconvenient thing about the job was that planning my life could get dicey since emergencies weren't scheduled events. But a regular paycheck was good.

I looked down to Poupon as we walked toward the east side of the building where I'd heard the tapping sounds. "We're done with inside for the day." It might be hot, but outside felt a whole lot better than my cramped office.

And the smell of stale coffee and burnt popcorn couldn't compete with the summer scent of cut grass and sun warming the earth. Maybe the heat would stir up a thunderstorm—at least, that was what I and all the citizens of Grand County hoped.

Not expecting to find anything except maybe a bit of rain gutter that might have detached to scrape and bump along the side of the building, I tilted my head to the sunshine and kept walking, thinking about getting on the road to Broken Butte.

I turned the corner of the building and stopped in shock. "What the heck?" I shouted.

My volume and tone startled the three boys, which made the two standing on the grass under the window stagger, causing the third boy, who stood on their shoulders, to lose his balance and topple to the ground. The one hitting the ground got his wind knocked out. He let out a hitching noise, but I didn't see any breaks or blood. Kids are kind of like rubber, so I took the Dad parenting approach and didn't panic.

The other two, my twin nine-year-old nephews Mose and Zeke, looked like terrified children carved from tree trunks by a sadistic woodworker. They didn't move, maybe didn't breathe.

The screen from one of the narrow windows in my office was bent, barely hanging on to the frame with the netting torn.

I narrowed my gaze on my nephews. "What are you doing?"

By now, the kid on the ground sat up. Tony Haney, Sarah's ten-year-old nephew. Garrett's son tightened his mouth and gave me a blank look, not exactly faked innocence, but more like he didn't care.

Poupon sank into the building's shade and watched the boys.

Mose, the taller of my nephews, said, "We weren't doing nothing." He wore a plain blue T-shirt a size or two too small. His jeans had holes in the knees, and his running shoes sported more than a few extra openings.

Zeke, only an inch shorter but with more charm, flashed his dimples. "Hey, Aunt Kate. We didn't know you were in town today." His clothes were equally as shabby as Mose's. Louise would take them school shopping next month. They were eking out the final wear from last year's supply, or more likely earlier this spring from the rate they grew.

Tony stood up and brushed himself off. Grass stains not only marked both knees of his jeans, but now the back of his logo T-shirt showed swathes of green. Maybe I could give Garrett a few pointers for removing grass stains. I imagined, since he'd been a busy attorney until recently, he didn't have a lot of kid-maintenance knowledge. Tony buried his fists in his pockets and looked away with an air of dismissal.

"You thought I'd be gone, and you were, what? Going to break into my office?"

Mose and Zeke stared at me with round eyes. Even Zeke seemed to understand they'd been busted. As the silence grew, Mose struggled to answer. "W-w-we thought you might, you know, have, um, you know, we thought, you know..." He trailed off and looked to Zeke for help, giving me no clue what they were after.

Zeke gave it a shot. "So, you know how there's a evidence room? Like in the shows, where they keep the money and drugs and guns and stuff?"

Kid stuff aside, this seemed more involved than Mose and Zeke's usual shenanigans. Previously, they'd been caught pretending to be on a cattle drive from Texas to Montana after seeing *Lonesome Dove* and tried herding Louise's chickens. Most of the hens scattered over the hills and had probably been eaten by coyotes. Once, the twins had gone on African safari with

Louise's broom and mop for spears, gotten lost, destroyed the cleaning tools, and ended up late for supper moments before Louise had called the family to form a search party. There was the time they'd dug a cave behind Mom and Dad's house and nearly killed themselves when it collapsed. But they'd never, as far as I knew, attempted a B & E, at the sheriff's office, no less.

I had an idea whose brain fart this was. Tony still gazed down the street, as if ignoring us. "Does your dad know where you are?" I asked Tony.

He slowly brought his attention to me. How does a kid that age get so cool? "Does your dad know where you are?"

Zeke gave an inappropriate snicker but clammed up when I gave him the evil eye, honed as an aunt but perfected as sheriff.

Tony was a good-looking kid, with thick chestnut-colored hair, like his father and Sarah, expressive brown eyes, tall and thin, but not gangly. I'd felt sorry for him when they'd moved back. He seemed lonely and unsure of himself. I'd encouraged the twins to befriend him.

But the last two months I'd come to see a side of him that made me wonder. Moving from a city like Scottsdale to the Sandhills had to be hard on a kid. I didn't know the details about his mother and what kind of relationship they had, supportive or absent. Sarah didn't like her, I knew. But Sarah also wasn't fond of her brother, and I wasn't sure she had a lot of affection for Tony, either.

Mose said, "Tony's spending the day with us. His dad had to go to Broken Butte."

When Mom had taken off, Dad didn't have the stomach to keep living in the house where they'd spent their forty years together. He'd given it to Louise and her clan of five kids, and they'd moved from the tiny ranch house they rented five miles outside of town to the two-story home sitting on the south side of the railroad tracks.

I imagined kid mischief would take the boys into the hills behind their house, not across the tracks into town. "What are you doing hanging around the courthouse?"

Mose took that easy one. "Mom had to do business. She didn't want to leave us at home."

"She said she didn't trust us to be good." Zeke showed the whites of his eyes in exasperation at his mother's unreasonable assumption.

When I tilted my head in a clear way that said she'd been right to doubt them, Zeke turned red and gave a sheepish shrug.

I held my arms out to shepherd the boys toward the front of the courthouse. "We're going to find your mother and let her in on your criminal activity."

Zeke, the fast talker, gave it a shot. "Aw, man, Kate. Can't we work this out? We'll do, like, chores for you or something."

Mose jumped on that. "Right. We can mow your grass."

"Done."

"Well, hoe your garden, then," Zeke said.

"Walk Poupon?" Mose sounded more desperate.

Tony didn't offer anything. He maintained that passive expression that seemed odd for a kid.

I wasn't a parent or a child psychologist. But I knew that little humans had lots of needs and if they felt scared or alone or at risk, sometimes the only way they knew to react was to get into trouble. Maybe I'd have liked to swat Tony's behind to knock that belligerent look from his face, but I doubted that would help anyone.

By the time we got to the front door, Mose and Zeke had left off pleading. They might have seen the futility of it, or they might be terrified out of words by the thought of what Louise would do when I told her about their tomfoolery. Tony got to the door first and stopped, making no move to open it. Mose and Zeke stopped behind him, and Poupon joined the group.

I had to reach over everyone to open the door and hover over them until they all entered.

Louise was rounding the corner from the west end of the hall, hair that was neither long nor short, a dark beigy non-color, shapeless against her head. She saw the boys, the dog, and then her eyes found mine. She stopped dead center in the hall, making her chins quiver, and slammed her hands on her hips with a force I thought might crack bone if she hadn't been so well insulated. "What in the Sam Hill is going on?"

I nodded to Mose and Zeke. "You want to tell her, or should I?"

Louise held up her hand. "I don't need anyone to tell me anything. I see you with my sons and their playmate and I'm speechless."

That made me pause. Not exactly how I expected her to react.

"I mean, I thought you knew better." Apparently not totally speechless. She hadn't taken her focus from me, so I figured she meant me. "You can't get to me using my kids. I'm going through with this, and you won't stop me."

I held up my hand. "Whoa. I don't know what you're talking about, but—"

She planted her foot in a powerful step toward me. The boys huddled in the face of her rage, probably as flummoxed as I was that she didn't seem to care about them. "I did it, got all the signatures. Okay? Are you happy? I filed the recall. I know you thought I wouldn't and that you and the whole family would laugh at me. Poor Louise, she lost again. But I did it. And do you know why? I did it to save this family."

I couldn't come up with an answer to that. Recall. Yeah, that was an issue. To save the family? Didn't know how to dismantle that messed-up narrative. But I hadn't even told her about her juvenile delinquents.

She took another step, and the boys moved to the side, leaving open space between me and Louise. "You thought, 'Oh, Louise will make some noise, but then she'll drop the recall and I'll go about doing whatever I want to do whenever I want to because I'm entitled to.' Well, no one ever showed you the consequences of your actions before. It's time you take responsibility for what you've done to this family."

Did she need therapy? For sure some anger management. What about delusions? Was she having a psychotic break? Did she need medication? Restraints? I'd discovered a while back that she'd had a breakdown years before; maybe she needed an intervention.

I tried to redirect and deescalate, techniques used in law enforcement but that I'd already worked out being the fifth kid in a string of nine. "Recall. Sure. But I think you need to know what Mose and Zeke—"

She snapped out her hand and latched onto Mose's arm. He let out a startled shriek, and she jerked him with her as she rolled toward me and the front door. "Don't try to change the subject and use my kids against me. Come on." She flicked her head back to let Tony know she included him.

Louise was like a tank rushing to a battlefield, and I stepped out of her way before she ran me down. She and the three boys barreled out of the courthouse.

I hadn't gathered my breath to sweep the shards of reason into a pile when Ethel Bender lumbered around the corner in her stretch pants, shapeless black shirt, and slippers—because her ankles were always swollen. She reached into the pocket of her pants and pulled out a plastic sandwich bag. "Who's my sweet boy?"

Poupon knew the answer to that one. He wagged that stumpy tail and held his regal head high, practically prancing to Ethel. The plastic bag crinkled, and Poupon waited patiently, even plying Ethel with an adoring gaze. The shameless suck-up.

Ethel pulled out a bite-sized bit of what looked like a medium-rare rib eye. There were several bits in the bag. "What a perfect gentleman." She seemed to appreciate the way he politely accepted the bite, wolfed it down, and waited for another.

Not wanting to witness my traitorous deputy, I skirted around Ethel on my way back to my office, even though I'd promised myself to spend the rest of the day outside.

The sweetness left Ethel's tone. "So that's it, then. Louise got the required signatures, and I'll have to set a date for the recall."

I'd assumed that was the business they'd conducted, but when Ethel spoke it out loud, it felt like a railroad nail driven into my gut.

"I'm going to have to schedule it in the next few weeks or it'll be too close to the general election." Ethel sounded put out.

Not sure what she expected from me, I tried to sound neutral. "I'm sure you know what's best."

She murmured to Poupon, maybe not bothering with real words before looking up at me with a scowl to pair with her wrinkles and hair so gray it looked bruised. "That's just it. I didn't know best. There hasn't been a recall in this county since I've been clerk. And that's over thirty years. So, I had to spend hours looking up the protocol and calling all over the state to find out how it's done."

Betty Paxton shot around the corner from her office. Today she wore a jersey dress with splotches in bright primary colors. Cinched at her waist, or what should have been a waist, and hemmed above the knee. I guessed she'd rocked it twenty-five years ago, about the time she'd first spiked her short blond hair. "You leave off that pity party. It takes about ten minutes to look up statute, and the only reason you called around to your NACO cronies is because you wanted to gossip and grouse."

NACO would be Nebraska Association of County Officials, of which both Ethel and Betty had their share of abettors and detractors. The association met twice a year for conventions, usually in the eastern end of the state. Betty and Ethel never missed one, but never attended together.

Ethel rotated her shapelessness around to address Betty. "How would you know? The treasurer isn't responsible for special elections."

Betty patted my shoulder. "Don't pay any attention to her. She gets owly when someone asks her to do any work."

Ethel wadded up the plastic sandwich bag and shoved it into her pants pocket. "Any work? You're kidding me. I have to schedule a date, solicit poll workers, get ads made up and scheduled, ballots printed." She narrowed her eyes to me. " Do you have any idea what this will entail?"

When I'd run against Ted over three years ago, Ethel had made it clear she camped under Ted's banner. Betty had unflinchingly supported me. I didn't question whether Betty's loyalty stemmed from her abiding animosity for Ethel. But over the last couple of years, Ethel and I had worked together out of necessity. I'd hoped maybe we were coming to some understanding, if not friendship. But this recall had set us back further than where we'd started.

"To be clear," I said to Ethel. "It's not me who filed the recall."

Ethel was so steamed she didn't seem to notice Poupon's rapt attention to her. She snapped at me. "That might be. But you could darned sure stop it."

I chuckled. "I just talked to Louise. I don't think I've got much chance to change her mind."

Ethel hmphed. "And why would she? Louise has a good head on her shoulders."

Betty swiped at the air as if swatting a fly. "Oh, quit being so hateful. Kate has been a marvelous sheriff."

This time Ethel put more verve into her humph. "This is going to cost the county a lot of money."

Betty sniffed indignantly. "I'll thank you to mind your own office. I'm the treasurer, and though I think there are better ways to spend money than on frivolous recalls based on sibling rivalry, we can afford to see justice carried out."

Um. Thanks?

Ethel zeroed in on Betty and looked exactly like the word I used for her in my mind, a battle ax. "If she had any dignity or cared about Grand County, she'd stop this sham."

Sham? Now we were getting poetic.

Betty dug her chin down in confirmation. "Exactly. I don't suppose you bothered to try to talk Louise out of it."

Ethel stepped back and considered both of us. "You're not getting it. The way to end this recall is for Kate to resign."

My mouth didn't drop open only because I didn't let it.

# 14

The hour-long drive to Broken Butte dragged by. Summer sun drilled though the windshield, and I could almost hear moisture evaporating from the hills, stealing the green the abundant spring rains brought us. We needed moisture to get us through the next few months or ranchers would be scrambling to find enough hay to last through the blizzardy months.

Maybe this was the perfect time to resign and leave Grand County in the bumbling hands of Ted Conner. Pack up my few necessities and take myself south somewhere. My undergrad degree in psychology wouldn't be useful, but I could find some kind of work. I didn't need much to take care of Poupon and me.

The voices of Carly and my family chattered in my head, everyone talking at once, and not one of them saying I should remain Grand County sheriff.

Trying to figure out my future reminded me of leaves in the wind. Gusts blew in every direction, and just when I reached out to close my fingers on a plan, a sudden burst blew it out of my grasp. This line of thinking carried me until I turned onto Bartelses' gravel road. It was coming on noon.

Meeting up with ranchers could be dicey. With hundreds, or often thousands of acres and endless chores, finding them wasn't as easy as catching up to an accountant in his office. But almost all ranchers made it to the house for dinner. At noon. Not everyone adhered to the old ways, but some traditions were hard to break.

Wrangler and Gidget lived in a brick single-story built in the early 70s. They had a sweeping front yard without a fence. A dirt road ran in front of the house and along the valley floor to the east, far beyond the barn and a few other outbuildings. I wasn't familiar with their ranch. Didn't know how many acres or what breed of cattle they ran. Of course, I knew *of* them. General information, such as Wrangler had graduated high school a few years ahead of me and apparently had a brother who lived in Rapid City that Roxy wanted to introduce me to. I didn't know where Gidget had grown up but didn't think it was in western Nebraska. They ranched on Wrangler's family place, and I didn't know if his folks were still alive and in the area. If it had been Grand County, I'd have known all those details, plus his grandparents' names and maybe even a favorite dog or horse.

Lucky for me, Wrangler Bartels kept up with custom. He was walking from the barn to the house when I pulled up. Probably not bad-looking when he was cleaned up, but now his dark blond hair was heavy with grease and sweat and the sharp cheekbones on his thin face were streaked with grime. He waited while I climbed out of my cruiser, leaving Poupon snoozing in the back seat.

Wrangler was tall and lanky. His jeans—Levi's of course, the same way my classmate Justin Boots always wore Tony Llamas—were dusty and grass stained, consistent with being in the hayfield. "Kate, isn't it? You're Robert's little sister?" He and Robert would have locked horns on high school football fields and basketball courts.

I hooked my thumbs in my utility belt. "Yep. Wondered if you've got a sec."

He glanced at the house, face all angles and lines. He smelled of diesel fuel, hay, and sweat, maybe not the finest cologne, but I'd smelled worse. "Gidget probably has dinner on the table. You're welcome to join us."

I thought about Maureen and could almost hear her rant. "Of course, the man would invite someone to eat the meal he hasn't prepared. Wouldn't occur to him it takes planning and effort and maybe there isn't enough for more at the table. But if someone's going to end up with a smaller portion, guess who that's going to be?"

Man, I needed to get these voices out of my head. I had my own issues with men thinking they rule the world. Being the first woman sheriff in Grand County, I'd been forced to deal with other sheriffs in our co-op who weren't always supportive of my right to be there.

Which made me wonder about Trey. I believed he respected my abilities as a sheriff. But he couldn't stand to date me because he wanted to protect me. So really, how much of an equal could he consider me?

Guess I'd have to figure out who killed Dwayne to prove myself...again. To Wrangler, I said, "Thanks, but this won't take too long. I'm here to ask about Dwayne Weber and what you might know about his death."

Wrangler shot a venomous glare toward the house. "I know he was a prick and I'm not sorry to see him go."

No sugar was sprinkled on that one. No need for me to ease into it. "Did you have an issue with Dwayne?"

His *ha* shot out like a bullet. "You mean did I take offense to him fucking my wife?"

Fair.

If he wanted to shoot that straight, I'd respond appropriately. "Can you tell me where you were Tuesday afternoon?"

Again, he frowned at the house. "I can tell you I wish I'd been in Hodgekiss to applaud whoever rung that jerk-off's neck. But I was at the country club. There was a scramble to raise money for the community center."

"Broken Butte Country Club? People saw you there?" Stupid question, but I needed to ask.

His brows dipped to hood his eyes as he focused behind me. I didn't hear footsteps, but I twisted my head to see if I needed to duck.

All five feet two inches of Gidget Bartels stormed up to me in bare feet, gym shorts, and T-shirt. Seeing most of the women in shorts on this wiltingly hot day made my uniform feel even stickier than normal.

Gidget squawked at me like a mad hen before she got close. Her face was puffy and blotched, and I inspected her closely to make sure the damage was from tears and not from fists. "What are you doing here? Trey Ridnour said you weren't investigating this case because you were too stupid to notice Dwayne had been murdered and arrest Kasey."

I doubted Trey put it in those terms, but I cringed inside to hear it.

Tension and barely restrained rage seemed to vibrate off Wrangler. I hoped it wouldn't spring free. He answered my previous question so quietly I almost didn't hear him. "Yeah, everyone saw me. I don't sneak around. Don't need to hide what I'm doing, like some people."

A flood rushed into Gidget's red eyes and spilled, as it had probably been doing regularly the last two days. Her mouth opened, and watery words slurred out. "I'm sorry, babe. It was a mistake. I told you. I was in Hodgekiss on July third to end it. I swear. But that's when I found him." She broke off in a gurgling sob.

I couldn't say if Wrangler believed her, but I had my doubts. But then, I tend to come down hard on cheaters. I couldn't accuse Gidget of murder simply because she had an affair. But she'd been awfully quick to condemn Kasey at the fairgrounds. "For the sake of argument, let's say Kasey didn't kill her husband."

Wrangler gave an aside, staring at Gidget. "Kasey had every right to kill that bastard."

Gidget bawled loud enough to give the blackbirds a headache.

Ignoring her as best as I could, I asked Wrangler, "Can you think of anyone who might have a grudge against Dwayne?"

Tears streaked down Gidget's face. She'd probably been described as "cute as a bug" all her life. Even now, in her late thirties, whenever I'd seen her, she'd been dressed in trendy fashions and had her hair fixed and face made up. The way she looked now gave an indication of how she'd age. And I'd bet no one would call her cute in a few years. That wasn't a generous thought, but I was still sour about infidelity, probably a flaw I should address at some point, but not today.

Gidget sniffed and swiped at her tears. "Everyone liked Dwayne. Except Kasey. She hated him."

Wrangler growled low in his throat. "No one liked Dwayne. He was an asshole."

I was Team Wrangler on this point. I addressed him. "Anyone in particular you think would want to do him harm?"

His face darkened, and he targeted me with a look like a January blizzard. "You're wasting your time here. Why not ask your brother?"

That came out of nowhere. "Robert?" Since we'd just mentioned him, he was the brother I thought of first.

Wrangler started walking toward the house. "Not that one. Michael. He and Dwayne were into all kinds of stuff together. Michael might be nearly as slimy as Dwayne."

Yowch. Michael wasn't one of my fans these days, but hearing family sniped at by outsiders ruffled my feathers.

Gidget watched Wrangler with desperation shining in her teary eyes. I'd guess she'd had visions of Dwayne continuing his climb in the rodeo stock world, divorcing Kasey, and Gidget and Dwayne enjoying the celebrity and income of successful bucking bull breeders.

Now Gidget needed to make amends with Wrangler or she'd be on her own. For a woman like Gidget, that could be a disaster. Maureen, and even Sarah, would probably school Gidget about ditching the role model of Sleeping Beauty and going more for Moana, but I didn't have the inclination to bother.

She started after Wrangler, then whipped back to me. "Kasey killed Dwayne. You need to talk to Michael. He'll tell you."

I wasn't sure Michael would tell me that cows moo. And going to see him might get me as dead as Dwayne, or at least rejected hurtfully.

# 15

---

By the time I made it back to Hodgekiss, my stomach was rumbling. Probably because it was well past dinnertime, but thinking about Michael and talking to him about Dwayne made me feel like rocks roiled in my gut. Michael had taken up residence in Louise's Camp Recall. He hadn't spoken much to me in two months, leaving a bruise so deep I didn't know if it would heal. How would I begin a conversation about a murder investigation?

Fredrickson's, on the west end of town, was like any modern gas station/convenience store on any rural highway in any town in the United States. Brightly lit, a few aisles of snacks and necessities, it had been built twenty years ago when the old gas station had blown up on a Tuesday afternoon because of the attendant's stray cigarette ash. Fredrickson's generally had a few slices of pizza in their warmer. That would work for me. "How 'bout it?" I asked Poupon, who didn't bother opening his eyes. "Could you use a Slim Jim?" That ignited his interest. He sat up and shook, taking stock of his surroundings and recognizing Fredrickson's, home of his favorite treat.

I pulled next to two Monte Carlos, manufactured sometime in the 70s.

It was one of those days in summer designed to make you long for fall.

The sun felt forty times closer to Earth, as if intent on burning life from the surface. Heat radiated from the pavement in front of Fredrickson's and amplified the smell of gas and oil. A day like today would best be spent on a lake somewhere, and my favorite somewhere was Stryker Lake in front of my house.

I let Poupon out of the back seat to water a tire. It was far too hot for him to hang out in the back seat, his preferred location, so I invited him to follow me into Fredrickson's. Since Poupon had become my family three years ago when Diane had me babysit him for two weeks and never reclaimed him, most folks in Grand County had become accustomed to him.

But not Newt Johnson, who happened to be standing inside near the drinks cooler when we walked in. Newt and Earl, bachelor brothers who'd done their tours of duty in Vietnam and returned to the Sandhills and, to my knowledge, never left again, were the only customers. Despite inheriting a big ranch house and a few acres from their mother, they mostly lived like coyotes, earning their living cleaning out ranchers' old sheds and junk piles. Like any feral animal, they weren't big on personal hygiene, but a few months ago they'd reconnected with an old flame from high school, and she'd managed some improvements. At least they washed their army fatigues every few weeks.

Newt started out with a wide grin for me, then caught sight of Poupon and beat a hasty retreat around the chips aisle to study the deicer and jumper cables. His buzz cut, identical to Earl's, looked like a dusting of snow on a bald hilltop.

Earl, older than Newt by less than a year, appeared from the candy aisle. Poupon didn't daunt him. Like Newt, he wore camo that appeared to be the exact same as what he wore in the service, only he'd shrunk as the years weathered him, so the shirt hung nearly to his knees.

Newt and Earl looked so similar that if you didn't know them well, you needed to check out their ears to identify them. When they were toddlers, Earl bit a chunk off Newt's right ear. With his ear whole, I knew it was Earl who said, "We ain't been out to Calley's place, so don't believe what Shorty says."

That was an interesting greeting. I threw my line in. "Shorty's pretty convincing."

From the back of the store, Newt shouted, "We ain't never. He tossed them lamps out, and he can't claim them now."

Earl shouted back, "Would you shut your pie hole." Then he pasted a pleasant expression across his grizzled face. "We got them lamps fair and square. Just because he saw them in the Antique Mall in Ogallala for a hunnert dollars don't mean he can come back on us."

I didn't even need to reel them in, they were swimming at full speed toward the boat.

This was all too much for Newt to stay away. Keeping his eyes on Poupon, he scrambled up the chips aisle. "That Tacy James shouldn't a told Shorty where she got them lamps."

Earl turned on Newt. "She didn't need to tell him where she got 'em. When she wouldn't just give 'em back to him, he knew where to come."

Newt's face had a few more dirt smudges than Earl's, but I'd give Earl the prize for the strongest garbage smell.

"Did you dig them out of his dump without his permission?" I asked.

Newt argued their case. "They had to've been out there for twenty years or better."

Earl joined in. "Long enough for the brass to get that good..." He hesitated and then spoke it slowly, as if he'd only recently learned the word, "Patina."

Newt nodded approval. "Yep. Patina. That's why Tacy paid us for 'em."

Earl again: "But only fifty each."

Newt registered outrage. "Then turned around and slapped a hunnert on 'em."

Poupon focused on the display of Slim Jims on the counter, giving no notice to the Johnsons, though Newt kept him under surveillance.

Louise's husband, Norman, who worked for Fredrickson, walked in from the garage bay in the back. Since he'd been married to Louise for close to twenty years and her love language was food, he naturally sported quite a spare tire around his middle. Whether he'd acquired his good nature as a survival skill or came by it naturally, he generally had a smile on his chipmunk cheeks. Norm had learned early on to give Louise her rein and not gallop after her grudges. "Hey, Kate."

I greeted him, then asked Newt and Earl again, "Did you have permission to be at Calley's dump?"

"Shorty knows we been out there before. He never said not to go." Newt verged on a whine.

I rested my hands on my hips and gave them both a steady stare. "I'll talk to Shorty. If you split your take with him, I'll see if he'll drop the charges." *Charges. Ha.* Chances were Shorty had been joking when he confronted Newt and Earl. He'd probably forgotten all about it and would be tickled with a fifty-dollar windfall.

They hung their heads and mumbled together, as if this wasn't a new situation, "Yes, ma'am."

Norman threw a few more hot dogs on the roller machine, making me wonder who actually ate enough of them that they had to be replaced.

While I had Newt and Earl contained, and since they liked to call themselves my CIs, confidential informants, I said, "You heard about Dwayne Weber?"

Newt's eyes flicked to Poupon to make sure he wasn't under threat of attack. Then he joined Earl in nodding. "We heard someone killed him and stuck him in with that bull."

No shock they'd heard the news.

Because Newt and Earl liked to scour ranchers' private dumps and were often hired to haul off junk, they had a way of being where people didn't expect them, learning secrets people might prefer no one knew. They liked to think of themselves as professionals covered by a sort of client-junkmen confidentiality clause and kept most of what they knew to themselves. But they'd proven surprisingly useful to me before.

"Were you at the fairgrounds on July third? Maybe see something unusual?" I pressed them.

Newt piped up first. "We was there early."

Earl added, "'Cause the stock folks brung the critters the night before, there's likely to be lots of beer cans around that morning. One year we got enough to get a tire each for our rigs."

Newt and Earl drove Monte Carlos they'd been given when they graduated high school in the 70s. Newt's was turquoise and Earl's an old gold.

"Was anyone else out there?" Since Dwayne's death was in the afternoon, I doubted they'd add anything useful.

They looked at each other for a minute, as if sharing the same brain, then Earl said, "Well, now that you ask, there was another guy there."

"Did you know him?"

Again, they made eye contact and I waited. This time Newt said, "We didn't think about it at the time. But yeah, it was that TJ Simonson from down by Ravenna."

Earl said, "Him and his dad got the lumberyard down that way."

I tried to place TJ Simonson. Ravenna was about 150 miles from Hodgekiss on the road to Lincoln. I'd passed through it a million times on my way to college or football games (Go Big Red), but I didn't know anyone there.

Earl said, "Yeah. He's got interested in bucking bulls. Probably here to see what the Webers had at the rodeo."

Newt elbowed him. "He was lurkin' around the stock pens and got all jumpy when we showed up."

Earl's face brightened. "That's right. Soon's we got there, he took off."

Newt put an ominous note to his voice. "Real suspicious. Like maybe he was up to no good."

Not hinky enough that Newt and Earl thought twice about it until they were questioned. Still, it gave me another lead to follow to put off seeing Michael.

I thanked the Johnsons, got my pizza and Poupon's Slim Jim, and visited with Norman about the chances of Grand County Consolidated High's eight-man football team taking districts this year.

After one more pee break for Poupon, I loaded him up.

Before I could slip behind the wheel, a pickup rumbled up and someone called out, "Where are you heading?"

I turned around to see Maureen with the passenger window down, leaning toward me. "Driving to Ravenna to talk to someone about Dwayne," I said.

"Climb in, I'll take you."

I considered it and discovered after a few lonesome days that company would be nice. "I've got my dog."

She waved for us to join her. "Bring him."

We drove away as Newt and Earl shot out of Fredrickson's, their mouths gaping open.

## 16

Poupon seemed as content in the back seat of Maureen's pickup as he did in the Grand County cop car, maybe not as impressed by the butter-soft leather as some of us, but certainly comfortable. He settled in without comment.

Maureen tucked a strand of her honey-blond hair—colored, conditioned to a sheen, and trimmed so not a speck of split ends frizzed—behind her ear. She turned the country-western music low, and off we sped due east on Highway 2.

I adjusted the AC, grateful for a break from the heat. "I went to see Kasey this morning. She doesn't seem too broken up over Dwayne's death."

Maureen gave a casual shrug. Even in this heat, her skin seemed perfect, her makeup so smooth and expertly applied it seemed natural. "You knew him. You shouldn't be surprised."

We had a long drive, plenty of time to get to know each other. "You worked with him with rodeo stock?"

Her face remained impassive. "I've known Dwayne for a long time. He's been shady the whole time. It seems like maybe karmic justice has prevailed."

"Do you have any idea who might have killed him?"

She inhaled. "Not Kasey. She needed him to deal with the men in the business. I know I told you I sent Trey away on a wild goose chase, but he might uncover something useful."

"If it helps clear Kasey, that will make her happy."

Maureen shrugged. "I can't see as Dwayne's death has made her too unhappy."

"What do you mean?"

She focused on the road. "She wasn't home last night when I went to check on her after dinner. She drove up before I left, wearing a sloppy grin. When I asked where she'd been, she made a crude gesture and laughed. I'm sure she was half-drunk, but I'd testify she'd been out getting laid."

I'd been sheriff too long to be shocked by skanky behavior. But it did curdle my stomach a little.

Maureen sat up straighter, as if to signal a change in subject and mood. "Sure a lot of open country around here."

I couldn't help the affection I felt for my home. "The ground is sand, so it doesn't suit crops. We grow grass, and the main point of that is to feed cattle. At about fourteen acres to sustain a cow-calf pair, it means lots of land to support each family."

"Hm." She looked thoughtful. "Plenty of places to hide the bodies, huh?"

I hoped she was joking.

"Who are we going to see?" she asked.

I filled her in on my visit to the Bartelses and Newt and Earl's information about TJ Simonson.

She looked interested. "You say these two junkmen saw TJ? And no one else?"

"Apparently not."

We rode in silence for a while. "It was pretty lucky you were in Greeley when all this happened. Seems like you found out really quickly."

Her eyes flicked over the hills on either side of the road as if she might be assessing the pastures, as I usually did. "I was in Greeley on business, but I'd already left to come here."

Interesting. "Why were you coming here?"

She glanced at me quickly, then back to the road. "There's a new breeder on the circuit. Wild Fire. Making a big name and getting really great placements. I've tried to find out who owns the operation, but I'm not having any luck."

"And you think it's someone around here? Something to do with Dwayne?"

Her gaze darted around, alert to her surroundings. "Their business address is in Oklahoma, but when I went there, all I found was a sandy pasture without water. You couldn't keep a cat alive there."

"What brought you to Grand County?"

"One of my stock haulers followed the Wild Fire truck out here, but he had to stop for fuel and lost them. I figured it was a good place to start looking. Especially since Dwayne is in the business and has a reputation for questionable practices."

About an hour into the drive, my phone rang. "Sheriff."

Always polite, Trey greeted me before starting in. "You're not supposed to be investigating Dwayne Weber's murder."

Can't say I hadn't expected this, but I played dumb. "What do you mean?"

Maureen nudged me and grinned. She must have been able to hear Trey, demonstrating the quiet ride of her fancy rig. I returned a smug look.

He exhaled in irritation. "Come on, Kate. Gidget called and said you'd been out to their place accusing Wrangler."

Before I became sheriff, I never lied. Now I was getting too good at it. It barely bothered me. Almost not at all, but I crossed my fingers anyway. "I was in Broken Butte and thought I'd interview a potential witness and save you a long drive in case it doesn't add to the investigation." Broken Butte was sixty miles west of Hodgekiss, and Ogallala, where Trey lived, was seventy miles south. He should thank me for saving him that trip.

His curt voice told me he conceded. "Okay. I assume you found out he's got a strong alibi."

"As a matter of fact, he does. I'll type up a report and email it to you. Check that off the list."

Again, the long-suffering exhale. "It does help. But you've got to back off. I mean it. Kasey's got a pretty strong motive for the murder."

"A cheating husband? It's a lot, sure, but killing someone is a big deal."

I'd bet Trey squirmed a little when he realized I'd stomped in the boots of a woman scorned and I hadn't killed anyone. "There's more than that."

That was interesting. "What have you got?"

"It's not your investigation, remember?" He paused for effect. "I'm not going to charge her until we can follow up on a few loose ends. I'll be out of town until late tomorrow. But I'm warning you. Let this one go."

Frustration tightened my chest. "You're wasting resources. I know the people in Grand County. I can be invaluable in this investigation." *For instance, I could be tracking down a possible witness or suspect in Ravenna at this very moment.*

"I've been with the state patrol awhile now. I've got contacts and plenty of resources."

That twanged a string in my brain, and I blurted, "Is Ted helping you?"

He hesitated long enough I knew I'd nailed it. Maureen was right. The good ol' boys were doing their damnedest to push me out.

"You jerk." I reached to punch off and heard him protest before it went dead.

Maureen tilted her head toward me in a sympathetic way. "It would have been nice to be wrong."

"Yeah."

She lifted a hand off the steering wheel and used it for emphasis. "You know what it is. Men are terrified of women. Even if they aren't aware of it, they have a visceral reaction to strong women and will do whatever it takes to keep us down."

I murmured agreement, and she went on. "When I was young, I thought maybe I could make it on my own. I had a champion bull. I worked hard on my genetics. Here's the thing, people think the bull is one to target. But it's the cow. She's got the characteristics you want to select for. And I had the best cow in the business."

She paused, clearly passionate. I urged her on. "What happened?"

She glanced at me, and a hard edge cut into her voice. "I fell in love. Thought it was the real deal. And that son of a bitch sold my cow and took off with the money."

No wonder she had a grudge against men. "I'm sorry."

A wistful smile tipped her lips. "That's not the worst of it. The pedigree for that cow is worth a whole lot today. Bulls out of her line sell in the tens or even hundreds of thousands."

"Ouch."

She shrugged, only a slight twitch at the corner of her eye showing resentment. "Yeah, well. It all worked out. I married Fred. He didn't have any qualms about smart, strong women, and we built this business together. That jerk got what he deserved."

For the rest of the trip, I mostly listened to Maureen lecture on suffragettes and women not being allowed credit cards as recently as the 1970s. It wasn't anything new to me. The bull business might be one of the staunchest holdouts against gender equality, but it wasn't the only one.

I wasn't sure where the lumberyard was located, but it didn't take too much driving to find it in the tiny town of Ravenna.

The fresh white paint and the old-timey font of Buffalo Lumber and Supply on the western wooden façade told us we'd found the right place. It looked straight off a movie set, boardwalk with a flat covering and posts all painted and spiffy. Gates to the side of the building showed an expanse of concrete surrounded by two-story open sheds with stacks of lumber and bags of feed and other supplies.

Maureen parked in front, and I turned to her. "I think it would be best if you waited out here. I've never met TJ and don't want to spook him."

She thought for a second. "Okay. But I want to know everything."

An old collie ambled toward us, wagging his tail. I stepped out and petted his smooth head, noting his tricolored coat shone with care. Then I opened the back of Maureen's pickup, careful to keep my hand on Poupon's collar as he jumped out, in case the two took a dislike to each other.

Both wagged and, when I released Poupon, sniffed. With the ease of longtime friends, they scuffled a bit and fell into line behind me as I approached the front door. The collie dashed ahead with Poupon in playful pursuit.

The plank floor creaked as I walked between tightly spaced shelving to the cash register in the middle of the store. Nothing beat the scent of fresh lumber, and with the heat, it seemed to swell around me. I inhaled deeply.

"Looks like Barney's got a new buddy." A friendly voice came from a room behind the counter, and a man appeared. In his mid-thirties, he was stocky, with a flap of greasy dark hair that fell across his forehead and wide-set eyes that looked trusting and sincere.

"Hi." Easing into the interview seemed like the best strategy.

"Hi." It sounded friendly and curious, pretty much what I'd expect from Sandhillers. When he saw my uniform, he sobered. "Can I help you with something?"

Since my uniform could be intimidating enough, I tried to sound nonthreatening. "I'm looking for TJ Simonson."

Despite my efforts, alarm paled his face. "I'm TJ. What's happened? Is Mom okay?"

I rushed in. "Everything's okay. I'm Kate Fox, sheriff in Grand County. Hodgekiss."

Instead of reassuring him, even more color drained from his face. "W-why are you here?"

The dogs scampered between our legs, their claws clacking on the board floor. TJ didn't seem to notice.

I watched him closely as I said, "Have you heard about Dwayne Weber?"

From the lumberyard in the rear, a door crashed open and an older man barged in. He wore farmer John overalls and had the same barrel-shaped build as TJ. Instead of dark hair, a snowy white mane draped exactly the same way as TJ's. He stomped toward us. In a booming voice, he said, "That's a fancy rig out front." He stopped and narrowed his eyes at me. "That yours? You a sheriff?"

I might have been sensitive about men taking women seriously, so I told myself that this old duffer wasn't skeptical of me and my ability because I was a woman, but legitimately asking because he'd come into the dimly lit store from the glaring sunshine and couldn't see me clearly.

"Kate Fox, Grand County sheriff," I repeated for him, but this time giving it more heft, offering my hand for a strong shake.

The older man, who had to be TJ's father, grasped my hand in a welcoming way. Where TJ looked peaked, this man's broad face was ruddy and rough, with a distinct whiskey nose as evidence of a drinker who'd gone beyond amateur status. "Sure. Sure. You're one a Hank's kids. Known Hank a long time. I'm Titus Simonson. We got ourselves into a few scrapes back when the world was young. How's he gettin' along these days?"

TJ hadn't gained any healthier color, and his gaze bounced from me to his father and back again.

I hadn't heard Dad mention Titus before, but he liked to keep his antics from his younger days to himself. From what I'd gleaned from his sister, my aunt Twyla, Dad had been a wild one. Titus looked like maybe he'd continued in their rowdy ways. "Dad's doing well. Still with BNSF."

Titus thrust an arm under the bib of his overalls and rubbed his big belly. "I heard about your mom's problems."

Who hadn't? CNN had done an hour-long documentary on Vietnam war protests after the media caught wind of her story. She got prime billing. I figured our family had weathered far more than fifteen minutes of fame, but here I was, facing down a recall. A mother's gift that kept on giving.

Titus's attention rested on TJ—those initials had to stand for Titus Junior—then he studied me before giving a cautious, "So, what brings you to Ravenna?"

"I wanted to ask TJ a few questions about the rodeo on July third." I glanced at TJ as I said it, but Titus's sudden stiffening caught my attention.

The affability drained from his face. He sniffed like a tweaker, though I doubted that was his substance of choice. "I got nothin' for you on that score."

I hadn't asked Titus, but his reaction was curious, so I followed up on it. "Why's that?"

He glowered at TJ, who shifted his attention to a rack of fuses. "I don't truck with nothing rodeo. And if my boy'd a listened to me, he wouldn't either and we'd both be a lot better off."

The dogs barreled through us again, buckling Titus's knee. He braced himself on a nearby shelf with bins of nails, bolts, and washers and cursed under his breath.

I swiped my fist along Poupon's back to grab his collar, but both dogs zoomed off before I got hold.

I couldn't pass up whatever flowed between father and son. "I'm looking for information about Dwayne Weber, and I wondered if TJ knew him."

Titus yanked on the side of his bib in a way that said a storm was brewing. His voice had a goading tinge. "I don't know, TJ. Do you know Dwayne Weber? Ever have anything to do with that SOB?"

A lump traveled down the length of TJ's pasty throat, and he blinked rapidly.

I let the silence stand for a few seconds. Titus's heavy breathing filled the store. When the tension had grown, I tried again, nailing TJ dead center. "How did you know Dwayne Weber?"

Titus sniffed. "Hold on. What do you mean *did*?"

I let the magnifying glass burn onto the younger man. "TJ?"

His hair drooped across his face but didn't hide the nervous tautness of his features. Finally, the words tumbled out. "Okay, yes. I was at the rodeo."

Titus sucked in and exhaled two wet breaths to build up steam. "What brand of stupid are you? I told you to stay clear of that snake."

TJ's eyes watered. He pushed his hair off his forehead, but it flopped back down. "I know. And I am. But I wanted him to get a taste of his own medicine, so I went up there to do some damage."

This wasn't what I'd expected to hear. I'd hoped TJ had seen something suspicious, not that he'd been the murderer. "What kind of medicine did you administer?"

With a pinch of skin around his eyes and a tightening of his lips, Titus raged without words, no doubt extoling the depths of TJ's stupidity.

TJ hunched his shoulders and lowered his face to the floor, only venturing one glance at his father.

Then, as if he'd had enough, TJ straightened his shoulders and locked eyes with Titus. "I was going to loosen the lug nuts on the trailer tires. It's what he did to me in Cheyenne, and it cost me everything I had."

Titus broke their stare-down by throwing back his head in disgust, which was a darned sight better than swatting his son, as I sensed he was tempted to do. "It's not enough to waste all you had and then some on two damned buckin' bulls. But then you're set on revenge. Son, haven't I taught you anything?"

"I didn't do it," TJ yelled, and the collie barked.

Then Poupon barked, and they both tumbled between our legs and took off on a dead run before any of us could stop them.

"Why would you want to loosen the lug nuts on the trailer?" Might have seemed obvious to the two of them, but I wasn't following it.

TJ pushed his hair back again only to have it flop forward. Seemed like it might be easier to cut it. He looked contrite and defiant at the same time, which had to be as confusing for him as it was for me. "You ought to ask your own brother about that."

With hope, I asked, "Robert?"

TJ shook his head, and his greasy hair whipped right and settled back on his forehead. "Michael. Dwayne's henchman."

Titus clenched the buckles of his bib straps, knuckles white. "Don't you go blaming anyone else. You did a dumb thing and then doubled down by being even stupider. I swear you take after your mom more every day."

TJ looked as if he'd like to argue, but he clamped his mouth shut. Probably practiced in that.

Apparently, Titus felt compelled to air all their dirty laundry. With a twist of his mouth below his veiny nose and a bitter tone to go along with it, he said, "She quit me a couple of years ago and lives over in Bryant now. Works at the café there. Has heart problems and said living with me was killing her. Swears she feels like a million bucks now that she's not 'under my thumb,' as she says. Like her bad genetics is my fault."

If he was looking for sympathy, he could walk on by me. I shifted toward TJ. "What do I need to ask Michael about?"

TJ focused on Titus until the old man waved his hand and gave a gruff, "You got yourself into this damned mess. Might as well let it spill."

TJ pushed his hair back again. He whispered two words before his voice strengthened. "I bought two buckin' bulls from Dwayne Weber."

Titus bit with venom, "Using the store's money and without asking a by-your-leave."

TJ swallowed again, his face still pale. He just barely kept a squeak from his voice. "I'd seen 'em buck, and they were solid stock. I started hitting the circuit, just local, mostly. Doing pretty good. But better than Dwayne thought I should. So, I was winning nice purses, and Dwayne was getting nothing. When we met up in Laramie, he put sugar in my gas tank so I couldn't haul the bulls to Rawlings, and I missed getting points."

Titus grumbled under his breath. "That's not the least of it."

TJ grew bold enough to scowl at his father. "But I made up for it at another couple of go-rounds. So, when we got to Cheyenne, I was neck and neck with Pecos. Dwayne got so mad at me, he loosened the lug nuts on my trailer. But not enough to make it so's I'd know right away and need new lug nuts and miss the event, like in Rawlings. This time, they didn't come loose until I was on the interstate heading toward Denver."

Oh no, I dreaded to hear this.

"The wheels came off, and the trailer jackknifed in traffic. It ended up head over teacup in the ditch, and one bull broke his neck. The other busted his legs, and I had to shoot him right there on the side of the road."

"Oh, man." I let out a moan. "I'm so sorry."

Titus's nasty smirk taunted TJ. "Oh, it gets even better."

"I guess I should feel lucky there wasn't a big wreck and people didn't get hurt." TJ's eyes watered. "The bulls were supposed to be guaranteed. No matter what, is what Dwayne told me."

Titus's voice could shred raw meat. "But that's not what the damned paperwork said. The contract you didn't bother to read."

TJ directed his words at his father and somehow dug up some steel to put in them. "That's right. I trusted Dwayne, and he lied to me. Turns out the bulls were only guaranteed for disease. So, yeah, he killed my bulls and then he stole my money."

That seemed like a pretty strong motive for murder. "What does Michael have to do with this?"

TJ's perplexed expression said he thought I should already know this. "Because Michael is always around to do Dwayne's dirty work."

Ground beef and curdled buttermilk. My Michael? He was the brother who always had a scheme going since he was a kid. He cut the Sunday comics up and sold them door to door in Hodgekiss when he was barely four years old. When his fourth-grade class sold wrapping paper to fund a new swing set for the school, Michael added a hidden premium of a dollar on each sale and made himself a tidy profit. Of course, he worked hard, enlisting me to drive him to Broken Butte on a Saturday, and raised more money for the school than anyone else. In fact, his record still stands.

He and Lauren had bred ostriches, sold supplements, they even got into a pyramid scheme for energy drinks for a short time. Some of his projects brought a windfall, but nothing lasted long. Michael told me once that he figured he could make ten risky deals, and if one of them succeeded, it'd pay for the rest. I hated the thought of him being involved with something deliberately criminal and dangerous. I wasn't sure I believed TJ. It was a topic I couldn't delve into now.

I steered it back to Dwayne. "And you were at the rodeo that day."

TJ blinked his eyes and scrunched up his nose as if fighting tears. He inhaled and got control. "But I didn't do it."

Titus watched me, probably figuring out what I'd meant by referring to Dwayne in the past tense.

"Do what?" I asked.

"Loosen the lug nuts. I mean, I wanted to hurt Dwayne, but the bulls didn't do anything to me. I wanted Dwayne to know how it felt to shoot an animal you love. But I couldn't hurt the bulls."

That TJ talked about loving the bulls surprised me. But with the amount of time breeders spent raising, feeding, training, and hauling them to events, it made sense they'd develop affection for them.

It made me think of the silly dog Diane had foisted on me and now I considered family. I swiveled my head and located Poupon and Barney standing by a giant silver water dish, both snouts buried and water sloshing on the floor.

TJ verged on tears. "I just couldn't do it."

"Did you hang around for the rodeo?" I asked.

A flash of fear sparked in his eyes before he turned away. "Yeah. I thought I might get a chance to do something. I don't know. Make him pay somehow."

Titus zeroed in on the inevitable question. "Why're you asking about TJ and Dwayne?"

I studied TJ as I answered. "Dwayne was murdered. Sometime in the afternoon."

TJ seemed to shrink into himself, but he didn't look surprised. He quickly shifted his attention to Titus with palpable dread.

Titus exploded like a volcano. "What the hell did you do? It's not enough you sink us into debt on a harebrained scheme, now you're running all over the country looking for trouble?"

I didn't think it was possible, but TJ was now ghost white. "You think I killed Dwayne Weber? Come on, Dad. I couldn't even put bulls in danger. I wouldn't do that."

"People deserve killing more than dumb animals." Titus spared a look of disgust for his son before turning to me. He thrust his chin my way. With a shaky hand, he pointed toward the door. "And now we're done talking to you without a lawyer."

"But I didn't do anything," TJ said behind me.

Titus shouted at TJ, his head close to mine so it sounded like a bomb exploding. "You keep your goddamned mouth shut."

He hustled me out the door and slammed it behind me. When I tried the latch, I found it locked. I raised my fist to bang on it when it suddenly swooshed inward.

TJ had hold of Poupon's collar and urged him out the door. He glanced behind him, then quickly up at me. "Michael is neck-deep in this. If he didn't kill Dwayne, he knows who did."

# 17

Maybe it was hotter now than when we arrived, or it might be I was stirred up. That was the second time Michael's name had come up in relation to Dwayne's murder. I needed to talk to him, and I didn't have another lead to follow, so putting it off wasn't an option. The pizza lumped in my gut like acidic ping-pong balls.

I took one step toward the pickup and felt like a flame had been thrown onto the acid in my stomach.

Ted's Chester County Bronco was parked next to the pickup. Maureen sat on the tailgate, swinging her legs in a girlish way. Ted leaned against the side of the pickup, arms folded, looking relaxed and so Ben Affleck hand-some even I noticed. But not in a good way. His charm dial was set on eleven, and it seemed to be working on Maureen.

Instead of drawing my gun and firing, as I wanted to, I pasted on a face Barbie would be proud of and marched over to them. "Teddy! What a surprise to see you here."

Ted jerked like someone stuck him with a hot poker. He gave a quick survey of the parking lot, no doubt looking for my cruiser. "What the hell are you doing in Ravenna?"

With a nod to the lumberyard, I said, "I'm considering renovating my front porch and wondered about wood versus composite decking. Maureen offered to drive me here."

Maureen transformed to young and naïve, not at all like the woman I was getting to know. She chirped, "Ted has been entertaining me with his exploits as sheriff. Quite the adventures."

It took Ted a moment to assimilate that I'd arrived with his new conquest. Then he had to backtrack to what I'd said and put it all into perspective. Finally, he caught up. "You're here to talk to TJ about Dwayne's murder."

I raised my eyebrows. "Oh my gosh. Does TJ have something to do with it?"

"Come off it, Kate. Trey told you to stay out of this. He's trying to protect you from making a big mistake before the recall. For once, let someone help you."

That cheesed me off in a big way. "Trey said? To you? And then he invited you to join in so you could solve it and be the hero. Coincidentally, in time for the recall."

He broke off eye contact and seemed fascinated by something above the cruiser.

Maureen's voice was three octaves higher and sweeter than what I'd heard from her. "Wouldn't it be a good thing to have Ted on the case? He's solved so many."

Huh. Ted's evasion struck me as odd until it dawned on me. "He told you to stay out of it, too."

Ted's face pinched together like he'd downed a tankard of lemon juice.

I pushed him. "So, what are you doing here?" When he didn't respond, I verbally punched one of his buttons in front of this pretty lady. "You don't know how to do real investigating, so tell me how you figured this one out."

He loomed over me. A decent dog companion would at least bark in my defense, but Poupon didn't stir. Ted glowered at me. "You're not the only one who can follow a lead."

I forced a guffaw. "Lead. That's rich. Let me guess, TJ's mom was at Odergard's with her coffee bunch this morning, and they were talking about Dwayne Weber. She complained about how Dwayne had screwed TJ over, and *voilà*, here you are."

"I didn't drive up here on a whim. I asked around and found out TJ was in Hodgekiss on July third."

"After you eavesdropped on a bunch of retired women."

He glanced at Maureen and growled, "A good sheriff keeps his eyes and ears open and gathers clues constantly."

I didn't need to force my laugh this time. "Thanks, Barney Fife."

Ted lifted his chin in a superior way. "You think you're such a great sheriff because you got lucky a time or two."

"It's not luck. It's called working."

He cocked the corner of his mouth in amusement. "Except you flubbed up too many times. Letting Marguerite escape was the nail in the coffin of your career. You should save yourself the embarrassment and quit."

"Yeah, you know about embarrassment, don't you? Like losing an election after you've had the job for eight years."

Maureen kept quiet, but I figured she was taking it all in.

He studied me as if evaluating, a spiteful glint in his eye. "You know, there were lots of things I loved about you. But your stubbornness is not one of them. It's going to ruin your life if you don't learn to compromise more."

"Oh? And compromise means what? I share you with your mistress?"

Again, he slashed his gaze to Maureen.

She scooted to the end of the tailgate and hopped off. "Let's load up, Poupon."

Ted gave me a fake sympathetic look that made me want to slap him. But the urge was overwhelming when he opened his mouth and said, "I've apologized a million times. You need to forgive me and move on. This grudge is only hurting you."

The sun couldn't burn hotter than I did right then. "You did *not* just say that to me."

"You know I only have your best interests at heart. Take Carly's offer and go out to the ranch. You know you'd be happier there."

I pushed around him to the passenger door. "I'll be happier when I nail Dwayne's killer."

Now he laughed. "That's why you're here? To pin it on TJ? Everyone knows Kasey killed Dwayne. I'm just gathering witnesses and motives."

"What can TJ contribute to that?" I knew Ted couldn't stand not to show off what he knew, and he might have something I could use.

"Just that he'd paid Dwayne in cash and Dwayne didn't tell Kasey. But she found out last week when TJ showed up at their place. TJ's mom said Kasey went after Dwayne with a pitchfork when she found out."

I cocked my head at Ted and pointedly said, "A husband can do a lot of things he ought to be murdered for. That doesn't mean a wife will go through with it."

He slapped his thigh with a pop. "Poor Kate. The victim. How long are you going to keep playing that card?"

That volley hit me in the gut. Victim? Did I see myself that way? Did I act like that? I'd thought I'd moved on. I had a job I loved—well, liked, anyway—and owned a house I really *did* love. And speaking of love, I'd found a man that flipped me on my head and turned me inside out and brought parts of me to life I hadn't known were dead.

And I'd lost him.

So, yeah, maybe I was letting the bitter flow in where it shouldn't. That needed to stop.

I poked my finger at Ted because when you're married to someone for eight years, you know what torques them off the most. "You have a nice day. I've got work to do."

Problem was, the work I had to do might be worse than exchanging insults with my ex.

## 18

The day would be ending if you were the kind of person who worked in an office and punched a clock. If you were a rancher working on the first hay cutting, you'd probably be at it for a few more hours yet. Since Michael and Lauren didn't have enough acreage for a livestock herd, they had no hayfield. But that didn't mean Michael, who stormed through life like the devil was on his tail, would be home. I decided to take the chance and drove north of Hodgekiss.

I'd offered to take my own car and let Maureen stop at the Long Branch, but she'd asked to come along. I agreed, reasoning Michael might not be as combative with a stranger as witness.

"There's a case of bottled water under the back seat. Grab us some."

I twisted around, patted Poupon because he was there, and wrenched a couple of bottles free of the shrink-wrapped bundle under the seat. I handed one to Maureen and unscrewed the top of my own bottle. It wasn't cold, but it was wet.

Maureen sipped her water and watched the endless prairie with its green, gold, and red grasses rippling like waves. "How big of a place does your brother have?"

The sun had an aggressive burn, like it was fighting for the last hours before being forced to release the day from its grasp. "Not a big place. They have two or three sections." She should know, but I added to make sure. "A section is a square mile. So, not enough for cattle. They were lucky an old rancher sold them the land, because finding small rural parcels in the Sandhills is a fluke."

She understood. "Sure. They wouldn't want to break up pastures. Your brother must be persuasive if he convinced someone to sell."

I laughed. "Actually, my youngest brother, Jeremy, is the charmer." The humor died when I thought of Jeremy's charm getting him into trouble three years ago. And that trouble fueling Dahlia's argument for recall.

Michael had other ways of getting his way. I always wondered if his friendship with Crank Misner, the old rancher who sold him the place, hadn't been based on Michael performing some sketchy chore for the old guy. Since Crank had died ten years ago, it was unlikely we'd ever find out.

Maureen still appeared keenly interested in the surroundings as we drove. "I can't believe I've never been in the Sandhills before. This is amazing cattle country."

I had to agree. "Most people who come here for the first time don't appreciate it. They see all this empty land that's only green for a few months out of the year. It looks barren and bleak to them. They don't understand the sea of grass is heaven for cows."

She laughed. "They ought to come to Arizona. I'm glad I only raise bulls down there. It's hard to graze cattle in the desert." She sighed. "Nothing like Montana."

We pulled into the immaculate ranch yard and parked in front of the double-wide Michael and Lauren had planted out here eleven years ago with the intent of building their own house across the yard, next to a three-stall barn and set of corrals. Sunflower stalks bobbed in the breeze, their pods full and ready to burst out in bloom.

I hadn't been to Michael and Lauren's for at least a year and was surprised at the progress on their new house. The outside framing looked complete and the subflooring on the two levels as well. The roof trusses were stacked against the elevated gas tank.

"You lived in Montana?" For some reason, I hadn't considered her being from anywhere except Arizona.

Her face closed up, obviously not terrific memories for her. "I was raised there. Thought I'd stay there forever. Beautiful country." She shut the engine off.

I unbuckled and leaned into my door. "What made you leave?"

She slid out and tossed off the question with a quick answer. "Needed to start over."

Michael's pickup wasn't parked out front, but Lauren's later-model Chevy S-10 Blazer was there. I let Poupon out of the back seat.

Maureen studied the construction project. "They're building a new house?"

"It's been a long-term project. We'd all helped them pour the foundation not long after they moved here. They've been working on the rest of the house bit by bit as they scrape together extra money. But it looks like they've had a big push recently."

As with everything, it seemed, Maureen carefully assessed the house. "It looks like it'll be a good size when it's done."

I pictured the sketch Lauren had shown me. "Hope they can move in before their girls get into high school."

"Privacy is nice at that stage."

She wasn't telling me anything I didn't know. "At any stage, really. We shared two bedrooms upstairs. One for the boys, one for the girls. One bathroom. I had to move back for almost a year after my divorce. I sure love my own house now." I didn't add that Dad was living with me. But I considered that temporary.

"What does your brother do for a living?" Maureen asked.

I hedged. "A little of this. A little of that." I pointed to the old barn positioned where two hills bottomed out, creating a narrow passage. The trail road in that V led to pastures hidden from the homeplace. "He works harder than anyone I know."

Maureen showed a skeptical grimace.

I laughed. "I know. But it works for him." I pointed to the barn. "For instance, a few years ago he did a deal and ended up with ten squeeze chutes about twenty years old. He sold all but one, and even though he doesn't have cattle, he installed it in the barn. He made a ton of money on them, then realized they were all pieces of crap. He refuses to acknowledge it and keeps that darn thing anchored in the barn anyway."

The whole steel apparatus stood about six feet high, with two gates that swung together at the front, like doors at an Old West bar. The sides were as long as a king-sized bed and at a slight V so the bottom of the chute was narrower than the top. Usually, a corral or holding pen contained the cattle who would be herded into a narrow alley that led to the chute.

A critter was forced through from the back and would see an opening through the chute's doors to freedom. But as it stuck its head through the open doors, a cowhand would throw his weight down on a long metal lever and swing the gates closed. They left an opening big enough for a neck but narrow enough the head was caught on one side and the shoulders on the other. The sides of the chute could then be lowered so the animal could be injected or branded.

In the case of Michael's barn, the squeeze chute was bolted to the floor slightly off-center in the barn alley. By opening stall doors and setting up barriers, one or two people could herd a cow into the chute. If he needed to work a few head, he'd probably have to rig up some portable fencing. It seemed like a poor arrangement to me, but you could never tell Michael anything.

A clatter from the double-wide made me spin around as my nieces Kaylen and Lucy bounded down the stairs and stampeded toward us.

Eight-year-old Kaylen had her mother's blond hair that poked out in every direction. In faded pink shorts and stretched T-shirt, she outran her six-year-old sister. "Are you staying for supper? Mom picked corn, and Dad's not here, so you can have his."

Lucy, who took after Michael not only in looks but also attitude, raced after Kaylen, determined not to be left behind and probably striving to get to me first. Unfortunately, she tripped on a bunch of bindweed and somersaulted to end up flat on her back.

I gave her a second to see if she was hurt. Kaylen spun around and hurried back.

Lucy jumped to her feet, shreds of grass and dust covering her tank top and cutoffs, her face crimson wrath. She took a swing at Kaylen, connecting with her chest, causing more noise than pain. "You should have waited for me."

Maureen turned an amused face to me. "Your nieces?"

To an outsider, they probably looked like scruffy kids bound to be loud and annoying. To me, they were adorable, a little unpredictable, and as attached to my heart as a tree is rooted to the ground.

Kaylen brushed the grass from Lucy's clothes. "You're okay, squirt."

And apparently she was, because they finished their trek to us holding hands. Lucy took up from Kaylen's invitation. "We don't know where Daddy is. He was 'posed to be here, and Mom's on a tear because of it."

Kaylen twisted her mouth in perfect imitation of her mother. "He's got a lot of work to do because of Dwayne Weber getting killed. So, we need to be patient."

Maureen stiffened beside me.

In an authoritative voice to let them know they needed to mind their manners, I said, "Maureen, this is Kaylen and Lucy. Girls, this is Maureen Steffen. She's a new friend."

Maureen surprised me with a warmth I hadn't seen from her before. "Very nice to meet you, ladies."

They both glowed with the attention and respect. Kaylen especially seemed smitten with Maureen's elegant demeanor. Lucy seemed more curious, but she was harder to please, angling to play situations to her best advantage.

The screen door smacked the frame, and Lauren, short spiked blond hair that looked as though she'd been working outside all day, plodded down the steps. We waited while she crossed the yard's green carpet. She seemed genuinely glad to see me. "What a great surprise."

I introduced Lauren and Maureen.

"Did the girls tell you to stay for supper? We've got plenty. BLTs and corn."

I couldn't deny that sounded like a bit of summer heaven and I'd have accepted in a heartbeat.

But Maureen said, "That's nice of you, but we need to get back to town soon."

Lauren took hold of my arm. "At least stay for iced tea or a beer. It's after five, you know."

I didn't wait for Maureen's approval. It'd be rude not to at least have a drink. "Iced tea would be great."

Kaylen's face fell in exact replica of Lauren's. "At least that's something. I'll get the glasses out."

Lucy shoved Kaylen to the side and got a head start for the mobile home. "I'll do it."

Lauren clucked as if annoyed with them, but her eyes twinkled, clearly amused. "They're so ready to go back to school. They go crazy when someone stops out. This is a real treat for them."

Guilt gathered like a rain cloud in my head. I loved spending time with my nieces and nephews. I didn't usually need to make a special effort to see them since we had regular family cookouts or school events, and I was the most reliable babysitter my siblings had, since, basically, I had no social life.

But with the whole Mom situation and Dad moving out of the house, not to mention the tension of some of the family blaming me, the get-togethers had dwindled. When Louise filed the recall, my participation had ended abruptly.

"I'm really glad to see you," Lauren said.

We meandered to the front porch, Maureen taking in the yard, the chicken house, the hills surrounding the place.

I said, "I've really missed seeing Kaylen and Lucy this summer. They're getting so big."

Lauren beamed at the house, as if she could see them. "They're such a pain in the butt, bickering all the time. But yeah, they're growing up fast. Kaylen is cooking now."

Maureen joined in. "Really?"

"Well, pizza and pigs in a blanket with refrigerator biscuits, and mac and cheese from the box. But she can do scrambled eggs and French toast."

That hit me like a fist. I taught Michael and Douglas how to cook those delicacies when they were a few years younger than Kaylen. We Foxes learned how to take care of ourselves since Dad was on the railroad for days at a time and Mom could disappear in her sculpture studio for long stretches. How had Michael drifted so far away from me?

I pointed to the home construction. "Looks like you're making real progress on the new place."

Lauren's gaze traveled to it, then back to me. She didn't seem particularly pleased. "Yeah. Michael's had some plans come together lately. He hired a crew from Potsville to do the framing."

The way she said it seemed clear she didn't want to go any further into Michael's plans.

"Michael's working late?" I asked.

Lauren cast a quick glance at Maureen, then back at me and sighed. "I'm sorry. I hate that Michael's been on Louise's side in all of this recall business."

Maureen's eyebrows shot up in surprise. But she didn't blurt out a question about my brother supporting a recall.

Lauren's face tightened in annoyance, and she waited a second. "I don't like it. But I promised Michael I'd stay out of it."

Lauren and Michael had dated in high school and married soon after. She'd been part of the family for eleven years. Once a part of the Fox clan, you're taken in and held tightly. Mom had been adamant about that, and Dad welcomed everyone. For the love of Cheez-Its, most of my siblings still referred to Ted as their brother-in-law and he was invited to all the get-togethers.

Part of me understood Lauren's loyalty to her husband. Domestic tranquility was a strong motivator. The other part of me felt like she poked a bruise. But because I was a Fox, or because I was the middle kid in a pack of nine, or for whatever dysfunctional reason—and the list was long—I didn't want Lauren to be uncomfortable, so I tried to let her off the hook. "It's okay. I guess maybe Michael feels my job is messing with his earning a living." I didn't succeed in sounding blasé. It came out more vinegary than understanding.

Lauren tensed up. "That pea-brained Stewie Mesersmith wouldn't sell Michael a horse because he thought you'd let your mom get into Canada, and he allowed as how she was a communist who deserved jail. If you ask me, Stewie is a little sketch, and we don't need to be doing any business with him."

If Michael was doing a legally questionable horse deal and my job as sheriff shut it down, I'd be pleased as punch about that. "Michael probably dodged a bullet there." I tried to make light of it.

Maybe Lauren and I weren't as tight as Sarah and I, but we were family and friends. She'd probably read me as well as I could read her, and she'd know I ached all the way down to my toes about Michael and Louise.

By the time we made it to the kitchen, the girls had filled a glass pitcher with tea and set out matching glasses of ice on the table. Obviously, this was their best serving set and they were proud.

Maureen brightened, as if impressed. "This is so pretty. Thank you."

The girls peppered Maureen with questions as she settled herself at the table. When they found out she was from Arizona and raised buckin' bulls, they wanted to know what Tucson was like. If there were rattlesnakes in the desert. Did she ride the bulls.

Lauren and I stood in the kitchen and chatted about the new vo-ag teacher at the high school and the Huskers' prospects of resurrecting their running game this year. It felt strained while we skirted around family issues, and I really wanted to talk to Michael.

Finally, Lauren raised her voice to bring Maureen into the conversation. "So, what brings you to the Sandhills?"

Maureen looked up from chatting with the girls. "I'm here to help Kasey out."

Lauren's intense and intelligent gaze fell on Maureen. "How is she?"

Maureen huffed in irritation. "She'd be a lot better if she wasn't being accused of murder."

Lauren's mouth dropped open, and she turned to me. "That's true?"

"Sadly, yes. But I'm hoping to prove that wrong."

Maureen's strong voice finished the thought. "That's why we're here."

Lauren narrowed her eyes as if confused. "I'm sorry. I'm not following you."

This felt like walking across a frozen lake with marbles on my soles. I tried for offhand, which sounded silly for a serious subject. "From what I gather, Michael's been working a lot with Dwayne Weber lately."

Maureen zeroed in on Lauren.

A pinprick of alarm flashed in Lauren's eyes, then vanished. She stuck her hands in her back pockets, pulled them out and shoved them in her front pockets. "Oh, some, I guess. He's kind of been all over lately."

The girls chattered at Maureen, telling her about the bucket calves they'd raised from birth and how they'd earned premiums at the fair and then sold them.

Maureen folded her arms on the table and leaned into them, as if not interested in me and Lauren. "What are you going to do with the money?"

Coward that I am, I welcomed the interruption. Lauren and Michael were tighter than peanut butter on pancakes. Schemes and secret deals sealed their loyalty, and I doubted I'd get anything more from Lauren about Michael and his relationship with Dwayne.

Lucy flopped back in her chair, her legs not touching the ground. She folded her arms across her chest and set her lips in a pout. "Daddy says we gotta save it."

Kaylen cast a mischievous grin at her mother. "But Mom told us we can spend ten percent on fun. We need to save ten percent. And then with the leftover eighty percent, we buy more bucket calves next year."

Maureen beamed approval. "Listen to your mother. She's a smart lady."

Lucy's big lips still showed dissatisfaction. "I don't know what a person cent is, and I don't want to have to bottle-feed more calves next year. I want to buy an electric car so I can go where I want to. I found them on Amazon, and they only cost seven hundred dollars. They're sweet."

Maureen's cool blue eyes looked stern. "A smart woman invests in herself. I'm a fan of livestock, myself. If you work hard and trust yourself, you'll be a success. Just don't let any guy tell you what to do."

Lucy didn't warm to Maureen's advice, and her attitude cooled. "Daddy tells Mommy what to do."

Lauren's face reddened.

Kaylen drew herself up. "Uh-uh. Mom tells Dad what to do."

Lauren left my side and stood by the table. "Your dad and I have what's called a marriage. We're partners, and no one tells the other one what to do."

Lucy tucked her arms close to her chest in defiance. "Then why did Daddy tell you to take Luke to the back pasture?"

Lauren's skin darkened even more. Her eyes flicked toward me and back in a move so rapid I barely noticed. "It was more like asking than telling. Like when I call him up and ask him to get milk at Dutch's before he comes home. Sometimes I just say, pick up some milk."

Luke? Back pasture. Was that any connection to Lucky Luke, who had been struck by lightning and hauled away before Kasey saw him dead?

Kaylen shoved Lucy's shoulder. "Would you just quit being so contrary? Goll."

A smile crept onto my face. I'd heard Michael use the term "contrary" with both his girls since they were tiny and colicky. As hard-driving as Michael was, chasing from one thing to another, I'd only ever seen him treat his kids with patience and humor. He took after Dad that way.

Maureen pushed back from the table suddenly. She strode from the table to the living room, her steps thundering through the house. She stopped in front of three floating shelves attached to the wall. I recognized them from a home décor party Louise had hosted several years ago.

Louise was for anything that allowed her to invite all her friends and relatives over, bake them dessert, and sell them whatever trend-of-the-moment direct sales was going around. All the sisters and sisters-in-law felt obligated to buy at least something. Which is why I had decorative candles, about five tubes of lipstick from various companies, a negligee I'd worn once, Tupperware that I'd lost lids for but never bothered with the lifetime guarantee to request a replacement, and a set of shelves just like these that might still be hanging on the bathroom wall in the house at Frog Creek. The most useful item I'd ever bought at one of Louise's parties was a pizza wheel. And that was one of the first things I'd thrown into a box when I left Ted. It was his favorite kitchen utensil.

Maureen picked up a family picture of Michael and Lauren and the two girls taken two years ago when the Episcopal church invited a photographer who promised a free eight-by-ten with an offer of packages as artful as any school pictures. "What a lovely photo," Maureen gushed, and I wondered if maybe she needed glasses. Kaylen's eyes were closed, Lucy looked to be on the verge of a fit, Lauren's tension was palpable, and Michael's smile made me think of Jack Nicholson in *The Shining...Here's Mikey!* "Is this your daddy?"

Kaylen jumped up and ran over, but Lucy, who could hold a grudge—again just like her father—scowled at Maureen.

Kaylen pointed at the photo in Maureen's hand. "That was before my hair grew out. I want to get it long enough for braids so it won't get in my eyes when I ride Buster."

"Good idea," Maureen said. She placed the picture back on the shelf and gave it a long look. She turned back to us with a thoughtful expression. "I probably ought to get back and check on Kasey."

Kaylen walked us to the door with her grown-up manners, saying how nice it was to meet Maureen and how she hoped I wouldn't be a stranger. Lucy swung her legs at the table, arms crossed, wearing a pout.

Lauren stood by the table, her face guarded and hard. Obviously, she didn't like me questioning about Michael.

If she'd been on my side before I'd shown up here, she had flipped. Another family member gone.

# 19

---

Feeling like I hadn't made much progress on solving Dwayne's murder and had lost ground on the recall slope, I picked up my cruiser at Fredrickson's and drove Poupon and myself home for another night of listening to frogs croak on Stryker Lake.

I rose with the sun and got an hour or two to enjoy the sweet dew and work in my garden before the furnace kicked on for the day. With Trey still out of town, I had a little more time to make some headway. But regularly scheduled sheriff duty needed taking care of first thing.

I pulled up in front of Blackie's Café in Edgewood for our monthly sheriff meeting. Since the temps were expected to reach a hundred today, I'd left Poupon at home with a humongous bowl of water and all the shade my elms could offer. My guess was he wouldn't venture far from the front door in hopes someone would return soon and let him in to sleep on the couch. The sun wasn't fooling around now. It hadn't slid too far up the sky, but it was blasting heat like it wanted to melt the sand.

Every month, the four of us sheriffs gathered in alternating counties for midmorning coffee to compare notes and discuss any issues that plagued our giant chunk of Nebraska that couldn't claim one stoplight among us. Most of time, we caught up with each other or gossiped. Today we were gathering in Choker County, directly north of Grand County.

A chill from the air conditioner spiked my arms when I stepped into Blackie's. Smells of bacon and fryer grease mingled with coffee. I asked the waitress, Velma Ray, who'd probably been waiting tables at Blackie's since the Eisenhower administration, for a cup of coffee to fight the frigid temperature of the café. I didn't want to be responsible for adding any steps to her day, so I waited at the front counter.

When she brought it to me, I thanked her and walked to the back to join Milo Ferguson, whose county we met in today.

Milo sat about three feet from the table to accommodate his belly. Good thing his arms were long enough to reach the table and the Frisbee-sized cinnamon roll he was working his way through. He paused his fork when he spied me. "How do, Katie."

I slapped his shoulder in greeting as I sat. "Finer'n frog's hair."

He picked up his fork. "Whoo-wee. It's hotter than the gates of hell out there. You getting any rain down your way?"

I'd finished telling him the sad tale of a withering prairie when Kyle Red Owl walked in. He waved to us and spoke to Velma. While he waited for her to pour his fountain drink, he said something that made her cackle so loud Milo swiveled his bulk around to see.

Milo chuckled at me. "That Kyle is a real Casanova. All the ladies love him."

I considered that. Kyle had served in Afghanistan as a Marine and still had that cut physique. Women were definitely attracted to him, but I thought it was more in the way a person felt seen because he picked up on something special in everyone.

Kyle brought his drink to the table and took in Milo's empty plate but, as always, kept his expression neutral. To me, he said, "Where's your deputy?"

I assumed he meant Poupon. "Spa day."

He nodded sagely. "Smart."

Milo patted his belly that strained his uniform and looked so tight and heavy it almost gave me a sympathy stomachache. "Ted's late."

I bit back my addition of "as usual." If I was allowing bitterness to pollute me, the least I could do was not make others smell it.

Kyle set his drink down and addressed me. "You've got some action down your way, I hear."

Recall or murder. They were both too much action for my taste.

Milo let out a rumbling belch, but he held his hand over his mouth at least. "I heard Trey Ridnour won't let you near the case. That don't sound like him. He's usually cooperative."

Okay, we were going with murder. That would be my preference.

Kyle agreed. "Last year, we worked together on a homicide outside the rez. Relied on me for the local information. Not like the trooper out of Scottsbluff."

I cringed. That trooper had acted as if Kyle had leprosy. It wasn't hard to figure out he didn't like indigenous people.

Milo laughed as if making a joke when he said to me, "What'd ya do to piss Trey off?"

I didn't laugh, and Kyle and Milo both sobered. Well, Kyle's expression didn't change much, maybe the hint of humor in his eyes faded.

Milo raised his eyebrows and said, "What?"

Did I really have to confess? But if I did it now, at least I wouldn't have to say it directly to Ted's smirking face. I gave them the rundown of how I'd missed the signs of snapped neck, and they listened with sympathy and respect that made me want to hug them both.

When I finished, Kyle took a big draw on his straw and swallowed. "Trey is convinced Kasey murdered Dwayne because she found out Dwayne and Gidget Bartels were sleeping together?"

Milo shook his head. "That don't sound right. You got a girl, Kasey, who had an affair with the guy she ends up marrying. She's known from the get-go a cheater doesn't quit cheating. In her world, this is just the way things go. She's not gonna kill for that."

Kyle said, "Yeah, I don't think she did it, either."

"Oh," Milo said, rapping the table softly. "I think she did it, all right. Look at that girl. She's not bad to look at, sure, but she's taller'n most men, and she's got muscle enough to win a tractor pull on her own. But she didn't kill him 'cause he's tomcattin' around."

Kyle looked interested. "Then why?"

Milo winced as if something—let's call it a cinnamon roll the size of

Kilimanjaro—shifted in his gut. He pulled a tiny plastic cylinder from his breast pocket and flipped it open for a toothpick, which he slid into the side of his mouth, and replaced the holder in his pocket. "I've heard a lot of rumblings about Dwayne Weber hanging around Edgewood. He's been buyin' and sellin' and making moves faster than a carny with the shell game. He's doin' it with cash, and I'm guessin' he wasn't tellin' ol' High Pockets about none of it. She got wind of his double-dealing, and Dwayne's a goner along with all that undeclared cash."

By now I figured Milo was speculating and outright making things up. I harbored a great affection for Milo ever since he'd jumped Elvis's battery on a snowy night in Edgewood after a basketball game when I'd been in high school. But after working with him for three years, I knew he loved a good conspiracy theory.

A tiny spark of skepticism played in Kyle's expression. "What kind of deals?"

Milo hesitated long enough it was obvious he had no concrete answer. "Livestock, of course." It looked like he had a sudden thought, and he said to me, "Ask your brother. I saw them two together all the time."

This time I didn't even hope for another brother. "Michael?"

Milo nodded. "Yep."

Kyle shifted and pulled his phone from his back pocket. He checked the time. "Wonder where Ted is. I've got a meeting with the school in an hour."

Milo chuckled. "Are they still doin' D.A.R.E. up there?"

Kyle turned those liquid brown eyes on Milo. "Working on a presentation about consent and women's rights."

It looked like maybe Milo wanted to comment but thought better of it. The world had changed the rules for men who grew up five or six decades ago, but some of them were trying to keep up.

Velcro squawked as Milo opened a flap on a pocket mid-thigh in his khaki pants. "I'll see if I can get Ted." We waited, and when Ted didn't answer, we concluded he was out of service or on a call.

Milo said, "Welp, might as well get on with it. Anybody got anything about a deputy?"

We kept each other updated on our perennial search for a deputy. Even with four counties joining in, the position was part-time. The deputy would alternate weekends in each county so the sheriff could be assured one weekend off a month. Our budgets were all so tight, any other dedicated days off were rare and required advanced planning. Right now, we relied on the other three sheriffs and the state patrol to fill in if we needed to be gone from the county.

The deputy position required completion of a twelve-week course at the police training facility, the same as for county sheriffs. With that kind of commitment and no guarantee of income, the get wasn't worth the give for most people.

"What about that Rick Hamner who runs in Grand County every election cycle?" Kyle said.

I shook my head. "He hired on the railroad last year."

"Finally decided to work for a living." Milo shifted the toothpick from one side of his mouth to the other. "If you don't make it through the recall, not havin' a deputy puts us in a squeeze."

And there it was.

Kyle showed a bit of sympathy in the quirk of an eyebrow. "I'm sorry about that. My uncle Lloyd Walks His Horse always says to watch out for family. They can hit where it hurts the most."

Milo sucked his toothpick and scratched his tight belly. "Was sure surprised to hear about Louise pullin' that on you. The Foxes always seemed so tight."

They both looked at me as if I'd contracted a dread mogus. "It'll be fine. I've done a good job, and everyone knows me. They're not going to vote me out." I believed that. At least, I thought I did.

We wrapped up the meeting and walked to the parking lot and the pavement-warping heat.

Kyle held his hand out to shake mine, something I'd never seen him do. His always-straight face looked more serious than usual. "Good luck on the recall."

It sounded more like a condolence than a rousing cheer.

Milo stood near my cruiser, waiting for me.

Big and burly, his belly hanging so far a person could only guess if he wore a belt, he stared at me with what appeared to be tears gathering in his eyes. "Oh, hell, Katie." He lurched toward me and engulfed me in a hug.

When he released me, he made a quick swipe at his eyes. "You been the best sheriff Grand County ever had. But if you repeat that to Ted, I'll call you a liar. You dang sure didn't deserve this."

I thanked him, and he moved out of the way for me to get in my cruiser. It was all I could do not to shout at them, "I haven't lost yet."

Maybe they knew something I didn't.

## 20

I hadn't made it more than a few miles from Edgewood when my phone rang.

I recognized Louise's voice immediately, and she sounded as if she'd shoved her frantic gear into overdrive. "You need to get here. Now."

A thousand disaster scenarios ran through my mind in a split second. Most involved nieces and nephews and lots of blood. It spiked all my systems on alert. "What's happening? Where are you?"

"Just hurry." She cut off the call before I could ask anything else.

I rarely needed to use lights out here because, on a busy day, I might pass one or two pickups. This time, I didn't want to mess around. I flipped on the lights and buried the gas pedal. My good ol' Charger had extra umph, and we were traveling close to 125 miles per hour on the straight road in no time.

Still with lights flashing, I swerved onto the street in Hodgekiss leading to the house where I grew up. I couldn't keep my thoughts from careening to two years ago when Mom shot a man in her basement studio. I hadn't thought so at the time, but now, with the note of panic in Louise's voice, I wondered if the house was cursed.

I barreled into the empty gravel lot connected to our two-story that we all used for parking and braked next to Louise's old maroon Suburban. I was halfway to the side door into the kitchen when my niece, Esther, hollered at me from the backyard where she stood with what looked like old saddle blankets in her arms.

I raced toward her. That was when I smelled something burning. It drove a splintered spike of fear into my belly. This time of year might not be as bad as late August when the grass is drier, but we hadn't had recent rains, so a prairie fire could eat up thousands of acres in the blink of an eye.

Now in her tween stage, she wore her blah-colored hair sawed off at chin level, and she carried her childhood weight but hadn't started to stretch or develop curves. "Over here," she yelled to me.

Esther took off racing out the back gate and up the hill behind the house. "Hurry."

She didn't need to urge me. As a kid, I'd traipsed around this hill a million and twelve times. The view from the top took in all of Hodgekiss spread along the railroad tracks. As a pup, I'd bring my plastic horses here, or I'd pretend to be a horse and gallop all over. But as an adult, racing up the sandy hill required a lot of effort, and my thighs screamed in no time. The growth, thick in some spots, matted with clump grass in others, didn't have much summer moisture left and swished in a reedy whisper as we ran. The skin-searing heat only added to the misery as I redoubled my effort to climb.

We made it about halfway to the top when I saw a thin line of smoke appear from the other side of the steep hill, and the smell of Granddad's pipe tobacco mixed with burnt popcorn grew stronger. I sprinted past Esther to the top of the hill.

A blowout had dug a hole on the other side of the hill. Blowouts are pockets of sand that are the result of erosion, usually at the top of a hill where the wind picks up. They come about because the Sandhills are made up of exactly what the term says: sand. Much less common now than they used to be because current land management practices are better, they happen when a tiny, exposed spot of sand—maybe from an animal digging—opens on the fragile hilltop and wind works it into a widening pocket until entire hills can look like ice cream cones without the ice cream.

Years ago, someone had tried to heal the scar of this blowout by tossing old tires and other trash into the loose surface to stabilize the ground and help grass get a toehold.

In our junior version of Newt and Earl, the Fox kids had excavated this dump throughout the years, and all that remained were a few cracked and decomposing tires with weeds growing through them. In another hundred years, probably more, the prairie would reclaim the area.

Louise was in the middle of a circle of tires flapping at flames in the sparse grass that struggled to grow around the deteriorating rubber. I froze at the sight of her frantic beating of flames that didn't seem to be making much progress.

The acrid smell of burning rubber overtook the burnt-grass smell. Mose, Zeke, and Tony stood on the far side of the blowout. Tears streamed down Mose's and Zeke's faces, mixing with what I assumed was soot and dirt, making them look like miniature coal miners. Tony's eyes were wide and his face pale. They stood close together, and I could only guess at the threats Louise had issued for them not to move a muscle.

Louise's eyes flicked to us, and she yelled at Esther, "Toss me a blanket."

I finally understood what shocked me most. It wasn't the fire gaining momentum, it was that Louise was fighting it in her mom jeans and bra. The thin bit of fabric she wielded was her T-shirt. Sure, it was extra large to accommodate her baked-goods-loving figure, but it was no match for the hungry fire.

I grabbed a handful of the blankets Esther held, recognizing them from a stash Uncle Chester and Aunt Hester (yes, that's right) had used to pack Grandma Ardith's furniture when we moved her to the home. Nabbing two, I jumped into the blowout. I threw one to Louise and began knocking the flames down with the one I kept. It had taken me ten minutes to get here after she'd called, so Louise had been at this for a while. The fire hadn't spread far, but it wouldn't be long before someone in town smelled it and the volunteers would come running.

If a brisk wind surprised us, which really wouldn't be a surprise since wind was a regular visitor on the prairie, this small incident could turn into an inferno taking out valuable grazing land.

I had no doubt Louise would call it in if it looked like it might get out of hand. But if she could get the flames out without alerting everyone in the county, it would save the boys from getting into serious trouble, or worse, acquiring a reputation as delinquents.

As if the day wasn't hot enough, add the heat from the flames along with the exertion of attacking the fire with a blanket, and I felt like I'd combust and turn to ash after only a few slaps at the flames.

With all three of us jumping between the crumbling tires and whacking at any stray sparks, we stopped the spread and managed to kill the fire within about ten minutes. At least before anyone else from town showed up.

Louise panted and rested her hands on her knees. Sweat glistened on her cheeks and forehead and ran down the sides of her face. In a weak voice, she said, "Esther. Go down to the house, and if anyone shows up looking for a fire, tell them we were burning trash and it's all okay."

Esther, now covered in soot and dirt, admonished her mother. "But burning trash in town isn't allowed."

Louise straightened and raised her voice. "Just do it."

Esther pursed her lips with a look that said she was disappointed in her mother's choices. But when she turned to start down the hill to the house, I had a view of her expression. Her eyes twinkled, and she winked at me.

I liked her style. With an older brother and sister and the younger twins, Esther had that spot I knew so well. The middle child. Esther, invisible and easily overlooked, had always been special to me. But that little wink went straight to my heart. Since Louise was back to hands on knees, trying to catch her breath, I offered Esther a quick thumbs-up.

I wandered around the lumps of half-buried tires and clumps of singed grass, looking for hot spots. This blowout had been nearly healed when I was a kid and really hadn't been in too bad of shape. Until the delinquents had set fire to it. Not only would the smoldering old rubber pollute the air for days, the fire had burned the grass and exposed bare spots again.

It was illegal to toss tires and trash out now, so we'd need netting or some other material to stabilize the damage. Technically, this land belonged to Troy Stryker, but he lived in Denver and wouldn't care. Between the Foxes, we'd take care of it.

I worked my way over to the boys standing as still as rocks, probably hoping we'd forgotten them. Mose and Zeke looked at the ground. Tony watched me in a challenging way. "Okay," I said. "Who wants to tell me what happened?"

Mose blinked in the harsh sunlight and spoke in a squeaky voice. "We got Mom when the fire started, and she came up here."

Zeke's voice was every bit as strained, like someone pulled his short hairs. "And then you showed up and, man, you two stopped it right away. It hardly burned anything."

Tony agreed with a smirk. "You guys are awesome."

Behind me, Louise flopped her blanket, probably dousing a spark. "You boys are grounded."

Mose and Zeke chorused an "aw," and then Zeke said, "For how long?"

I gave Louise credit for not saying forever, which would have been my reaction. "Until I say so. But it's going to be a long time. Long enough for you to think about what you did."

I kept my eyes on Tony. "What *did* you do?"

He didn't look away. "Nothing."

Mose and Zeke side-eyed Tony with identical pleading expressions. I imagined they might be trying to convince Tony to confess.

Tony didn't.

Louise lumbered over. She'd managed to tug her T-shirt over her head. Not only was it smudged black and covered in bits of grass and weeds, it had several burn holes. I could probably speak for all of us that it was better than seeing her nearly naked.

She stopped in front of the boys, huffing and puffing, her face glowing like a furnace. I was one heartbeat away from diving for cover.

But then she sort of...crumbled.

It started when the wrinkles across her forehead shifted from angry downhill slashes to the shape of waves. Then her hands fell from her hips, and her arms dangled as if she had no bones. Her eyes drooped and her mouth twisted. In a sudden swoop, she burst into tears.

Mose and Zeke gave one horrified gasp, and both started to bawl like baby calves abandoned in a storm. Even Tony looked alarmed.

With nothing else available to avert the disaster, I did the only thing I could do. I stepped forward and put my arms around her, pulling her into a tight embrace. "It's okay. Everyone is safe. The fire's out."

She hiccupped and her sobs tapered off, but then she sucked in a breath that sounded like a three-hundred-mile gust in a wind tunnel and let loose again, clutching me.

I felt like I was being smothered by a giant ball of bread dough. The last thing we needed was for me to panic. Patting her back, I murmured reassurances and worked at loosening the arms that trapped me.

When that didn't help, I whispered, "You're scaring the boys."

She gulped, and a strange series of clicks sounded from the back of her throat, but then she gained some control. She straightened and stepped back, lifted the hem of her stretched T-shirt, showing her pasty skin, and wiped the tears and sweat from her face, leaving smears of dust and soot across her flushed cheeks. Sue me, but I thought: What's black and white and red all over? My sister after fighting a prairie fire.

"You okay?" I asked, keeping my stupid joke to myself.

She lifted her chin, already signs of my bossy sister reemerging. Her face did an awesome transformation from defeated to commanding. "You two." She pointed at the twins with a finger that looked as dangerous as a gun. "Get your butts to the house. I want you in the shower and every speck of dirt washed off in five minutes. After that, Mose, you go to the basement. Zeke, you go to my room. No talking. No games. You sit there. I'll be in to deal with you later."

This time they didn't protest or ask questions. They took off trotting down the hill. I wasn't sure they'd ever seen their mother break down, and the fact that she'd used the word "butt" and not "rear" showed them she was still unpredictable.

She narrowed her eyes and aimed her smoking finger at Tony. "You're not allowed at my house again. Kate will take you home. Wait in her car."

What? Well. I guess I could drive him home. It was only twenty minutes, but it would have been nice to be asked first.

A trace of hurt passed across his face before he tensed his mouth in a defiant way. With his brown eyes, thick hair, and full lips, he looked so much like his aunt Sarah that it cracked my heart. I didn't know if he took after her in that she'd rather shoot you than admit she felt pain. I knew Sarah would cut off her arm if it would help me, and I felt the same for her.

So, seeing even a hint of vulnerability in Tony made me want to protect him.

"Right behind you," I said. But at Louise's murderous expression, I didn't add the "buddy" that had been on my tongue.

When he was halfway down the hill, Louise's shoulders slumped again, and she closed her eyes as if struggling for control.

I waited for her to say something. An explanation. A thank-you. An apology. I'd run to her side, no questions asked, fought a fire beside her, held her when she broke down. Didn't that count for something?

But she didn't offer a word.

The stench of scorched rubber crawled into my nose, and I turned from the fire. I'd been given my orders. If the mission hadn't involved a kid, I might have walked away and let her deal with whatever happened. Oh, who was I kidding? I probably would have done what she asked if I could. That was my job in the Fox family.

The sun burned as hot as any prairie fire. I thought again of the legendary Santa Ana winds that spiked crime rates and apparently made people go crazy. Maybe the heat was doing the same for the Sandhills. Men were getting murdered, kids were starting fires, family was turning on each other. What was next?

If it involved Louise lecturing me about anything, I didn't want to hear it. So, I plodded down the hill.

"Kate." Louise's voice struck the back of my neck like a poisoned dart. I didn't want to turn around, but of course I did anyway.

She looked like a circus clown. Stretched T-shirt hanging over baggy jeans, her hair in a mangled nest, and everything covered in soot. "Thank you for being here. For helping me."

A hen's egg sat in my throat, and I spoke around it. "You're welcome." When she didn't say anything else, I started down the hill again.

"Wait."

I waited.

She obviously fought herself over what to say. "You know I love kids. And I know Tony is having a hard time making friends here because it's summer. I tried to include him. I really did." She choked up and gave herself a second. "But the truth is, he's a bad seed. No matter how nice I was to him, he wouldn't soften up. He kept dragging the twins into one stupid stunt after another."

I didn't want to agree with her, but what she said might have merit. Especially if the boys had something to do with letting Slim into the arena before the mutton bustin'.

She kept on. "Mose and Zeke won't say anything bad about him. They always stand next to him and take equal blame. They never snitch. Norm thinks that's admirable, but I think it's stupid. What I find hard to take is that the boys seem more and more drawn to Tony. He's exciting, I suppose, where vacation Bible school can't compete."

*Well, duh.* "Is Tony responsible for what happened here?" I asked.

She swiped her palm up from her forehead, plastering her hair down with sweat from her face. "Zeke told me when he came screaming into the house. But I won't get him to admit it now. All that honor and boy code Tony has them swearing to."

Before she bolted off on a rant, I dragged her back. "What did Zeke say?"

She puffed out a disgusted breath. "Tony had a fuse he'd found in his granddad's shed. Thank heavens Alden didn't have any dynamite lying around. I'll bet he was clearing ditches at some point, and this is what's left."

Of course, she couldn't drive from A to B, we had to circle around the parking lot.

"And who knows where he found firecrackers. We're lucky he hadn't gotten hold of bottle rockets or the whole town would have burned down. I guess we need to thank the Good Lord for that." She closed her eyes and mouthed a thank-you.

When she opened her eyes, she looked up to the sky for emphasis. "They came up here to play bank robbers and blow the safe open. Set the fuse and the firecrackers, and of course they set the grass on fire."

For the second time in a minute my response was, *Well, duh.* "Do you want me to lock them in the cell for a few hours?" It was a joke but not really.

Louise jerked her head toward me. "Oh, sure. Now you want to be all legal and take it out on my children."

Why had I thought Louise might miraculously develop a sense of humor? "I wasn't serious."

She stomped past me on the way to the house. "What is it with you? I give you an opportunity to show your loyalty. To do the right thing and help out the family. And you act like it's all a big joke. Don't you care? Are you deliberately trying to destroy us?"

*Are you deliberately nutso?* "Hang on a minute. You're not making any sense."

Sure, when she tells me to wait, I freeze. When I tell her to hang on, she keeps moving.

I jumped after her and grabbed her arm, my fingers sinking into the folds. "I don't get it. You file a recall because I'm not doing my job. But now you act like you don't want me to do my job. What is going on?"

Louise jerked her arm out of my grasp. "I want you to not be sheriff anymore. I want everything to go back to the way it was."

"Nothing will ever be the same. Mom left us for her soul mate." I couldn't help the sourness when I used that term.

Tears gathered in her eyes, and she looked toward Hodgekiss. "You chased Mom away. And now Dad is running around like a bull after everything in heat. Jeremy hardly comes to town anymore because he's embarrassed. Michael and Douglas are fighting—"

"Whoa. The twins are bickering? No one said anything to me about that." Their bond was unbreakable. Like bacon and eggs, chili and cinnamon rolls, the Huskers and red.

She huffed. "Because you barely acknowledge us anymore. You don't want anything to do with us."

"That's not true."

"Oh? When was the last time you called me?"

"I've hardly ever called you."

"See?"

I rubbed my forehead. "Why are Michael and Douglas fighting?"

She smashed her hands on her hips. "Why do you think? Michael agrees with me that you being sheriff is not good for you or any of us. Douglas thinks it's dandy if you want to be sheriff."

The way she said it made it clear she was on the outs with Douglas as well. With only eight of us Fox kids, we were building fences and taking sides. My stomach twisted like a tornado on the open plains.

When I didn't reply, Louise continued. "You're so determined to do exactly what you want with no concern for anyone else. You've always been that way, and I blame Diane and Glenda. They spoiled you rotten."

"You're wrong," I said, not specifying on which count because nothing she said was true.

"You're so stubborn. You won't listen to someone who has your best interests at heart. If you won't stop taking yourself down the toilet and the rest of the family with you, I'm going to."

"This isn't your decision."

She cocked her head, her face still a Jackson Pollock mess. "You're right. Now it's with the voters." With that, she spun around and continued her bobble down the hill. Over her shoulder, she called out, "Unless you want to do the right thing and resign. Then it's *your* decision."

# 21

I trudged back to the cruiser, slimy with sweat, grubby with grit, and like my niece Lucy, wanting to take a swing at the nearest victim. As I got closer to the back fence of the house—it was still hard to think of it as Louise and Norm's house instead of ours—the gate opened and Esther walked out.

She held a quart-sized pink Tupperware tumbler. Louise had taken Grandma Ardith's set years ago, and those suckers might even outlive the cockroaches and rats after the Apocalypse. Water beaded on the side, and my throat closed up. Esther held it out to me when I got close. "The boys got a drink inside. Thought you might be thirsty, and I figured you wouldn't want to come into the house."

My fingers closed on the cold plastic with relief. "You are an angel."

She offered up a shy smile. "I'm building up credit so I can come live with you when Granddad moves out."

I chugged so quickly I worried I'd get brain freeze. "You're welcome to come visit any time. But we both need to get permission from your mom." As much as I loved my nieces and nephews, some more than others, I wouldn't undercut their parents.

Her face fell, and I wished I could take it back. "You know her. She's intolerable. And Ruthie is even worse."

Ruthie was Esther's older sister, and I agreed with Esther, though I wouldn't tell her that.

I finished my water and plopped my arm around Esther's shoulder. "No one could love you more than your mother does, so hang in there. And honestly, you can visit any time. It's a bike ride away."

Her pout held a smile inside. "A really long bike ride."

"If it's raining or snowing, I'll come get you."

She took the Tupperware cup from me and waved before turning back to the house.

I climbed into the cruiser. An early incident in my sheriff's career made me habitually remove my keys before leaving the vehicle, but luckily, I'd been driving with the windows down. Tony sat in the passenger seat.

He seemed chipper, not like someone who nearly burned down the county. "Can we stop at Fredrickson's for a Coke before you take me home?"

I put the keys in the ignition and cranked it. "No. You're in trouble."

He laughed. "Ooooh. The big sheriff is gonna arrest me."

Arresting him would be too peaceful. I really wanted to backhand him. "I'm taking you to your father, and we're going to tell him what you've done."

He flopped back, still not cowed. "Big deal. But I don't see why we can't get something to drink first."

I ignored him and looked out the window, saying a silent prayer this heat would break and we'd get some rain. A glance at the cloudless blue overhead and a gust whooshing up the hill dashed my hopes.

We drove in silence for a while. I thought about what Louise had said, that she'd tried to help him out and he'd turned her away. What made a kid act out like that?

Before I could think about it too long, my phone rang. I punched it on. "Sheriff."

"Kate." Michael's voice made my heart jump. Maybe he'd called to work things out with me. "I'm out by Bill Dooley's old place, and you need to get out here."

Again. Another sibling backing my recall needing me to help out. "I'm busy right now."

"Don't give me that. This is important."

Well, dang. This didn't sound like family business. I glanced at Tony before replying. "What's going on?"

"It's Ted. I'm not sure what happened. But he's not in good shape."

"Is that the Double Bar T or the Pullman?" Bill Dooley had a couple of ranches, but he'd gone to live near his daughter in Rapid City. The old trailer at the Pullman place was left to slowly erode and get buried by the sand. One of Dad's cousin's sons and his wife, Phil and Amanda Derby, lived in the brick house at the Double Bar T and leased the ranches.

"The Pullman," Michael shouted. "Careful when you come out here. The Autogate's out."

Most Autogates, known as cattle guards in other parts of the country, were about eight to twenty feet wide, depending on the road they guarded, and five feet across. They were made up of a half dozen or more metal bars that ran perpendicular to the road, spaced a hands-width apart. A rectangular hole, maybe four feet deep, was dug underneath. This contraption kept cattle from crossing, but vehicles could drive over it. When the hole filled with sand, as it eventually would, a rancher could drag the Autogate off or flip it up and dig out underneath it. "Autogate" originally stood for "automobile," meaning the vehicle could drive over it but cattle couldn't cross. Now it meant "automatic gate," which was a real gate that swung open when tapped with a vehicle.

When the Autogate was removed and the hole cleared of sand, it left a crater in the road. A dangerous situation for a speeding, unsuspecting driver.

I wanted to ask way more questions, but Michael hung up before I could say anything else.

I flipped on the light bar and whipped off the road to make a U-turn from the direction of Haney's ranch to where Michael was waiting.

"Hey," Tony shouted, because boys, in my experience, never spoke if they could yell instead. "Where're we going?"

I was used to hauling Poupon to accidents and on investigations, but even I had to admit a kid is different than a dog. I didn't know what to expect and what shape Ted would be in. But I needed to reach the scene as soon as possible. Sure, Ted was my ex-husband, and it was true I often wanted to kill him myself, but if he was in trouble, I would be there. I held up my finger for Tony to wait a second, and I punched in dispatch in Ogallala.

Mary Beth answered, as I was sure she would. "There's been some kind of vehicular accident north of Hodgekiss. Get the emergency crew called."

Mary Beth grunted. "Location?"

"Not sure the mile marker. Tell Eunice it's Dooley's Pullman place. She'll know. I'm heading there now."

"Got it." We could talk in the more formal 10 codes, and I did if some other dispatcher was on duty. But I'd known Mary Beth for years, and when Ted and I were married, I took plenty of sheriff calls. It was easier for me not to have to translate to another language, especially since when I talked to Mary Beth it was usually an emergency.

When I disconnected, I spoke to Tony. "I don't have time to drop you off anywhere, so you need to come with me. You can't leave the car, and I need to keep it running for the air conditioner. That means you're going to have to sit in the back."

His easy cooperation was too much to hope for. "Aw, man. I don't want to wait in the car. I want to see the accident." Of course. Most boys were ghouls at heart.

With one hand on the wheel, I reached behind me and whipped out my cuffs. Before he knew what hit him, I'd slapped the cuff on his wrist and with a quick lunge, locked it to the "oh shit" bar by his door. I blessed all the practice I'd gotten by cuffing my nieces and nephews in one of their favorite variations of tag, called Cuff 'Em.

Tony fought the restraint. "Wait. You can't do that."

I kept my eyes on the road, knowing the turn was coming up shortly. "I just did. If you're not careful, I'll whip out my piggin' string and tie your feet to your hands."

He ruffled up. "What's a piggin' string?"

Obviously, a city kid. "You know when they wrap a rope around the legs of a calf at calf ropings? That's a piggin' string. I'm pretty good at it, and I carry one around with me."

"Why?"

With a meaningful glance, I said, "You never know when you'll need it."

Actually, I'd hoped I'd be able to fill in for someone at the rodeo and hadn't taken it out of my utility belt pocket.

The position had his arm above his head, dangling by the wrist. "But it hurts."

"It doesn't hurt." I tapped the brake when I saw the heavy wood posts and Autogate leading to a one-lane gravel road. It followed a wide valley floor with a series of green hills on either side. Since I didn't see any damage to the fence or gate, I assumed this wasn't the Autogate Michael warned me about. "Your alternative is to sit in the back."

He tugged on the cuffs I'd tightened around his wrist. "You know my dad's a lawyer. He's going to sue you for abusing a minor."

Wind gusted across the prairie, flinging dust and chaff in front of us. Good thing we'd staunched the fire before the wind had picked up again. I wanted to call to make sure, but I felt certain Louise would send someone up to monitor the blowout and beat back any flames that might flare up again. Although I loved summer and could take quite a bit of heat, a hot wind like this rivaled the blusteriest day in January for unpleasantness. Thank the thoughtfulness of Esther that she'd brought me water, or I might have withered like a mummy.

I fought the washboard road but registered Tony's overly adult threat. "Guess your father and I will have a lot to discuss."

What I wouldn't risk was leaving him alone with the keys in the ignition. He might have reasons for acting out, and I might want to show compassion, but that didn't mean I was stupid.

Michael's blue Chevy pickup was parked at the start of a blind curve. A fence ran up the hill and I assumed down the other side, bisecting the road where it would be convenient to have an Autogate just around the bend. I braked and slid a couple of feet on the loose gravel. I flipped toward Tony, not wanting to waste a second. "What's it gonna be?"

When he didn't answer immediately, I opened my door and jumped out.

"Back seat!" he shouted.

With lightning speed, I ran to his side, yanked open his door, unlocked him, and shoved him into the back seat. I popped open my trunk and extracted a couple of water bottles from a case I kept there and tossed some into the back seat. Michael had been smart to park where he did as a warning so I wouldn't hit the Autogate. It was also good to keep Tony from witnessing whatever it was I sprinted to find.

My legs wouldn't pump hard enough to carry me as fast as I wanted. Michael's voice had sounded strained, and I dreaded finding Ted in a mangled heap in the middle of the prairie, bleeding out or crushed under a rolled vehicle. Beau was only two, and he needed a daddy, even if that man was Ted.

The fence line opened for the road, with the metal wing anchors that attached to the Autogate still intact. But what I saw turned my stomach. Taillights of the Chester County sheriff's Bronco were pointed to the sky, the nose buried in a gap in the road where an Autogate should have been. My immediate assessment was that Ted had been barreling down the country road, took the curve at a good clip, didn't notice that the Autogate was missing, and rocketed headfirst into the five-foot hole.

Michael's head popped up from the narrow space in the pit next to the driver's side of the Bronco. Good thing Michael was trim, because it wouldn't have been wide enough for someone like Milo.

He called out to me. "Here!"

I tried to read everything in Michael's expression. But I was too far away. Were his eyes frantic? Were they horrified? He looked flushed, but was that heat, exertion, or reaction from witnessing a grisly scene?

Michael bent over, disappearing from sight until I dashed to the side of the hole. My prayer—*please let Ted be alive*—repeated over and over.

Window glass covered the hole with some pellets of the windshield's safety glass sparkling in the metal anchor wings. Michael leaned into the driver's window. His voice came out calm and strong.

That meant Ted was alive and could hear him. My knees nearly buckled with relief. I'd have jumped down with Michael, but there wasn't room. "How is he?" I maneuvered around the barbed wire fence so I could view the Bronco from the front.

Michael straightened and stretched his back. "I think maybe he's okay. But he's trapped inside, and we can't open the doors."

I couldn't see anything but a slice of Ted's brown uniform. It didn't look tattered or soaked in blood. "Ambulance is on the way."

In fact, I made out the thunder of an engine and tires on the country road above the caterwauling wind. The engine cut, and truck doors slammed closed. Michael must have heard it, too, because he bent down to talk to Ted.

In a matter of seconds, Eunice Fleenor and Harold Graham dashed around the bend. Eunice waved a hand in the air and shouted something to Harold. He skidded to a stop and switched directions to run back. I was sure she told him to bring the ambulance. She never slowed her pace.

Michael used the grill of the Bronco to propel himself out of the hole in time for Eunice to start asking questions as she slid in to take his place.

When Michael finished telling what he knew, which wasn't much, Eunice took over. She spoke in a loud voice, maybe to make sure Ted heard her in case he was shocky. "Hi, Ted. Got yourself in a predicament, didn't you? Hold tight, and we'll get you out. But I'm going to ask you some questions. Can you talk?"

Even with the gusts boxing my ears, I heard the irritation in Ted's voice, if not his words.

Harold backed the ambulance inches from the upended back of Ted's Bronco and ambled out to stand over Eunice.

Michael and I watched and waited to help.

After a second, he gave me a curious look. "You smell like smoke. Is there a fire?"

I rolled my eyes. "Just Louise's kids. It's one of those days." Since he was speaking to me now, I said, "What do you suppose happened to the Autogate?"

It took Michael a while to respond, and I supposed he was still in a snit and didn't want to talk to me. He scanned the prairie. "Looks like someone dragged it off." He pointed to the north. Grass had been trampled in an eight-foot swath for about twenty yards to where the rusted metal of the Autogate rested.

If Phil had been digging out the sand, he'd probably flip it up. At any rate, he wouldn't have dragged the gate that far off. That was only the first question. I waited while a blast of wind buffeted me, then said, "What do you suppose Ted was doing out here?"

Michael, the guy who could hold a grudge longer than Grandma

Ardith's fruitcake got passed around the family, seemed irritated to talk to me. "Couldn't guess. There's nothing out here except that old 'coon-infested trailer."

It hurt that Michael wouldn't look at me. "Do you think maybe Phil and Amanda are doing some roadwork? Maybe installing an automatic gate?" That wouldn't make sense. This pasture was probably only used for a couple of months out of the year.

"Phil doesn't lease this place." His answer was terse.

Huh. A hot gale tore at my ponytail and sent tendrils to tease my face. "Who does?"

He thrust his hands into his pockets and stepped closer to the edge of the hole, intent on Eunice and Harold. "How's it going down there?"

Harold sidled closer to us. "Eunice is evaluatin' him. Think he's not more'n banged up. Gonna have a couple of shiners. Sore muscles."

Michael let out a breath. "That's a relief. It could have been bad."

Wind roared, forcing us to raise our voices.

Harold rocked on the heels of his cowboy boots. "He's lucky, that's fer sure." His gaze rested on me, and he seemed to remember something. "You know, there's a kid sittin' in the back of your cruiser."

It was true, but I wished people didn't have to know it. "I was taking him home when I got the call."

"I see." He let that sit. "He seemed mighty anxious to get let out."

My heart dropped. Harold might have let him loose. It would be too much of a temptation for a kid like that not to take off in a cop car.

Harold watched Eunice and said to me, "I told him you'd be along shortly and left him there. Didn't know what we had here in this mess that a kid that age didn't need to see."

Whew.

Harold wrinkled his nose. "Is there a fire around here?"

Apparently, I hadn't aired out much. "All taken care of."

While Harold and I were talking, Michael had skirted us and took up Harold's old position above Eunice. Explosions of hot air walloped us, driving sand into our eyes and depositing grit everywhere. It chased around my ears like a dragon's warning.

Eunice stood up, her cropped gray hair contrasting with the green and beige of the landscape. "Okay. We're going to have to get Ted out of the vehicle. We could get the Jaws of Life and cut off that door, but that'd create a whole other set of problems. The better way is to get him out the window."

Harold and I inched around to stand next to Michael, and we all gazed into the hole.

Eunice brushed her hands together. "Kate, you're the only one tiny enough to slip into the Bronco. I'm gonna need you to climb in the passenger side and make sure there's nothing snagging up his legs. You help him get out. Michael, you got more muscle than me and Harold. You get down in here and hold him up. Me and Harold will lift him from here."

Now that I knew Ted wasn't dying, I'd just as soon have nothing to do with him. I didn't have much choice, though, so I shimmied down the other side. My back slid against the bank, sending a curtain of dirt down my neck and pants. Along with the sand that had blasted new wrinkles into my face, I now had grit in my most private places. And it was all Ted's fault.

The broken safety glass glinted on the window frame and covered the interior. I had a moment of burning annoyance when I thought I might be forced to take my shirt off to use as a broom. But bless Eunice's capable mind, she tossed a surgical drape down to me before it came to that.

I brushed at the glass and, when it looked clear, snaked into the window and plopped on the seat beside Ted. Between my anger at myself for being so concerned about him and my aggravation at Ted for getting in this pickle, and what I imagined was Ted's pain, embarrassment, and humiliation at me having to help, we hadn't said a word to each other until now.

The Bronco smelled of Irish Spring soap and his sweat, a scent so familiar and wrapped in eight years of marriage memories it made my head swirl. Or else it was the heat of the airless SUV that made me dizzy. I wriggled until I was upright and assessed the situation.

He sniffed. "Is there a fire?"

"No."

The steering column had been compressed toward him, and though it hadn't impaled him, it had him wedged tight. The driver's door was crushed inward so that it pinned his arm on that side. The right sleeve of his uniform had caught in a bit of crushed radio equipment, rendering him helpless. I kind of liked that.

On my knees, I leaned over him and hit the lever to pop up the steering wheel, more than a little surprised when it clunked up, giving Ted room to wiggle free. "Wondered why you didn't show up for the meeting."

He winced. "I was on my way." He yanked his right arm, clearly frustrated to still be trapped. "Can you just…"

Lying across his lap, I probed around on the floor to make sure nothing hindered his legs. "The route is three times shorter if you'd driven directly from your county."

"Less talk, more getting me out of here." He seemed to have lost his sense of humor.

I stretched until I found the seat button and pressed it to move his seat back. If it had been me, that would have created a lot of space. But since Ted was over six feet tall, it didn't move much. "I'm happy to help you out, but seems like you could be a little nicer. Why are you here?"

He closed his eyes as I braced against the driver's door with my palm and pushed back to kneeling.

"Thought I'd enjoy the sunrise," he said.

The Ted I knew hated getting up early. "You've been here a long time?"

He started squirming, easing himself out of the tight spot. "Since before dawn."

That would account for his ripeness. The sun probably hit his windshield for a few hours in the morning. He'd have been like a bug under a magnifying glass. "What brought you down this road?"

"It's been a long time since I've been over here. Thought I'd check it out."

I might have been blind during our marriage, but he'd schooled me since then. A blink of his eyes, a studied casual tone, and a stupid response told me he was lying. "Really? Because experience has taught me that when you end up in unexpected places, it usually means you're meeting a woman."

Honestly, I was only trying to poke him. Much as I hated it, I believed Ted and Roxy were made for each other. But his reaction knocked me backward.

His mouth clenched tight, and a lightning flash of panic hit his eyes. He looked nauseated but managed to grunt. "Your bitterness is showing again."

I might have been sniffing around before, but now I had the bone in my teeth. "Who is she?"

"You're crazy."

"Michael says there's nothing down here except an old trailer."

Here was the Teddy I knew so well. If he didn't want to answer a question, he'd lob one instead. "What is Michael doing out there?"

Good question. But not what I wanted to know right then.

Michael's boots, jeans, T-shirt, and finally his face descended outside the driver's window. "How's it going?"

Ted shook his head. "My legs are numb because I've been sitting here for hours. And I might have dislocated my shoulder, so I'm going to need a lot of help."

Ted was lots of things, a philanderer, a liar, narcissist, for instance, but he was tough. I admired the way he'd handled the pain but didn't feel too badly he'd suffered.

With grunts and nudges, shoves, pushes, tugs, and plenty of cursing, we set to work. Ted twisted enough to get his shoulders out of the window. I succeeded in leveraging under his rear to get him going. With Michael working to ease him out the window, Eunice and Harold were able to grab him under his arms, only bumping his shoulder once, making his face turn gray and eliciting a groan of pain. I pulled his legs free, and eventually, we had him sprawled on the side of the hole.

While I struggled to free Ted, I vacillated with so many emotions it was like driving three hundred miles an hour in a roundabout with twenty exits and not knowing your route. Justification that it wasn't my fault Ted had an affair and ended our marriage. Disgust at him for being such a monumental jerk. Sadness for little Beau because Ted would eventually mess him up. Irritation because I felt sorry for Roxy. But mostly, consuming curiosity about who would be stupid enough to have an affair with Ted.

Not to mention frustration because I couldn't follow up on any of it. Like the rest of Grand County, I'd have to wait for the rumors to dribble out. Except in our county, it was never a dribble, it'd be a gusher.

Michael worked his way out of the pit, and I slithered from the driver's side and followed him up.

By the time Michael and I brushed off the loose sand and weeds, letting the wind spirit it away, Eunice and Harold had Ted loaded onto the gurney and were lifting him into the ambulance.

Michael smelled like a locker room at halftime, and I was sure I wasn't any better.

I swiped at sweat on my forehead and pulled the ponytail holder loose to try to capture the escaped locks. My hair smelled of prairie fire and was such a tangled mess it'd take a whole bottle of conditioner to tame it. That is, if I ever found my way to a shower again. "You never told me who leases this place and what you're doing out here."

He wouldn't look at me, exactly the same way he acted when he was Mose and Zeke's age and I'd caught him putting a garter snake in Susan's backpack.

"You're not going to tell me?" I badgered.

He strode away so fast it startled me. "You're the sheriff. You figure it out."

## 22

By the time I got back to the cruiser, I'd had about enough. I felt like I'd been in a prize fight with the wind all afternoon. And if it wasn't a TKO, my worthy opponent was wearing me down.

I started up the big engine of my Charger, and Tony knocked on the Plexiglass between the front and back seat. "What happened? They took somebody away in the ambulance, but the lights weren't on. Does that mean he's dead?"

Over my shoulder, I said, "Put your seat belt on."

"I bet he's dead. Did you see him? Was there a lot of blood?"

I slammed on the brakes, and Tony hit the partition. Not hard, because I hadn't accelerated yet. "Ow! I'm telling my dad you tried to hurt me."

A gust pelleted the cruiser with sand.

I twisted in the seat to give him the mom stare. "Put. Your. Seat belt. On."

He must have seen danger flaring in my eyes, because he clamped his lips shut and sat back on the passenger side, as far away from me as possible. I didn't relax the stare until the seat belt clicked.

I hated to give Tony the satisfaction of knowing what had happened, but I needed to call Roxy. It probably wouldn't hurt to quash Tony's ghoulish delight when he heard no one died.

When she answered with a singing hello, I could tell she was smelling particularly Roxy this afternoon. "I was going to call you. What would you think about next Saturday for that bowling date?"

I glanced in the rearview mirror, terrified Roxy would mention Garrett, and Tony didn't need to know anyone was trying to set me up with his father. That might be why I was so abrupt. But I might have been anyway, since shocking Roxy was one of my hobbies. "Ted's been in an accident."

Her gasp ended in a squeak. "Oh my God. Oh my God." Typical Roxy chorus.

There was a limit to my mean, so I hurried on. "He's okay. Banged up. On his way to Broken Butte in the ambulance."

"Ambulance. Oh my God. Is he going to make it? I need to get there." A clatter sounded on her end, probably plugging in her curling iron. "Oh, no. Beau. Where are you? I can drop him at the courthouse on my way through Hodgekiss."

And now was as good a time as any to practice a new word. "No." Diane would be so proud.

She squeaked again. "He's up from his nap. And you don't have to do much for supper. He likes mac and cheese."

I tried again, with feeling this time. "No."

Her chatter halted in a moment of silence. "But I need to get to Ted."

"And I need to work."

She sniffed. "But it's your fault he's hurt. The least you could do is help me out."

I got blamed for plenty of things. Mom leaving, for instance. But Ted having an accident on his way to a tryst was—to use a bowling term Roxy might appreciate—over the line. "I had nothing to do with this."

She spoke in the fits and starts of someone racing around her house. "He was really mad at you guys. I mean, why would you plan a traffic stop so early in the morning? It didn't make sense. He said it was your idea. And now look. Ted's been hurt. Probably hit by someone speeding through the stop because no one expects anyone out there—"

Our four-county sheriff co-op got together every few months in a joint mission to conduct random traffic stops on Highway 2 or 61 or 97. Once or twice we'd intercepted drug runners. Mostly we caught speeders or issued fix-it tickets.

Before I could say anything, Roxy ratchetted up. "He already got shot in the spine, and it took him so long to heal up and he's still got a limp when he's tired. I don't know if I can go through that again."

I hadn't thought about it until then, but Ted received his last major injury while he was conducting an affair with Roxy. Maybe he'd figure out infidelity wasn't good for him.

Roxy sounded like she jumped on the panic wagon, where she had a season pass. More rustling and pounding in the background, as if she were throwing things against a wall. Maybe packing a bag for Beau? She muttered and fretted. My guess was that she wore headphones to free her hands and hadn't gotten around to hanging up.

I gave it a moment, then said, "Where did Ted tell you he was going so early?"

"Around Potsville. I said, 'Ted, that's just crazy to start before dawn.' And he said that's what he told you." She sucked in enough air to let out a sarcastic comment. "But no, Kate always has to get her way."

When was the last time I got my way? But that wasn't the topic now. "There was no traffic stop. We had our monthly meeting at nine thirty in Edgewood."

Her voice wavered. "That's not right. Ted left before light. He said he had to be in Potsville when the sun came up."

She might repeat the lie he told her a million times, but eventually she'd come to the truth.

"He drove his Bronco into an empty Autogate hole at Dooley's Pullman place. Been there since dawn."

"But. That's not even on the way to Edgewood." She stopped, maybe in stunned silence. Beau started fussing in the background. She didn't say anything. Beau protested louder. Finally, she said, "That son of a bitch." And hung up.

Part of me knew how she felt. The ground beneath you shakes. The table tips over, glasses shatter, there is a sound like a freight train between your ears, and the scene in front of you freezes while you coax your heart to keep beating. But every marriage is different, and every betrayal is unique.

While I'd believed Ted and I had a solid union that worked well for eight years, I admitted after the fact that maybe I hadn't spent enough time and attention on the marriage.

But Roxy was convinced she and Ted were soul mates. They had a child together, and Roxy acted as if Ted was a vital organ that kept her alive.

I didn't think of Roxy as a friend, but I wondered if I could do something to help her through this.

Right now, though, Roxy wasn't as big a concern as Dwayne's murder and Ted's accident and Michael's mysterious presence there. It was all connected somehow. Santa Grand County winds or not, this couldn't be random.

## 23

When we made it to the highway, I put on my blinker and turned north.

Tony piped up from the back seat. "Hey. This isn't the way home. Now where are we going?"

My snoozing hound would have been better company than this nagging boy. Poupon might be haughty, but at least he gave me his attitude without a sound. "I need to talk to some people before I take you home." It didn't make sense to drive him all the way through town and out the other side, only to drive back here later. Fuel being one of my biggest budget items, it was always best to conserve when possible.

Tony griped. "This isn't my job. I don't want to be locked up here like a criminal."

I glanced in the rearview at his aggrieved face. "Arson is a crime. So that makes you a criminal. Be glad I don't toss you in the jail cell and make your father pay bail."

He flopped back. "He can afford it. We don't have to live out here in old houses that are falling apart and smell like crap. We've got a mansion on a golf course in Scottsdale. This place sucks, and we won't be here long. So go ahead and throw me in jail. It might make Dad decide to go home sooner."

That told me a lot. Did Garrett know how unhappy Tony was living here? I thought the Sandhills was the greatest place on earth to grow up. But a kid used to sports leagues, play dates, and fast food might not agree.

After five miles, I took a right onto a dirt road. It led to Dooley's homeplace, where Phil and Amanda lived. We didn't need to traverse the several miles on the twisty, bumpy road all the way to their house because we were lucky enough to come across a center pivot sprinkler that covered an alfalfa crop about the size of three football fields.

While a cheery yellow swather mowed down green alfalfa, leaving endless windrows of cut hay on one side of the circle, an old red International H tractor with not even an umbrella cover dragged two side delivery rakes on windrows that were already down, probably cut the day before and cured overnight. Amanda sat atop the old tractor in a ratty feed cap and billowing long-sleeved shirt. The rakes turned two flat stripes of cut hay together to make one knee-high windrow that would be sucked into the baler, probably this afternoon or tomorrow. Wind whipped the hay she raked, creating a dust storm of leaves and dirt.

I assumed Phil sat in the air-conditioned comfort of the swather, the sweet smell of fresh-cut alfalfa swirling into the cab, radio playing. Staying clean and comfortable.

I bumped from the dirt road into the stubble of the field, avoiding the hay down on the ground, and made my way to Amanda.

She got to the end of her rows and made a wide turn to reposition the rakes and come back on the next rows. She spotted us and braced herself on the brake and clutch, leaned forward, and cut the engine. The metal flap on the top of the stack clanked to a stop. She waited while I climbed out.

"Hey," Tony shouted from the back. "Let me out."

I ignored him and shut my door. "Looks like a good cutting," I said in greeting.

Amanda was in her early forties. She wore her hair bunched under the cap, and her face was streaked with dirt and sweat. She wore a T-shirt under the oversized button-up that flapped in the wind. Everything about her looked dirty and itchy. Even so, a part of me envied her. I loved putting up hay, the smell, the feeling of satisfaction as I watched winter's supply stack up.

Amanda pulled the hem of her T-shirt up and swiped at her face. "We've watered the shit out of it. The wild hay won't be good if we don't get rain. What's brought you out here?"

No reason not to tell her the story. "I was out to the Pullman. Ted Conner had a little accident out there. Fell into a dug-out Autogate."

Her mouth dropped open in surprise and humor. "That's not what I expected. What's he doing out there? And the gate was completely gone? Like, a big hole in the road?" She reached around and unhooked a grungy red-and-white water jug from the seat stem and tipped it up to her mouth.

She seemed clueless about the Autogate and not that concerned about someone being on their place. "Were you having some work done on the road?"

She recapped the water jug. "I don't know what he's got going on over there. But now I'd like to."

Wind tossed bits of hay at me, and I inhaled odors of tractor grease and sun-warmed alfalfa, a smell familiar and nostalgic. "What who's got going on?"

She propped the jug on her knee and wiped at her neck, which I was sure had to feel like a thousand tiny River Dancers with spikes on their heels performing on her skin. "Dwayne Weber. It's his place now. Well, was, I guess. Thought I'd give Kasey some time to adjust before I ask if she's going to keep it."

I must have looked confused, because she said, "Dwayne subleases the Pullman from us. Not sure what he's doing. Your brother is mainly the one I see. I didn't know they were working on that Autogate. Phil dug it out last year, so I can't imagine it's full. And to take it out completely instead of flip it up, well, that doesn't make sense."

Now I wanted to check it out. I considered Tony in the back of the cruiser. I should take him home first. Kids put a crimp into my investigating. I waved at Amanda. "Thanks for the information. I'll keep praying for rain."

She twisted around to secure the water jug on the seat. "You do that. Thanks for letting us know about Ted. I can't wait to tell Phil. This is gonna be a good story, I'll bet."

Good grist for gossip, not so good for Roxy and Beau.

Still not my problem. Poor Tony was about to go for more of a ride than he cared to.

## 24

I let Tony out of the back seat when we pulled up to the decrepit single-wide house trailer at the Pullman place. We'd had to follow the fence line a ways to find the gate into this sweeping pasture since the Autogate was out. But the Charger didn't mind a little cross-country trek, and it made Tony squawk, which I counted as a bonus.

He headed straight for the front door of the pale blue single-wide with peeling siding. Since I thought it might be Ted's love nest and who knows what might be left in plain sight, I intercepted him. "You wait out here." There might have been a fence around a yard many years ago, but it had been torn out, leaving this eyesore sitting on the prairie. You could see where there had been a yard of sorts because when they quit tending it, the area never reseeded the natural grasses and left a dried-up dirt patch all around the trailer. A scarred example of why it was never a good idea to plow up the delicate Sandhills.

About fifty yards away, a windmill clanked with the brisk wind, pumping water faster than the overflow pipe could drain it, and water sloshed over the sides of the tank. "Go get a drink from the windmill, and I'll meet you over there after I check out the trailer."

Tony eyed the windmill and then frowned at me. "Ew. It's dirty."

This kid. "Catch the water in your palm where it comes from the pipe.

That's straight groundwater and probably the best you'll ever taste. It'll be cold, too."

Thirst must have won out over hygiene concerns, because he trudged toward the windmill.

My fear of finding something disgusting in the trailer was for nothing. Aside from quite a bit of dust and a mouse nest or two, the place was empty. Skunks hadn't even claimed it. However, if Ted had used the space, he hadn't left any lasting marks. My guess was they brought a sleeping pad or blankets and spread them on the floor.

I joined Tony at the windmill, where he'd decided to stretch out in a patch of green grass fed by the overflow. "About time," he said. "What are we even doing out here?"

I leaned over and cupped my hand under the icy flow of water and sucked it in. "Taking a look around."

He lifted his head and made a show of surveying the whole valley. "There. I looked. Don't see anything. Can we go? I'm starving."

"We may not see anything now, but it's obvious there are cattle in this pasture, and I want to know whose they are."

"How do you know that?"

"The hoofprints in the mud here by the tank. Let's go see if we can find them."

He didn't move.

"That means now."

He grunted and groaned worse than Ralph Stumpf as he pushed himself to his feet and dragged behind me. "I'm telling my dad that you forced me to walk in the heat and didn't feed me."

"You can tell him anything you want to." We made it to the cruiser, and I found a protein bar in the cubby so he wouldn't die of hunger. I let him ride up front with me, warning him not to touch anything or I'd lock him in back again.

Luckily, we found a bunch of cows over the next hill under two scraggly cottonwoods. Some poor homesteaders had probably planted the trees by a soddy and tended them with love and hope. The cottonwoods had survived. Who knows what happened to the old place and the people who'd dreamed here.

There were only six head. Not uniform Angus or Black Baldy that would make good beef cattle; these seemed rangy. They raised their heads when we came over the hill and trotted from the cruiser. I braked and watched them.

Tony clearly wasn't impressed. "Cows. Big deal. There're cows all over Nebraska."

I focused on the brand visible on a few of them. It resembled an equal sign with a ball in the middle. I'd seen that brand before.

Tony whined. "I'm so bored. Let's go."

There didn't seem to be much to see out here. Michael and Lauren could accommodate a half dozen cows on their place. If he'd wanted to lease a place and raise cattle, these certainly weren't ideal. I was still puzzled why Michael had been out here. And why was Dwayne leasing a whole section for a few head?

I drove back over the hill and onto the gravel road but hadn't gone more than half a mile when the dust from an approaching vehicle rose. I pulled to the side of the road and waited. When I was sure it was Michael's pickup returning, I climbed out. "Don't touch anything," I warned Tony again and whipped out my piggin' string to back up my threat.

Michael ground to a stop and rolled down his window. His sweaty and pinched face proved he wasn't happy to see me. "What are you doing out here?"

We might be adults, but I still pulled big-sister attitude. "The question is, what are *you* doing here, and what have you got going with Dwayne Weber?"

He hit me with a dead stare. "It's not your business."

I hadn't expected him to roll over easily. "Here's what I think. Dwayne is wheeling and dealing. Some kind of bad business with TJ Simonson. Probably buying and selling livestock for cash and skimming money from Kasey. Most of it illegal or questionable. And I want to know what you've got to do with it."

The color drained from his face. "I-I-I had nothing to do with that." He only stuttered under extreme stress, such as when he was ten years old and the principal threatened to expel him, and Dad said he'd have to send him to military school. As I remembered it, Michael and Douglas spent the rest of the school year helping in the cafeteria instead of getting recess, and they didn't get into much mischief the rest of the year. Of course, Douglas hadn't been in trouble, but he wouldn't leave Michael to suffer alone.

The wind sent another curtain of grit, and I blinked to keep it out of my eyes. "You're taking care of livestock on land leased by Dwayne. Lauren is worried. Douglas isn't talking to you. Obviously, you're in some kind of trouble."

He gritted his teeth. "I can handle it. You don't need to come to my rescue."

I pressed him. "You got spooked when you saw Maureen's rig at Webers' right after Dwayne died. You've got some cows with her brand over that hill. Explain that to me."

His shoulders sagged, and he dropped his head. "Can you let it go? Dwayne made some borderline deals. That wasn't me, I swear. But I'm in deep, and I need to get myself out."

My heart sank. "People were swindled, and you're partially responsible. I can't let that go."

"I swear to you, he was the cash, and I was the sweat equity. I had nothing to do with the other side."

"Did you have anything to do with Pecos's and Luke's deaths? With the lug nuts on TJ's trailer? Come on, you had to know Dwayne was dealing dirty." Plenty of people thought Michael was neck-deep with Dwayne, and I wasn't sure they were wrong.

He looked miserable but still didn't make eye contact. "I didn't ask where the money came from."

I swept my arm to encompass the prairie. "What was the plan here?"

Head down, he creaked his neck to look at me. "Rough stock. Wild Fire Buckin' Bulls. WF, for Weber-Fox. Dwayne had the connections. There is a whole group of guys that work together, help each other out."

"What do you mean?"

"It's hard to break into the game, you know? A guy like me might get a good bull, but he's not going to get good draws or make the best performances. Won't get to the National Finals. But if you know the right people and do the right favors, the gates open up."

This was what Maureen was fighting. "Why all the secrecy?"

"It's a really competitive business. Our plan was to get established before anyone could come after us."

"But everyone in the business knows Dwayne. It's a small world, so it won't be long before they see you with the bulls."

"Dwayne's got a cousin who hauled the bulls for us. I took care of them here and at my place. Dwayne supplied the initial investment. We've done great, and the money is starting to come in. It was a good plan."

"Except Dwayne was breaking about a hundred laws."

"That wasn't me."

"When did you plan on letting people know who Wild Fire is?"

A fizzle of frustration crossed his face. "If it was up to me, we'd have come clean this weekend at the big Fourth of July events. But Dwayne wanted to keep it under wraps because he didn't want Kasey to know."

"No one knows you're involved in this?"

He looked so much like Zeke when I caught him breaking into my window at the courthouse. "I only made one trip for Wild Fire. That was to Arizona to buy cows."

"From Maureen."

And like Zeke, he talked fast to explain. "Dwayne said they were the best breeding stock around. He's been watching them for years."

I'd bet he had. "Maureen Steffen knows your face. That's why you wanted to avoid her."

He nodded, looking sick.

After seeing his picture at their trailer, Maureen knew who he was now. "Dwayne and Kasey were doing fine. Why would Dwayne want to start over with Wild Fire?"

He lifted his head and gave me a look like I was stupid. "He needed to get away from Kasey. But they have assets together, and he didn't want to split it all up."

"So, he was going to use up the assets to start this new business and leave her broke."

Michael shook his head. "You don't get it. She's one crazy heifer. She started treating the bulls like puppies. According to Dwayne, she's got a violent streak and came after him with a pitchfork more than once. He wanted out, but he didn't make his move fast enough."

I didn't want to defend Kasey again but did anyway. "Dwayne was no prize. He was lying to her, stealing from their business, sleeping with Gidget Bartels, sabotaging competition in a really dangerous way, and who knows what else? And you want to make him out to be a victim?"

His eyes held a hint of desperation. "Do you think that Autogate thing was an accident?"

I didn't but hadn't come up with a theory.

"That was meant for me. Kasey killed Dwayne, and she tried to kill me."

"Even if she knows about Wild Fire"—I was pretty sure she did—"how would she know about you? And why would she care enough to try to kill you?"

"Didn't you hear me say she's crazy? I doubt she knows I'm involved in Wild Fire. She was laying a trap for whoever came out here. Dwayne was smart and careful." He rested his head on the steering wheel. "But he's dead."

I tipped my head to the trailer. "What are you planning to do?"

He sat up. "I'm going to move the cows."

"Why?"

"Because I'm a partner in Wild Fire, and they're mine. But if Kasey finds out, she'll make trouble. I need to get them out of here and sold before she can stop me."

"As his widow, she's entitled to whatever he owned."

"You don't understand. I owe a ton of money for the new house. Wild Fire was starting to take off, and I was sure we'd keep making money. So, I got all that work done. If I don't sell the cows and pay the contractor, I'll be sunk."

"Where were you going to take them?"

He took a second, as if he didn't want to say. "The Bar J. They aren't using that west summer pasture."

"Did you ask Carly?"

He didn't answer.

"Turn around and go home. You're in too much trouble the way it is without stealing from Kasey. This is underhanded and lousy, and you know better."

He tightened his lips as if wanting to fight me.

"What's Lauren say about this?"

The skin drooped on his cheeks, and he looked about ready to cry. "She's furious. Took the girls to her mother's." He closed his eyes and looked like he fought off a wave of panic. "I've got to make this right or she might leave me."

Lauren had a right to be steamed, but I doubted she'd end the marriage. "You've got some problems, but don't make it any worse."

I stood in the road, watching him drive away. Maybe he was right that whoever killed Dwayne wanted Dwayne's partner out of the way as well.

The cruiser door opened, and Tony shouted, "Are you gonna stand there all day?"

## 25

We drove the next half hour in silence, Tony maybe pouting, me hating on Ted, worrying about the hole Michael had dug for himself, stewing about Trey cutting me out of the investigation, and calculating the chances of Louise actually swaying the recall vote in her favor. Then there was the whole question of Kasey and her role in all of this. When we pulled into the ranch yard at Haney's homeplace, I shut off the engine.

Alden and Ellie had four good-sized ranches, but Alden's great-granddad had settled here first. When he and his wife earned enough to tear down the old soddy, they'd built this lovely two-story that now sat shaded by a line of blue spruce that towered with all the years they'd been coddled and loved. Trees didn't make it in the arid, sandy land unless someone tended to them like family.

The wind had joined forces with the sun, and both seemed intent on showing how powerful they could be. With weather this grievous, it was a wonder there weren't more murders this week.

The gray Ford pickup Garrett had been driving since he came back to the Sandhills was parked in front of the gaping doors to a huge pole barn. A building this size could house two or three full-sized tractors and various implements and still provide work space. Something like this cost as much as Diane's opulent home in Denver's tony neighborhood.

It looked like a swather was disassembled inside, probably taking advantage of the sunlight from the opening. I wasn't sure I'd rather work in the dark than deal with the wind, but maybe it wasn't so bad inside. By the looks of the swather, I figured Garrett was probably taking care of a hayfield casualty.

The wind shoved the cruiser and made it rock. While Tony climbed out, I pulled the ponytail holder from my hair and smoothed the waves back, hoping to make myself a little less wild and wooly. Then I got out and spoke to Tony. "Go to the house while I talk to your dad."

Tony held his ground. "I have the right to defend myself."

'Possum pie and tater tots. This kid tested my temper. Out came the fire-breathing mom face again. "You really want to play it this way?" I was seconds away from grabbing the piggin' string and hog-tying him in the yard. I almost hoped he'd try me and end up being sandblasted or maybe blown into Choker County by the time I was done talking to Garrett.

He didn't press me. With arms folded and a heavy tread, he marched across the yard and up the porch steps.

When I was sure he'd gone inside—no assurances what he'd do in there or if he'd stay—I wasted no time going to the metal building. Hopefully Alden or Ellie were home to corral the miscreant in the house.

The wind rehearsed for its hurricane finale, so I didn't think Garrett could have heard us pull up. I stepped to the twenty-foot-tall sliding doors, ready to announce my arrival, but a booming man's voice stopped me.

"I've never seen anything so lame-brained. I shouldn't have to tell you not to use the swather on the wild hay. Now look. This is going to cost a fortune. But you don't care about that, do you? Always the lazy way for you. You haven't changed at all."

The vitriol in the voice burned like acid. It had the vague reminiscence of Alden's voice, but this one was so loaded with loathing my stomach curdled.

Though I always suspected Alden's overly friendly attitude was a put-on, it hadn't mattered to me. He was someone I said hi and bye to when Sarah and I had run in and out of their house.

I considered backing out into the wind and driving off before anyone knew I was here. But I couldn't leave without talking to Garrett about Tony.

There was a mumbled reply that must've been Garrett.

Alden's voice rose. "What am I thinking that you can run this ranch? You're an idiot." A whack, like a canoe paddle on a smooth lake, made me jump. It was followed by another and a soft grunt.

This took away my option of leaving. I sped toward the altercation, shouting in false chirpiness, "Garrett? Are you in here?" I made a point of smacking my footsteps on the concrete as I hurried to the back of the building where the tool bench and shop area were located.

Behind an old International M tractor, Alden and Garrett stood about five feet apart, their faces turned toward me in a mix of curiosity, embarrassment, and horror.

Fortunately, Sarah and Garrett had inherited their good looks from Ellie, who came from a long line of beautiful people back East where she and Alden had met at college. Sarah suspected Ellie had been shocked by the realities of the Sandhills and had tried to shrink herself so small no one would notice her. I thought maybe Alden was too dominating to allow Ellie her own space. However it came about, Ellie was soft and quiet and didn't venture out much.

What he lacked in beauty Alden made up for in authoritarianism. Bulky but not tall, blotchy skin, and an expression that perpetually looked dissatisfied had made me keep my distance, even though he'd always been the type of parent who would greet you enthusiastically, then dismiss you quickly.

Alden's craggy face rearranged itself into clownish welcome. "Well, Katie Fox. Been a long time since you were out here. Maybe with Sarah for Mom's sixtieth birthday."

It always creeped me out the way Alden and Ellie called each other Mom and Dad. I tried to keep my tone light and surreptitiously survey both men for damage. "Yeah, I guess that was the last time."

Garrett wore a faded and grimy pair of Wranglers and grayish Converse with so many holes it seemed impossible they stayed on his feet. His T-shirt was stretched and faded until it had no identifiable color and was darkened with sweat under his arms and around his neck. Basically, the hayfield uniform. Still, he had the Haney good looks that I'd always envied in Sarah. His hair, with bits of straw from being in the wind, still lay perfectly as if arranged for a photo shoot. But there was a bright patch of red and swelling starting just under his right eye.

His effort to appear casual fell short, and his gaze roamed around the shop but not quite landing on me. "What are you doing here?"

A shop rag rested on the concrete floor. It was twisted in just the way we'd worked kitchen towels when I was a kid. Every Fox had towel-snapping expertise, and our epic battles left contusions on our arms and legs.

Now I recognized the whacking sound I'd heard earlier. The white welt encircled by crimson growing riper on Garrett's face was evidence of Alden's proficiency with snapping a towel. When we'd been warned we could take someone's eye out, I hadn't considered it a real possibility.

I didn't try too hard to present a friendly face. "I brought Tony home from Louise's. He's in the house."

Garrett leaned over and whipped the shop rag from the floor and wiped his hands. "I'm sorry. I'd planned on getting him. Louise told me this evening would be fine."

Alden's face tugged into an expression that looked more grimace than grin. "Welp, guess I'll head to the house and see what Mom's got planned for supper. That's if I don't get blown away first." Even his guffaw was strained.

Garrett and I watched him stomp out. I didn't know whether to let Garrett know I'd heard the fight or let it go. On the one hand, families fight and say awful things to each other all the time. On the other, it appeared that Alden had attacked Garrett, even if it was with a nonlethal weapon. Maybe I should reach out like I would to a friend or family member, let him know I supported him. Probably I should keep my mouth shut since I didn't know Garrett well.

Garrett stopped my internal debate by breaking the silence. "That's a sad thing about Dwayne Weber."

Small talk. Okay. "Sure is. Did you know him?"

He shrugged. "Not really. When we moved back, he came around. Tried to sell me a half share of a bull." He laughed. "Lucky Luke. Guess Dwayne thought I didn't know anything about livestock or rodeo. After I turned him down, I didn't see much of him."

"That sounds about right for Dwayne." We stood awkwardly for a minute.

Garrett inhaled and said, "Well, thanks for bringing Tony."

As if getting shredded by his aging father wasn't enough, I was about to drop more manure on him. "The reason Louise asked me to bring Tony home early is because he's caused some problems."

Garrett lost all expression, but the welt by his eye looked angry enough to compensate. "What kind of problems?"

Being sheriff, I'd had to deliver my share of bad news. I'd given out tickets, served papers, and knocked on doors to inform people their loved ones had died. I'd never been able to deliver news of calamity without a hard walnut of angst in my gut. So, I took a breath and sucked it up. "Today he brought a fuse and firecrackers to town. If Louise hadn't been so quick, and the wind hadn't come up yet, they'd have burned the whole town down."

Garrett turned his head a half inch and looked at me askew, as if cross-examining a witness. "But there was no damage, is that right?"

"This time. I have no proof, but I think they might have tampered with a trailer gate that let a bull into an arena of little kids at the rodeo."

He turned to the workbench and picked up a monkey wrench. "Okay, I'll talk to him." Except it didn't sound like Garrett intended to do anything.

I stepped closer to the workbench and spoke to the side of his face. "Day before yesterday I caught them trying to break into the sheriff's office to steal evidence they thought I'd store there, like a TV cop show."

He coughed out a *ha*, as if he thought the idea was funny. "You don't have an evidence room, do you?"

I put my hand on the cold metal surface of the bench and leaned to where I saw his face. "The point is, Louise says she won't have Tony at her house anymore and the twins are not to play with him."

Garrett whipped his face to me. "What? Because he's spirited? Because they misbehaved, without any dire consequences? Correct me if I'm wrong, but the Foxes have caused their share of mischief."

"Mischief Louise can handle." Not the way I would, but she had a method. "This has gone beyond that."

He drew himself up. "How do you know it's Tony's doing? Those twins aren't angels, you know."

I did know. "No one is letting them off the hook. They're taking responsibility, and there will be fallout. They aren't squealing on Tony. But I believe he's the mastermind, and I thought you should know."

Now the welt on his face didn't look nearly as agitated as the fire in his eyes. "You thought I should know? Well, thank you. Mission accomplished." He glared at me with such force it nearly pushed me outside.

The wind rattled the steel walls, and something banged against the side with a loud whack. Probably a tumbleweed.

It was my MO to avoid conflict when possible. And I had a firm belief in minding my own business, so stepping into the muck didn't make sense. But I did it anyway. "Look, Tony being isolated isn't going to help him with the divorce and moving to a whole new place. He needs to deal with what's really bothering him and not be allowed to keep acting out."

Garrett turned his head to the bench and stood stock-still for several moments.

I'd definitely overstepped my bounds, but maybe he needed a nudge and some backup to be firm. Parenting wasn't easy—I knew that even if I didn't have kids of my own. I thought Garrett was thinking this over, reviewing the logic of what I said and would come back with an apology for me and a parenting plan for himself.

I was wrong.

When he looked up, the handsome had drained from his face, leaving unmasked rage. He didn't raise his voice as his father had; he seemed to corral it inside to swirl like a corrosive whirlpool. "You're another one of those 'spare the rod, spoil the child' types, aren't you? And you think you can come in here, with no kids of your own, and tell me how to raise my son?"

"Well, no, I—" Except, yes, I had.

He stepped back from me as if eliminating the temptation to take a swing. "I refuse to dole out punishment like some sadistic tyrant. Maybe you Sandhillers don't understand reasoning and loving parenting, but that's your problem. Don't you dare tell me how to deal with my own child."

It was true I only had an undergraduate degree in psychology from the University of Nebraska (Go Big Red), but figuring out Garrett's overreaction hardly required a PhD. I didn't answer, just stood in front of him while he caught his breath and calmed down.

With skill he'd no doubt honed in court, he regulated his breathing and lowered his shoulders. He still looked like he wanted to squeeze the life out of something, probably me, but at least he looked under control.

I spoke only loud enough to be heard above the complaints of the wind. "I understand you don't want to be the kind of parent you had."

He glared at me.

"But having no discipline can be nearly as bad as getting the stuffing beat out of you."

He broke eye contact and turned back to the bench and that trusty wrench. "I don't know what Sarah told you, but she doesn't know what she's talking about."

"Sarah didn't tell me anything."

His voice lost that hard, lawyer edge. "Because she wasn't around and didn't see anything." He tapped the wrench on the metal surface.

I didn't move. "I was in the shop before I spoke up."

He kept tapping the wrench.

"I know he attacked you."

"You don't know anything. I did a stupid thing and wrecked the tractor. He was mad. Completely understandable."

My feet felt welded to the floor, afraid I'd make a false move and slam closed the opening into Garrett that let a tiny speck of truth out. "I'll bet he was understandably mad a lot when you were growing up."

The wrench tapping quickened.

I remembered Newt Johnson saying something about how good Garrett had turned out, considering what he'd been through. I hadn't understood it at the time, but I did now. "It's not your fault, you know. Any man who hits a child is wrong. Any man who only hits a child on parts of his body where no one can see is a very sick man."

Garrett tapped away for a moment. He set the wrench down and turned to me, his eyes red but dry. "So, you see why I can't discipline Tony."

"There are ways to discipline him that don't entail physical pain."

He didn't seem to hear me. "We never wanted children. And then Sheila got pregnant."

Since I'd crashed into his secrets, I needed to hear him out.

Garrett squared off with the bench and spoke to the pegboard, the outlines of missing tools like chalk around phantom bodies at a crime scene. "I loved him from the moment I saw him, of course. But I was so afraid of screwing him up I kept my distance. I worked all the time." He twisted his head to look at me. "I may be a shit rancher, but I'm a damned good attorney."

I nodded encouragement, only giving a nanosecond to consider I probably smelled from sweating inside Ted's Bronco, my face was probably streaked with grime, and my hair looked like the perfect home for a family of muskrats.

"Sheila took the lead with Tony, and she was the one who doled out the discipline. But now it's up to me."

I had a fair amount of curiosity about why Sheila was out of the picture, but I'd already stepped too far into his business for one day.

He dropped his head to the bench and braced his arms. "I'm all he's got, and I don't want him to feel abandoned if I punish him. He's been betrayed enough."

With the tension evaporating, I leaned on the bench next to him. "Kids need boundaries, or they don't feel loved." It looked like us Fox kids hadn't had discipline the way Mom and Dad had let us run amok. But Dad insisted on courtesy and manners and doing the right thing with family and neighbors. They had expectations for us, and I'd never felt a lack of love, though Susan had some issues on that score.

He didn't respond, so I butted in another step. "It could be Tony is trying to get your attention." Or, as Louise and Sarah said, he was simply rotten. "You don't have to wallop him, but maybe give him a nasty chore, say cleaning the chicken house. And then maybe after he's got a good start, you help him."

With his head hanging low, he twisted to make eye contact. "That's not a bad idea. We don't keep chickens, but the house at the Blume needs cleaning out."

The Blume was the Haneys' ranch several miles south of Robert and Sarah's place. If Garrett was cleaning it up, it might mean he planned to stay in the Sandhills and move there. That wouldn't make Sarah happy.

"There you go." We listened to the wind for a few moments, until I felt squirmy and uncomfortable. "I need to get going."

Garrett straightened and offered up a genuine smile. "Thank you. Really."

I waved him off, embarrassed, and made a stupid reply just to say something. "Lots of kids in my family."

He laughed as if I'd told a joke. This was the awkward kind of situation you'd expect in junior high. "I remember you as this skinny kid always hanging around with Sarah. If I noticed you at all it was because you guys were annoying me. I'm glad to get to know you better now."

My chuckle was genuine and easy. "Whatever happened to that girl you dated in high school? We used to spy on you and were convinced you'd get married."

He slapped his forehead. "I haven't thought about her in a long time. She went to Chadron State College when I went to U of A, and we lost touch. I think she's teacher in South Dakota with a husband and three kids."

We walked toward the doors. The wind had let up a bit and now sounded more like a fishing boat with a trolling engine.

When we got to the cruiser, he held the door open and leaned inside. "How 'bout I take you for a steak at the Long Branch to thank you for bringing Tony home and...everything."

Oh. Huh. That sounded like a date, and my thoughts slammed to Sarah. She'd have a thing or two to say about that, and none of it would be good.

He charged ahead. "I need to talk with Tony." He seemed to realize his state and purposefully looked down at himself and up at me. "And clean up. But I could meet you there in a couple of hours."

Wasn't I trying to stop rearranging my life to make everyone else happy? His schedule would give me plenty of time to finish my day and clean up. Maybe even wear a dress, something rare for me. I slapped the steering wheel. "That sounds great. See you there."

I drove away thinking how proud Dad would be of me stepping out. Diane would congratulate me on not letting Sarah's opinion shut me down. The good feeling lasted...

All the way to the highway, when Baxter's face flashed through my mind and my heart felt as charred as the blowout behind Louise's house.

## 26

On my way back to town, I dialed Douglas. The wind abated some, and the relief of it not battering me and roaring in my ears helped ease the tightness in my shoulders.

Douglas sounded like himself played on half speed, low and slow. "Heard you had an eventful rodeo down there."

Douglas managed the University of Nebraska (Go Big Red) research farm in the northeast corner of Grand County. The brother I always thought of as a teddy bear, he didn't venture to town often, preferring to steer clear of rifts and wrangling in the family.

I talked about Dwayne's murder and Trey wanting to keep me out of the investigation. He asked pointed questions about the cause of death, the time of day, and what bull, ending with, "Was there anyone unusual at the rodeo?"

I gave him the rundown. "Gidget, of course. TJ Simonson. But I already checked him out. There was some doctor from Denver who Roxy said had invested in bulls with Dwayne."

"A doctor, huh?"

I laughed. "You know how they're notorious for making bad investments. Guess Dwayne knew an easy mark when he found one."

After a round or two of me talking about Dwayne's death and him telling me the latest antics of his grad students conducting their research, I got down to business. "I hear you and Michael are crashing antlers."

He let out a sigh so deep and long it could have filled a hot air balloon. "Since Michael's not talking to you, and you didn't hear it from me, I assume Lauren told you."

"What's going on?"

Again, that epic sigh. "You know I'm not going to tell you. What happens between Michael and me stays there. But I'm worried and mad, and that's all I'll say."

I didn't want to mention Michael's association with Dwayne in case Douglas didn't know about it. But that could be what was eating at Douglas. Maybe I could find another way to sneak in. "According to Kaylen, he's been gone a lot lately."

Deadpan. "Yeah."

The green of the prairie seemed to have faded from earlier today. We really needed a good gully washer. "I know he's usually got a lot going on, but Lauren seems worried."

As if he couldn't help himself, he said, "She probably should be."

Now I jumped in. "Should I be?"

He didn't say anything, and I wanted to shout at him, but I didn't. "Give me a hint."

He let out a small puff of air, like an almost chuckle. "It's not Twenty Questions. But yeah, I'm worried about him. He might have gotten himself in too deep this time."

Too deep in debt with contractors? Too deep in Dwayne's schemes? "With dangerous people?"

His frustration pushed through the line. "I wouldn't say dangerous so much. Unless you think clueless doctors with cash to burn are dangerous."

Thank you, Douglas. He didn't say that carelessly. He let me know that whatever was going on with Michael involved a doctor from Denver, probably one who'd been to the rodeo.

We bantered a bit more because we liked talking to each other, and hung up. I still had more driving to do, so I braced myself for the hurdle.

The call took swallowing down nausea and some plotting to get Roxy to cough up the name of the doctor. Guilt banged at me for bothering her when she was probably dealing with some heavy emotions. But maybe it would distract her from what a crappy person she'd married and how she'd get herself and little Beau free.

It bothered me that I had Roxy's number in my contacts. When she'd gone missing two years ago, I'd needed to add it, and more than a few times I'd nearly deleted it. Now I was glad I'd kept it.

She answered with much less bounce than usual. "I just put Beau down and we're in the pickup outside the hospital, so I have time for a visit."

She probably wanted to share war stories about Ted and affairs and maybe get advice about divorce lawyers. Though I had sympathy for her, she'd been the woman on the other end when I'd experienced it all, and I didn't have a heart big enough to share my divorce expertise with her.

So, I girded myself and dove in. "Now that this is happening with you and Ted, it reminds me how lonely it is being divorced." They were preparing my room in hell as I spoke.

She sounded sad. "Believe me. I know how hard being single can be."

And now she was going to find out how hard being a single mother could be. "That's why I called you. You really get it." Gag.

She sounded upbeat, diving into the distraction of fixing Kate. "I understand completely. And I'm your best weapon against loneliness. First of all, we're going to do a major makeover."

Ick. This wasn't the direction I'd planned. "That would be wonderful. But even if I look good, who would I date around here?"

Now I had her. "There's Andy Butterbaugh."

"I don't think he's my type." Unless my type was someone who'd been married twice and had a couple of kids with each ex.

"Well, there's Dillon Misner."

We could go at this all day, or at least for twenty minutes until she'd exhausted every single man in the Sandhills and probably a few with unhappy marriages. I needed to redirect her. "I'm thinking maybe someone not from around here. You know, like that doctor who was at the rodeo on the third."

She sounded shocked. "Bruce Grynder? Oh no. He's definitely out of your league. He's a rich doctor, for heaven's sake."

"Do you know anything about him?"

"Well, Kasey told me he's divorced. But he lives in a fancy neighborhood in Denver. Littleton? Has a big house. Let me think about this a minute, and we'll find the perfect guy for you."

I had what I wanted, now I needed to call her off. "I'm excited about this. But let's wait for a couple of months. I want to drop a few pounds before I go on the market." It took all my will to channel the whole Roxy thing.

She hesitated. "I wasn't going to say anything because I didn't want to hurt your feelings, but, honestly, I think that might be for the best."

"Oh, rats. Someone is speeding. I've got to go." I hung up before my stomach gave out and I threw up all over the cruiser.

I found a turnoff and pulled onto a gravel road. The wind had tapered off enough I rolled down my windows and shut off the engine.

There are tools at a law enforcement officer's disposal. With a phone call I could ask the state patrol to help locate Dr. Bruce Grynder. But with a name like that, plain old Google worked fine. I found his clinic, a family practice in Aurora, a suburb of Denver. Getting through to a doctor could be tricky. In my experience, they rarely called you back. But that was when I was merely a patient, and most information could be related through a nurse or assistant. This time, I made sure the person answering the phone understood it was a personal matter involving the sheriff of Grand County, Nebraska.

I sounded much more important than I felt, in light of Trey shutting down my involvement in the investigation. Still, Dr. Grynder called me back in fifteen minutes. Not even enough time to make it to my next stop.

He sounded curious but not overly concerned. After introductions in which I had to explain where Grand County was located, his voice carried enthusiasm. "That is some lovely country you live in. I'd never been up that way before some buddies invited me deer hunting last fall. All that isolation and peace. I really envy you."

Some people got it, and I appreciated Dr. Grynder's viewpoint. "Is that when you met Dwayne Weber?"

He laughed. "He's such a character. Dwayne was our guide and a pretty fine one at that. We all got our deer."

No doubt. Dwayne could make good money on a side hustle of hunting guide, and I wouldn't put it past him to have been feeding corn to the deer for weeks, priming them for easy pickins when the hunters came around. "You and Dwayne became friends? Kept in touch?"

Again, that friendly bounce. "Oh, I don't know about friends. He was entertaining, and the whole idea of bull riding fascinates me. After I met him, I started watching the rodeos and PBR performances. Those bulls are real athletes, for sure."

"You were in Hodgekiss for the July third rodeo..." It wasn't a question, but I trailed off to give him an opening to explain.

"Oh, sure. Dwayne said he had a young bull performing that day. Since Luke died, I thought maybe I'd buy shares in another one." He laughed. "I admit I don't know much about what makes a good bull. But I trust Dwayne. He's had some success, and I thought it would be fun to have ownership in something. You know, I have friends who have shares in race-horses. This is kind of my thing."

I could pity a guy who trusted Dwayne, but I'd have to forgive his massive stupidity first. "You invested in Lucky Luke?"

His voice dipped. "That was a blow. I bought half interest and then to have that tragic accident. It's not only the money, although it was a big loss, close to forty thousand dollars. But it's like a friend died, you know? I thought maybe getting back in the saddle, so to speak..." He guffawed at his lame joke. "...Might help me get over it."

I scribbled notes, keeping track of the details for Trey. "You lost a chunk on Lucky Luke. Didn't that make you mad?"

He seemed carefree about it. "Not mad so much. As Dwayne always said, there are no guarantees in this business."

"But the bull was insured, right?"

A little groan, but not like the shriek I would make if I'd lost forty grand. "We thought so. But insurance companies always have an angle, don't they? Dwayne gave it his best shot. He really fought with them. I ended up with about a third of my initial investment. Something about only being insured for medical and not accidents."

This stank of the same dead carp Dwayne had fed TJ. "Do you know what company Dwayne had the policy with?"

Dr. Grynder sounded so unconcerned, I understood why Dwayne had picked him. "No. Dwayne handled all of that. He felt so bad about it. I suspect the company didn't pay at all and Dwayne coughed up his own cash to pay us back what he could."

I picked up an interesting word. "Us?"

"My buddy. Another guy on the hunting trip. He bought the other half share."

Hold on a minute. "Dwayne didn't own any part of Luke?" Garrett said Dwayne tried to sell him shares of Lucky Luke. Wish I knew if that had been before or after he'd already sold to Dr. Grynder and his buddy. Were there others? How many "halves" had Dwayne peddled?

"See? That's why I trusted him. He loves the business so much, he sold his favorite bull just to keep doing it. We paid for training, feed, board, and the entries fees, of course. But taking care of animals is hard work, and Dwayne did over and above on that score."

Or Kasey did, at least. Dwayne collected the cash. Did Kasey know about this? More notes for Trey. "Did Dwayne sell you shares for another bull?"

He gave a little click of his tongue. "It's embarrassing to admit, but I decided I don't really want to invest in another. Losing Luke kind of broke my heart. It was fun to watch him compete, and even though it was only a few times, I got attached to the guy. I think I'll invest in art or something that can't die on me." He chuckled again. He might not be bright, but he seemed like a cheerful sort. "I'm sure you know how persuasive Dwayne can be."

"Oh, yeah." I laughed to encourage him to continue.

"In all fairness, even when he told us about the four million in payouts at places like Duncan, Oklahoma, he always said that not every horse wins the Kentucky Derby and running bucking bulls was the same."

"It's a risky business."

Now he laughed. "But if you get a good one, you can sell semen for thousands a straw. There's a lot of money in the business. But I realized it wasn't all about the money, so I left the rodeo before he could talk me into giving my heart away again."

I collected the name and contact information of Dr. Grynder's buddy who had also invested in Lucky Luke. Then I broke the bad news about Dwayne's death.

There was a moment of silence. Then a quiet, "Oh. I'm really sorry to hear that."

I believed him.

# 27

I searched the cloudless sky, hoping for some sign of rain. Today's wind had wicked moisture from everything, and if we hoped to have enough grass to feed the cattle until late fall, the sky had better open up soon. Of course, a sheriff doesn't need the grass to grow to pay the bills. But maybe I wouldn't be sheriff much longer. I might be out of a job come fall. I didn't think so, though. Recalling a sheriff was extreme, and they couldn't want Ted back.

With a snap of my fingers, I could be back on a ranch. Maybe live in the fancy house Carly's father had built for Roxy. Wouldn't that be a fun turn of the tables, for Roxy to be living at Frog Creek with Ted, and me in the house she'd spared no expense designing and furnishing? She'd have a cramped stucco Sears house built in the 1930s with closets as big as phone booths. And I'd have high ceilings with log beams, river rock fireplace, and windows opening to meadows. That almost made me smile.

But I was still Grand County sheriff. And I didn't feel like letting Trey Ridnour, Ted Conner, or anyone else tell me what I could do in that capacity. For most of my life, I felt as though I called my own shots. People didn't tell me what to do. Or so I'd thought. I'd only started to realize how that might not be true.

Of all my siblings, Diane probably had the most accurate take on my problem. I had an overdeveloped sense of responsibility to my brothers and sisters, my friends, my job, and pretty much everyone but me. That needed to change.

It was going to start with me going out on a date and liking it. I darn sure was going to wear a nice dress, even if the date was only a steak at the Long Branch. And I was going to wear the blue one with the plunging neckline. Not only that, I'd also wear the push-up bra and maybe give myself cleavage to rival Roxy's. That was a reach, but damn it, I needed to seize the moment.

As soon as I followed up with Kasey.

The sun wouldn't throw in the towel until nearly nine o'clock, and it celebrated extended summer hours by continuing to blast heat. It was uncommon for nights not to cool down in the Sandhills, even on the hottest summer days, but tonight was going to be the exception. I parked in front of Kasey's house next to her pickup and built up a sweat climbing the porch steps. It slicked all the dust and dirt that had accumulated on this long day. I banged on her door.

She didn't answer, giving me time to study her crunchy and dying front yard and consider starting a sprinkler that sat next to the porch. When she didn't answer my second knock, I tromped toward the barn. The corrals were empty, so I assumed the bulls were turned out in the pasture and had wandered over the hill.

Kasey's voice floated out of the open barn doors. A country song with a sweet lilt that shocked me.

I followed it in to find Kasey in a stall beside a striated brown-and-gray bull that looked half Brahman and half whatever the bull term for mutt is. His head was down, horns about knee-high to Kasey. His massive shoulders hit her chest-high, but the distinctive hump rose to her shoulder. He looked relaxed, though his breath chugged in and out because of his size, and his eyes were at half-mast.

She must not have heard me because she continued to sing and sweep her arm along the bull's back with a curry brush.

I took a moment to relish the perfume of the barn, sweaty horse blankets, fresh straw, manure, and comfort, then cleared my throat. "That's not something you see every day."

She abruptly stopped singing and brushing and scowled at me. "What?"

I tried to sound friendly in hopes of keeping her off the defensive. "Someone singing a lullaby to a two-thousand-pound beast while combing his hair."

If I'd expected Kasey to look grief-stricken, maybe dark shadows under her eyes or a puffy face from tears, that was not what I found. She looked strong and put together as usual. She reached over and scratched his neck, and he tilted his head like a puppy. "Sam's not such a beast. And he likes it."

"I'd think with the way Slim mangled Dwayne you'd be skittish about getting into a pen with a bull."

The low sun shone through the open barn door, highlighting specks of dust and hay that floated like snowflakes.

She scoffed. "I thought you and Trey established good ol' Slim didn't kill Dwayne."

"Maybe not, but Slim sure roughed him up afterward."

She stood in the hay-strewn stall that had obviously just been cleaned and rubbed the bull between his eyes. He closed them, looking completely at peace. "Obviously someone stuck him with a Hot Shot or something. These guys wouldn't kick a kitten if they could help it."

"But they're bred to fight."

She coughed out a derisive sound. "They're bred to buck when they're given the right stimulation. It's their job. And if you train them right and have the right genetics, they'll twist and tangle and do their damnedest to throw a cowboy. If the fool gets hurt, that's hardly the bull's fault. They fight just as hard when they have the flank box on."

Dwayne and Kasey had won some nice payouts taking their young bulls to bucking futurities where they had no rider but only an electronic box strapped on. She'd bragged about it one night in the Long Branch how they'd won close to $50,000 in two years just for one of their bulls bucking a ten-pound dummy.

She zeroed in on me with a malicious gleam. "They like to buck. Same as we like to fuck. It's all in the genes." She chuckled. "Genes, jeans. Get it?"

Not the most genteel of women. I'd bet she liked to shock and did her best to offend people. That trait wouldn't help her out much now, with half the county ready to string her up. If folks had liked Dwayne better, they might have already gotten the job done.

As abrasive as she was to people, she seemed to have a real way with the bull. "He looks like an oversized puppy."

She scratched his ears. "They're way better than any guy I've ever known. You love them and treat them right; they love you back." She leaned in and kissed between his eyes. "Ain't that right, Sam?"

The stall they occupied looked way too small for safety. If he startled or got a bee sting, he'd crush Kasey against a wall before she could move. "He's sure gentle with you."

She talked baby talk. "You still get the job done, don't you?" To me, she said, "They won't hurt me because they know I'll protect them. I've raised them from the time they were born. I feed them, work with them, pet them. And I won't let anything or anyone hurt them."

Kasey was a tough nut. No wonder people had no trouble believing she was capable of murder. They might soften up a bit if they could see her coddling the humongous bull.

She shoved around him to the stall door, her boots swishing in the hay. With a note of challenge, she said, "What are you doing out here?"

"I'm kind of surprised to find you alone. Did you get the funeral arrangements made? No family coming in? Friends around?"

She unlatched the gate and stepped out onto the concrete alley and into a beam of sunshine. "Those damned church ladies and their questions. I kicked them out. They were driving me crazy. Maureen went into town to grab something to eat, not that there aren't a million casseroles in my freezer. And Roxy." She stopped and flashed a sly smile. "Well, she's got problems of her own."

What did Kasey know about that? You could go straight at some people, ask direct questions and get answers. Then there were people like Kasey. The only way to get information from them was to come in the back door, and sometimes, you had to crawl under the threshold. "I'd like to ask you some questions about Dwayne."

She turned away from me and strode to the back of the barn, pausing at an open wood door that probably led to a tack room. "I told that dipshit

Trey Ridnour, and I'll tell you. I didn't kill Dwayne. So, leave me the hell alone."

I followed her to where she'd stepped inside the gloomy six-foot-square tack room. "I don't think you killed him. That's why I'm here. I want to find out who did and get Trey off your back."

She swung around to me, making her braid fly behind her. "And how do you think you'll do that? They've already decided I did it."

"Can we talk?" I indicated a couple of hay bales stacked neatly in the alley.

She clacked out of the shadowy tack room and flounced past me to plop down on a bale in the shade. "Fine."

I sat on one in the spotlight of sun from the open door and leaned forward with my forearms on my thighs. "Do you have any idea what Dwayne was up to?"

"What do you mean, 'up to'?"

The ray of sun heated my brown uniform. "Milo and a few others said he's been in Edgewood a lot lately."

She dropped her head to the back of the stall and looked up at the ceiling, as if too exhausted to go on. "Sure. That's where he and Gidget Bartels meet up."

Now it was my turn to be surprised. "You knew about that?"

With effort, she pulled her head up and nailed me with her gaze. "I'm not like you, thinking love is the be-all, end-all. I quit caring where Dwayne wet his willy a long time ago."

That wasn't my idea of marriage, but everyone got to make their own bed, and if they liked sleeping on messy sheets, well, that was their choice. "According to Milo, Dwayne was doing a lot of livestock deals. Mostly with cash."

She sat up, looking alert. "Milo can mind his own county, fat jerk. But who did he say Dwayne was doing business with?"

"Milo was sketchy on the details. I wondered if you could fill in the gaps."

She fingered the thick braid draped around her neck. "Here's the truth. I knew Dwayne was diddling that midget. And I suspected he was working on something behind my back. That's why I took out the life insurance on him. I thought it was a good bet Wrangler'd come after him and take his head off. And if not Wrangler, then someone else. And they did, didn't they?"

Seemed like a sad way to live. "If you didn't trust him, why stay with him?"

"I can tell you why." The voice from the doorway startled us both. I hadn't heard her pull up, so she must have parked at the house and walked down.

Maureen moved from the bright light of the doorway to where we could see her. She looked like an ad from *Cowboys & Indians* magazine, all glossy and fine. "It's the bull business. All men, all the time."

I pointed out the obvious. "You seem to be making it."

She acknowledged that with a nod. "Yes, but Fred died. If we'd have been divorced, he'd have had the name and the reputation. I know genetics and training, but it takes connections and money to get past the men who guard the gates. They run the shows, pull the strings, and set things up. A good bull is only the beginning, and it took Fred's insider status to get them where they could win."

I gave her a skeptical frown.

"You think I'm full of it. But it's true. I promise you, if Kasey had divorced Dwayne, she'd be waiting tables at a twenty-four-hour diner and Dwayne would be sitting pretty." Maureen's face tightened. "It's time to make changes."

Kasey snorted agreement.

I turned to her. "So, why didn't he divorce you?"

She stared at me as if I'd just declared two and two were five, then she shifted her gaze to the gate and Sam. "Because I know the genetics. I can train the bulls. It's my business."

A vicious symbiotic relationship. How sweet.

I had a few more questions for Kasey. Right now, she still looked like the best suspect for Dwayne's murder, and she wasn't doing much to help herself. "If you don't know about Dwayne's deals, then you probably don't know about him leasing the Pullman from Phil and Amanda."

Kasey's eyes popped open for a split second, then settled back to bored and belligerent, what could be defense or might just be her personality. "No."

Huh.

Maureen came closer. "Dwayne leased some property you didn't know about? Where is it?"

I kept my focus on Kasey. "It's several miles northeast of Hodgekiss. A place called the Pullman." I gave it one beat, then watched Kasey closer. "In fact, Ted Conner had an unfortunate accident out there this morning."

That disinterested look was replaced by surprise. "What kind of accident?"

If she was faking her surprise, she was good at it. "Drove the Chester County sheriff's Bronco into a dug-out Autogate hole."

She stood up. "Is he hurt?"

Maureen didn't say anything.

"Well, he's not any better for the wear. I think Roxy's a lot more hurt, even though she wasn't in the Bronco."

Her face closed up, and she narrowed her eyes at me. After a few seconds, she said, "I didn't have anything to do with any Autogate or with Ted on that road today."

Now we were getting somewhere. "Today?"

She picked at a bit of hay on her jeans and didn't answer.

I raised my voice to let her know I wasn't stopping. "Did you have something to do with Ted at other times? Maybe at the trailer on the Pullman? Maybe you knew about Dwayne leasing it?"

She dropped one hip in an aggravated stance. "Okay. Yeah. I was sleeping with Ted."

Maureen pursed her lips as if Kasey's words were bitter, but she didn't look shocked.

Even though I'd suspected as much, I did feel appalled. "Isn't Roxy your best friend?"

Kasey blew a dismissive raspberry. "What are we, in junior high? It's not like I wanted to steal her boyfriend. Ted and I were scratching an itch."

I looked away, not sure what to say.

Maureen took over for me. "We're all struggling to make it in this business, and in life. Women need to support each other. Have some loyalty and respect. This thing you're doing, that erodes a foundation."

Kasey shook her head. "Sit right up there on that throne of yours with all your money and connections and look down your nose at me. I work damned hard. Why shouldn't I have some fun?"

It might not be fair to gang up on Kasey, but that didn't stop me. "Fun is one thing. But Roxy really loves Ted. This'll devastate her."

Kasey laughed. "You, of all people, should know Roxy better than that. All she's ever wanted is to be Ted's wife. She'll forgive him."

There was never a time when I felt affection for Kasey, but now I thought if I could toss her in front of a speeding hay mower and let it rip her to pieces, it would serve her right. "But Roxy's been here for you lately, greeting people, taking food, writing thank-you notes."

Maureen focused her attack on me. "There you go again. Putting the blame on the woman and defending the man."

Whoa, where was I defending Ted in this?

Kasey walked toward the open doorway. "There's no blame. Sex is sex. Roxy's had her share of affairs, so don't go thinking Ted is her only one."

She made me feel slimy being in the same barn as her. Her husband was murdered, and she acted unconcerned, even flip.

This was an investigation, and I was beginning to think Trey might be right to think Kasey might have done it. She had muscle enough. She could break a man's neck. With her Bull Whisperer skills, dragging Dwayne to Slim's pen wouldn't be a problem. She even suggested a Hot Shot to get him to buck.

I didn't want to be like the rest of Grand County and accuse her simply because she was a despicable human being, but it didn't seem as if she mourned Dwayne, or had feelings for anyone, really.

I caught up to her outside, next to Maureen's pickup. "You say you had nothing to do with Ted's accident and that you didn't know about Dwayne leasing the Pullman. And yet, Ted was on his way out to meet you before dawn."

She snickered. "He wasn't on his way to meet me."

"But you knew about the Pullman?" I glanced at the bumper of

Maureen's pickup. The silver paint was scratched and chipped in one spot. Someone had probably backed into her on Main Street.

Again, Kasey's hip dropped, showing her irritation. "Okay, sure. I found out about the Pullman when I went through Dwayne's files. Jesus, Kate, you were right there when I saw it."

The folder that made her cheeks flare. Sure. "So, you invited Ted to meet you there."

"The one time. Right after I found out. I thought it would be fitting to f—" She curled her lip at me. "*To make love* to someone else out there while Dwayne was cooling on a slab at the mortuary. He shouldn't have hidden things from me."

As awful as what she did, and even worse how she said it, she hadn't found out about the lease until after he was dead. It couldn't be a motive for murder. She wasn't too concerned about his affair with Gidget, so no motive there, either.

Her voice carried a hard note. "Let me make this easier for you. I couldn't have been responsible for Ted's accident."

I leaned on the bed of Maureen's pickup. "Why is that?"

Kasey smirked at me, and I tried to appear casual, not as if I waited on her explanation. I glanced into the bed of the pickup. Maureen must be helping Kasey with chores. A shovel and sand marred the pristine lining.

"I got tired of sitting around here and fed up with the constant flow of people bringing me food I don't want and hugging me. So, I took myself to Ogallala for a steak. That asshole sheriff's deputy stopped me on my way home on the north side of the lake and tossed my ass in jail for DUI, which is so bogus. But there it is. I didn't get out until after breakfast."

## 28

When I pulled up in front of my house, not only was Dad's old Dodge there, but Trudy Drake's white Taurus was also out front. Trudy had spent thirty years in Spearfish, South Dakota, before her husband had passed away last year and she'd moved back to Hodgekiss.

Wasn't Dad making time with Deenie Hayward? What was Trudy doing here?

Poupon sauntered from the backyard and wagged his stumpy tail. Shocked he'd show that much enthusiasm for me, I hurried to him and scratched his floopy head. "How was your day?"

He answered by sitting down beside me. Strange behavior, indeed.

I made my way to the garden to set the water and see if maybe Dad and Trudy were in the backyard. He could have rigged up the lights and table like he'd done for Deenie, even though it would be two or so hours until dark.

I wasn't reassured when they weren't back there. That meant they were inside. On the chance they hadn't heard me pull up, I spoke super loud to Poupon, who had followed me. "Who's a good boy?"

He pointed his nose away from me, clearly not liking my tone.

I needed to shower and get ready for dinner, so there was nothing to do but make my way to the house. Normally I'd go in the back door. But I wanted to take more time and make more noise, so I shouted at Poupon when I passed by Dad's bedroom window. "I'm going to get something from my car and then go inside." Although I felt silly talking like that, and there was nothing I needed in my car.

I took my time, and as I was climbing the steps to the front porch, the door to my house opened. Trudy Drake stepped out, a living example of guilt if I ever saw one. For an eighty-year-old woman, Trudy looked pretty good. Problem was, Trudy had to be in her early sixties. She had the comfortable body and curly white hair of the stereotypical Mrs. Claus. And with her red face and curls all whipped up like fur around a hood, it made the image more apt.

She leaned back in the doorway. "Thank you for the iced tea, Hank. It's been good to catch up." When she faced forward, her surprised face couldn't have been more fake. "Oh, my goodness. You're home."

Dad stepped out behind Trudy. He wore a chambray shirt with unraveling cuffs, untucked from his Levi's. Worse, he was barefoot. The idea of Dad dating was fine. Seeing him have dinner with Deenie had been fun. But this. No, this was more than I could handle.

I'd like to say I tried to be hospitable, but that'd be a lie. In a flat voice, I said, "Good to see you." And made my way past her into the house, Poupon close on my heels.

Now it made sense why he was happy to see me. They'd kicked him outside. The dog version of being handed a nickel to go to the corner store for candy. This was Poupon's house. I was indignant on his behalf, even after I remembered I'd left him outside today.

Dad tried for some levity. "What happened to you? You look like you dug a hole to China. Or more like you blasted your way."

I didn't turn around. "I need a shower."

I heard Dad talk to Trudy. "I apologize for that. She's obviously had a bad day."

Trudy hurried to reassure him. "Oh, don't worry. I should have left before she got home."

"I didn't expect her this early," he said.

Then I did something I'd been raised never to do. I got downright rude. "It's my house, and I can come home whenever I want." Okay, I didn't shout it. And Dad and Trudy probably didn't hear it. But I said it and meant it.

Dad walked Trudy to her car, and I did everything I could not to watch. Seeing him kiss her goodbye might send me into orbit.

By the time Dad returned to the house, I had my robe on and was heading to the bathroom, which was through the kitchen at the back of the house. He caught me in the area of the front room I called the dining room.

I'd never heard him raise his voice. He didn't have to, and he didn't now. "There's never any reason to be rude. Especially to Trudy. She's a nice lady, and you could tell she was uncomfortable."

When I was a kid, Dad talking like that to me would cause me to burst into tears and sink in a sea of remorse so deep it could drown an elephant. Heck, last week it might have done the same thing. But not today. "What has happened to you? You've always been a good guy. Not like a Ted or a Dwayne. But this..." I waved my hand around to indicate his bedroom. "This tomcatting around is not like you, and it's wrong."

He took in a breath as if I'd slapped him, then let it out slowly. "First of all, what I do with my personal life is not your business."

I thrust out a hip, a move worthy of Kasey. "It's my house, and you're my father. So yeah, it's my business. And how do you think your 'making time' with Trudy is going to make Deenie feel?" I had to use the euphemism of "making time" because who could say the real deed when talking to and about their father?

"I never made any promises to anybody. All the ladies know I'm dating around."

All? Were there others? It was so weird to be standing in my house talking to my father about his poor behavior. "What they know and what they feel might be different things. I saw the way Deenie looked at you. And you should be honest with yourself, because I saw the way you looked at her."

His gaze flicked away. "I'm not getting serious with anyone ever again."

That hit a sour note. "Sure. I get it. Your heart is broken, and the life you built is gone. You have every right to dig a hole and pull it in after you. But the fact that you're dating, or whatever you want to call it, tells me you want to keep living. And here's this really great woman who lights you up, and you want to put up a waist-high fence and only let it get so far. Well, Dad, that's just stupid."

I'd never seen him mad at me, but I read it in his face then. "You were married for eight years. You never even had kids. What do you know about true love?"

I almost blurted out Glenn Baxter's name. But part of me believed if no one knew about him, I could pretend he never existed. I started for the bathroom. "You're right."

Before I made it through the kitchen, he followed me. "Katie, I'm sorry. I know you're hurting now. This thing with Louise and Michael and the recall. It's hard on everyone."

I turned around and leaned on the counter. "I don't understand why she's doing it."

He pulled out a chair from the table and dropped into it. "She's hurting, too. It makes no sense, but she somehow thinks if you aren't sheriff anymore, we'll all go back to our roles, and everything will be good again."

"What roles?"

He considered something and gave me a sad smile. "For instance, your role has always been to pick up all the pieces of this family and hold them together."

I shook my head.

He nodded, arguing his point. "You babysit, are free labor, loan money, and are always the one they go to with problems. But you didn't fix their mother. Now the truth is, you're starting to stretch and grow, and the dynamics are changing. Some of the kids don't want that to happen. You can go back to the way things were, and maybe everyone will be happy. Maybe you will be. But if you keep on this path, there're going to be bumps."

He ran a hand along his graying hair and stood. "And this conversation has made me realize I've been putting you in that same savior role as the rest of them. I'll move out as soon as I can find a place."

I suddenly felt selfish and lonely. "Dad, no. I love having you here."

He hesitated in the doorway, and he rested eyes full of sympathy on me. "Maybe. But we all have to make changes."

## 29

My stomach tightened, and I thought of Dwayne, Ted, Kasey, Carly, Dad, and a quick rundown of my brothers, sisters, nephews, and nieces. Then I realized it was not tension or worry but plain old hunger. A juicy steak, Uncle Bud's thick fries perfectly crispy on the outside and hot and tender inside, an obligatory salad, all accompanied by an icy beer...the image nearly made me pass out.

I even looked forward to sitting across the table from a handsome man. I flat-out refused to think about how Sarah would feel. And blocked out my argument with Dad. Although I didn't need to worry about giving Roxy the satisfaction of me on a date with someone she'd handpicked, because she'd be distracted with sweeping the pieces of her life into a pile.

This was me doing something I wanted without worrying about coddling anyone else. And I looked damned fine doing it.

The sun had dimmed to smoldering instead of red-hot flames. And I saluted the sky for tamping down the wind. I wouldn't even complain about the lack of rain, though we'd need to get some soon. Dust rose behind me as I drove away from my bungalow.

When the phone rang, I punched it on to Trey. He didn't waste time with greetings. "I told you to stay out of the investigation."

I ignored that. "Are you back in Nebraska? Find anything out in Texas?"

His turn to ignore me. "You shouldn't have gone to Ravenna. I already planned to talk to TJ tomorrow."

Ted must be tattling on me. "Now you don't have to. I'll send you my notes. By the way, you won't be able to rely on Ted to keep tabs on me."

I heard a grin in his voice. At least he never held a grudge. "Did you finally shoot him?"

"Someone else saved me the trouble." I told Trey about the accident. "Turns out he and Kasey Weber are having an affair."

There was silence broken by the pings of gravel on my undercarriage. Then, "Huh." That might have included acknowledgment of my experience with Ted's affairs, Kasey's involvement and how it related to Dwayne's murder, or disbelief in Ted's sleazy behavior. Probably all three.

He let that sit for a second. "Here's some interesting information I learned in Texas. Wait. How did you know that's where I went?"

Why hold back now? "Maureen told me she tipped you off."

"I suppose that was your plan to get me out of the way so you could investigate and clear Kasey."

"I had every intention of letting you muff this investigation on your own. But then it seemed you were ready to throw the cuffs on Kasey without looking into it."

I could picture his face pinched in exasperation. "That's really what you think of me?"

Now I felt sheepish. "I guess not. Might have let myself get carried away." He didn't need to know I'd recently been tossed a wheelbarrow-full of man-bashing and I might have accepted it.

He let it go. "*Now* what do you think about the chances that Kasey killed Dwayne?"

I gave Trey the rundown of what I'd found out. "I wouldn't put it past her, but what would be her motive?"

"Because she's vicious and scary isn't good enough?" He laughed.

When I didn't answer, he continued. "For the record, I still think Kasey did it. But I learned some interesting things about the buckin' bull industry and about Maureen."

"Do tell." I topped the hill that led away from my house.

"There are rumors going around, and enough I think there might be something behind them, about rigging the draws and placements of bulls in competition. Apparently, there is a real art to being situated at the performances. If you get in the beginning or end you can get on the road to hit the next performance. If you get juggled or held up, it can mean not making a competition and you lose points."

"TJ talked about that some. He said Dwayne tampered with his trailer to keep him from making a performance."

"Dwayne didn't seem to be well known, but people who knew him didn't have much good to say. He played dirty, and everyone knew it. But he's not the only one. And certainly not a big deal. At least not up to now, but they said he was aggressive, and it seemed like he was on the way up."

"So, no smoking gun there. Here's something I learned." I told him about Dwayne selling shares in Lucky Luke, the bull tragically dying, and Dwayne giving pennies on the dollar to the investors. "Maybe Dwayne swindled the wrong guy."

"Hm. Maybe." Trey took a moment, probably thinking that over. "Here's something else that caught my attention. Maureen Steffen has been making a big stink. She's demanded auditors look into the software that draws bulls for competition, and she's threatened lawsuits. The big boys do not like her one bit."

"That doesn't surprise me. She thinks men have unfair pull in the business—she's probably right. And she's built up a load of resentment."

He scoffed. "I said the big boys, but there's plenty of women in the top tiers. Most everyone I talked to said Maureen is on a mission against men."

I countered. "She's worked hard to get a place in the business. She swears she'd never have made it if her husband hadn't been the public face and hadn't glad-handed the other men."

"They may not have liked Dwayne, but Fred Steffen was everyone's best buddy. And they weren't shy about their suspicions."

My stomach tightened. And not for steak. "What suspicions?"

"They're pretty sure Maureen killed him."

"No. That's only because they don't want to be challenged."

"Here's some food for thought. Fred Steffen died five years ago. He was found in a pen stomped to death by a mad bull."

On that note, we signed off, with Trey reminding me once again that this wasn't my investigation.

Dressed in my blue dress with my lingerie-enhanced cleavage, makeup and hair ramped up to date mode, I steered Elvis onto the highway and headed to town. I wanted to dream about medium-rare steaks and sparkling banter. The fantasy of having the proverbial nightcap at my house or maybe a series of passionate kisses would have been great to dwell on.

Instead, my head swirled about Dwayne's murder. It occurred to me if I had a ranch job, I might be obsessing about rain and grass, calculating the weight of our steer crop and the price of beef on the hoof. Those topics seemed cheerier than dwelling on death. But murder it was.

Bulls are big and rank and unpredictable. Except when they cuddle like kittens. Maureen was a strong woman who'd built a business and learned to work around the confines of the old cowboys. And when she'd grown big enough and powerful enough and didn't have her husband to take the limelight, she'd decided to elbow some space for the women coming behind her. That didn't make her a murderer.

Not at all. Except her hatred of what she called the patriarchy was so passionate it burned if you stood too close. Except she said it was time to make changes. Except her husband died in the same way Dwayne had. And we knew Dwayne's death wasn't an accident.

What about Ted's "accident"? Maureen was helping Kasey out. Maybe she heard Kasey make plans with Ted. She'd done a fine job flirting with him, frothing him up like a dancing grouse in mating season. Ted knew of a place they could meet.

And what about the scratches on the tailgate of Maureen's pickup? The kind of scratches that could be made by a chain. A chain used to yank an Autogate free and drag it away. And the shovel and sand in the bed of her pickup. Did Maureen kill Dwayne and then set her sights on Ted? A regular serial killer. With no motive except she hated men in the buckin' bull business.

And that was when I tapped Elvis's steering wheel and blew out an impatient breath. I was traveling down a conspiracy hole like pundits on cable TV. None of that made sense.

*Take the night off.* This was Trey's case, after all. Let him figure out if Dwayne was murdered by his wife, a woman with a grudge against men, or someone who Dwayne had wronged. That last category could include anyone from an angry husband to someone he'd cheated in the bull business, to anyone on the receiving end of his malicious plots.

I parked Elvis on Main Street in front of the post office and brushed my hands together to show myself I was done with this investigation. Tonight was pure fun.

I might not have looked like a Kardashian as I pushed my way out of Elvis. He was a low-slung beauty, and I wasn't used to wearing heels, and the combination resulted in a few grunts and a quick tug on my hem when it rode dangerously high. But once out, I threw back my shoulders and strutted down the sidewalk.

Garrett's gray pickup was parked farther down the street in front of the tack shop. The Long Branch wasn't a reservations type of restaurant, more the kind of place you hoped didn't run out of the meatloaf special before you could make it in on Tuesday night.

The Long Branch sat on the corner of Main Street and the highway, with the front door facing the highway. I rounded Main Street on my way, still fighting the parade of suspects following the marching band through my brain. A black pickup parked on the opposite side of the highway caught my attention.

It looked like...it *was* Carly's pickup. She'd left for Lincoln yesterday. What was she doing—

A white flash of shock, a tsunami of panic, all the oxygen sucked from the air. I was momentarily blinded, but my eyes focused on him. He was a living ghost, and my soul felt snatched from inside me, leaving me paralyzed, not even able to gasp for breath.

I didn't know how long we stood there, but I heard Carly's voice from far away. "You clean up nice."

I tried my best not to gulp in air. Maybe I succeeded, but probably not.

Glenn Baxter stood in front of me, a bland expression on his face, looking for all the world like a man who barely remembered my name. "This is a surprise. I didn't think I'd run into you." In a town of five hundred? I'd say there were pretty good odds he'd see me.

I probably looked like a bass hooked through the mouth and tossed on the bank to wheeze my last breaths. I glanced at his hand, aching to grab it, to feel his skin, his warmth. I didn't want to stop there. My arms itched to encircle his neck, and only the thinnest thread held back my urge to press myself against him. Who knows what guardian angel stepped into my head and opened my mouth, giving me a lilting chuckle. "Wow. I wouldn't have expected to see you in Hodgekiss."

Carly thrust her chin out in a defiant way she'd done since she was three years old and insisted she could round up at branding. "I asked him to come help me with the Bar J."

Whatever words she said rebounded off my head without sinking in. "That's nice. I hope you had a good trip here."

He hadn't changed his expression, making him seem like a mannequin. "I got a smaller plane so we can land at the airstrip here instead of having to land in Broken Butte and drive from there."

"That's nice." Apparently, the angel taking over had a limited loop of dialogue.

Carly sounded pointed when she said, "I'm thinking of putting the ranch into an environmental easement since Rope won't stay on longer and no one else will help me."

Baxter's eyes, so much like a lion's, kept their focus on me. "There are some programs, but most of them require at least a five-to-ten-year commitment."

Carly's tone poked me like a sharp stick. "And I only have two years to finish my degree. But I don't see that I have much choice."

Somewhere deep inside I understood what Carly was saying and that she was trying to force my hand to resign my office and take over the ranch. But it made as much impact on me as knowing the sun was sinking lower. I didn't know if I was breathing, but I must have been because I didn't pass out. Nightmare or fantasy, whatever, it couldn't be real that Baxter stood only a few feet away from me. Close enough to touch. Close enough to detect his unique scent of aftershave and skin, and I hated what it did to my heart, my flesh, my brain. "That's nice."

Carly drew her head back in astonishment. She opened her mouth to say something, but I headed her off.

"Well, it's really good to see you. I need to get going. Enjoy supper." I spun around on the slick sole of my high-heeled sandal.

Carly's voice ricocheted off the back of my head. "But weren't you just getting here?"

The good ol' guardian angel kept right with me, so I executed that confident strut I'd had earlier and whipped around the corner on my way back up the hill. I had one moment to glance in the side window of the Long Branch.

Garrett sat at a two-top in the bar side. He was watching out the window, and I locked eyes with him for a second. He smiled and raised his hand in a wave.

I should have felt bad for him. I should have turned around and joined him. Or at least stopped in to make an excuse.

But some things are impossible.

For me, being in the same county as Glenn Baxter fit that category.

All I could do was get to Elvis before I collapsed in a bloodless pile of skin, blue dress, and push-up bra. Or spontaneously combusted, all of which would be better than thinking how I stood like a Sandhills version of Talking Elmo, repeating "That's nice," and probably slobbering out the side of my mouth.

In an emotional coma, I sat petrified behind the wheel of Elvis, knowing I needed to get out of town before Baxter appeared or Garrett came to find me. But I couldn't get my limbs to take commands and stared into the post office window at the row of mailboxes and their ancient combination locks.

*Bang, bang, bang.*

They might have tapped on the window, but it sounded like a sledge-hammer on pavement. The surprise made me jump, and that got the blood flowing enough I could turn my head to see Newt and Earl standing outside of Elvis.

My fingers closed around the crank, and I lowered my window. "What's up?" My voice sounded as if it climbed out of deep well.

Their smell of mildewed trash, decomposed critter, and dirt drifted into the cab, acting like smelling salts. They wore their usual camo, looking overdue for a wash, of course. I figured they were coming up on their regular visit to their friend, Mona, down in North Platte. They always backed up before they took a run at cleaning up to impress her.

Earl began, leaning closer, much to my discomfort. "We was wondering who that girlie was you got into the rig with the other day."

It took me a moment to scrape my brain together, actively shoving away the image of Baxter, lean and tall, on the sidewalk in front of the Long Branch. In Hodgekiss, Nebraska. Did he look paler than the last time I'd seen him? Thinner? What if that lung ailment was making a return visit?

Newt shoved Earl aside and poked his head into the opening. His particular perfume of dead varmint, garbage, and absence of soap made my eyes water and my brain focus. "'Cause when we seen her drive up, we remembered something."

I sounded like I had a cold as I tried not to inhale. "That's Maureen Steffen. She's a friend of Kasey Weber's." I looked to my right, exhaled, and inhaled slightly fresher air.

Newt and Earl snapped their eyes to each other, and then both uttered, "Huh," at the same time.

What now? "You boys have something to tell me?"

Earl scratched at his buzzed head, making me itch all over. "She was to the rodeo grounds that day Dwayne Weber was kilt."

She said she'd been on her way when she'd heard about Dwayne. "Okay, thanks."

Newt nodded with enthusiasm. "She wasn't there in the morning, which is why we didn't think about it. 'Cause you asked only about when we was working."

Earl continued. "But we seen her later, during the steer wrestling."

Newt: "We remembered 'cause we thought she looked like a movie star, and we wondered why she'd be at the rodeo. Then we thought she was acting squirrelly 'cause she was lookin' over the bulls pretty good, but when Dwayne came around, she ducked behind the crow's nest like she was hidin'."

No one else had remarked about seeing her or her pickup at the rodeo. "Did you see her pickup?"

Newt's eyes widened. "That fancy rig? Sure did."

Earl said, "That's the other thing we noticed that was weird. She parked that thing on the other side of the east hill. Like maybe she didn't want anyone to see it."

"But you did?"

Newt puffed up a bit. "We keep a eye on things."

They could be helpful at times. "Did you see her leave?"

Newt and Earl made eye contact again and communicated wordlessly, like maybe they shared a combined vision. Earl broke it off and spoke to me. "She might've been there during the big kerfuffle. When everybody was at the trailer. Can't say. That Willy Calley and Tuff got into some fisticuffs over by the exhibit building."

Newt took it up from there. "They was pert near even matched, and took a while before Tuff got the advantage."

Earl nudged Newt. "Shorty's kid woulda stayed in it, but Tuff bit his finger."

"He ain't never." Newt pushed Earl from the window, and I drew a breath of almost clean air.

I raised my voice so they might hear over their escalating argument, but I doubted it. "Thanks for the good work. Keep your ears and eyes open."

I backed out and headed Elvis up Main Street so I could go around the block and avoid passing the Long Branch.

I should have been thinking of Dwayne's murder, the growing case against Kasey, and the new information about Maureen.

What filled my thoughts instead was only one thing.

Glenn Baxter.

# 30

The dimmer switch on the sun had finally started to turn, and dusk loomed. It made no difference to me if it was day or night, summer, fall, or spring. My world felt like nuclear winter.

Even *I* thought my reaction was melodramatic. People get their hearts broken every day, probably every minute. They survive. They find joy again.

For the love of butter. I'd survived my sister's tragic death, a divorce, my mother's nearly lifelong lies and abandonment. I could move on from Glenn Baxter. We'd only shared one night together. If you didn't count the two years we'd talked almost daily on the phone. I was better than this.

Not able to stand my own thoughts and assuming Poupon was the only one to talk to at home, I dialed Diane.

She picked up on the third ring, sounding more relaxed than I'd heard her in a decade. So unlike her, in fact, she spared time to greet me. "Hi, Katie. What's new?"

It took me a second to confirm I'd really punched her number and this was my sister speaking. "Did you know Carly is thinking of putting the Bar J in an environmental easement?"

She giggled.

Wait. Diane. Giggled. Had I ever heard her do that before?

"Sorry." It sounded like she sipped. "We're into our second bottle of Cabernet and thinking about opening a third."

"We?"

"Greg. He came over to light fireworks with Kimmy and Karl."

He had a name now. And was spending time at Diane's house. With her kids. A warm glow helped chase away a bit of the icicle that had formed with the first "That's nice" I'd uttered outside the Long Branch. Pushing past the lump in my heart, I forced the smile I felt for Diane in my voice. "I'd like to meet Greg."

Speaking at about half of her normal speed, she said, "You get your butt to Denver, and we'll make that happen. Now, what is this about Carly and the Bar J?"

"She says since Rope is leaving, she's got to do something with it until she's done with school."

A bit of the real Diane reared its head. "She sure as hell better finish school. And you sure as hell better not abandon any hope of a real life and bury yourself out there. So, what's the problem?"

"It's a terrible idea. An environmental easement would restrict grazing and could lock up the ranch for a decade or more. Maybe she'd never get it back. Glenn Baxter is here now trying to talk her into it, I'm sure."

She gave a low-throated chuckle and sipped some more. "So now we get to the real issue."

It had been a mistake to call a tipsy Diane. Though who would have thought she'd be cutting loose. "What real issue?"

"Glenn Baxter."

About twenty-five curse words crossed my mind, but I clenched my jaw and held them back.

That sultry chortle again. "Come on. You can fool Louise and the other sibs, but you aren't likely to get anything past Carly and me. We've been lied to by the best."

That was a topic I would've liked to explore further, but not now. "I don't know what you're talking about." I knew exactly what she was talking about.

"I've got to hand it to Carly. She knows how to play a good game."

It felt as though I was being sucked into the mud and I had to lift my chin to keep my nose clear. "If you and Carly are so tight, will you tell her to call off this easement plan? I can help her find a ranch foreman."

Diane sipped. "Don't get all twisted. Carly knows what she's doing."

That was exactly the problem.

"Do you think it's an accident you ran into Baxter in town? His being there is no more random than you standing outside his office tower when we were in Chicago."

She knew about that? Damn it. Diane and Carly had mad skills I had no clue about. I wasn't sure I liked it. "Never mind. I'm done trying to help everyone out."

She whooped. A decidedly un-Diane sound. "Hallelujah! I knew you had it in you."

"Eat worms."

A hearty laugh preceded, "And good night to you, too." She hung up.

## 31

The crickets chirped. The frogs croaked. Poupon snored, the sound winding its way from where he slept on the couch to the porch steps where I sat sipping a beer and eating Cheez-Its from the box. It wasn't exactly the medium-rare steak and fries I'd anticipated, but the crunch kept me from chewing my insides out.

There wasn't much of a moon, so the stars took over, filling the night sky with a brilliance more valuable than all the diamonds at Tiffany's. This sky was something Baxter, with all his millions, couldn't see in Chicago. Would he be watching it somewhere now? I so wished I didn't care.

A rumble of an engine warned me of someone driving down my road. Damn it. Why did my heart have to pray it was Baxter? Headlights topped the hill and pointed down, and in a few seconds, they swept across my picket fence and yard, shining for a moment after the driver cut the engine of the big Ford.

When she opened the door and the cab lights flashed on, my heart dumped a few feet into my gut. Roxy. She hopped out and pushed the door closed instead of slamming it, letting me know Beau was probably sleeping inside. Her feet crunched on the gravel before she opened the gate and clacked up the sidewalk in her high-heeled cowboy boots.

I had to admit she looked Roxy-fine. Long legs, jeans puddled on the tops of her boots, low-cut sleeveless top, and earrings dangling in her mussed curls. She must have wanted to look good enough to make Ted regret his cheating when she confronted him.

She sounded downright chirpy. "Glad you're still up. I know you go to bed as soon as it gets dark." Of course, Ted would have told her that. It wasn't true...not all the time, anyway.

I patted the step beside me. I didn't want to commiserate about broken hearts with her. I wouldn't let on that my mudhole was as deep and sloppy as hers. Better to act like I was lending her a sympathetic ear. "Want a beer?"

She plopped down next to me. "No. Beau's in the pickup, and I need to drive home. Not like Maureen, who doesn't worry about anyone else. I've got a little man who needs his mama, and that's about the most important thing in the world."

Mentioning Maureen seemed a little odd, but good for her for focusing on what she had in her life and not what she'd lost. She'd come all the way out here without calling, so I assumed she wanted to talk. "How are you doing?"

We stared at the darkness toward the lake. Trees cast shadows around the grass, and an occasional glint of stars reflected on the water, but the night was calm and warm and closed around us in an intimate way.

"To be honest, I feel like a fool. I've been trying to be a good friend to Kasey, and here she was, ruining my life."

"That's rough." I felt bad for Roxy but didn't want to share notes about Ted.

She sniffed, and I hoped to all the angels in heaven she wouldn't climb aboard her tragedy train. "Kasey and I have had our ups and downs, for sure. But through it all, I thought we were friends. Like you and me."

Yikes. If I was the best she had, I did feel sorry for her.

She sounded sad but not ready to burst into tears. "It's hard when a friend disappoints you. And it really hurts."

But not as bad as losing a husband. When was she going to get around to that? And what kind of waterworks could I expect?

Roxy propped her elbow on her knee and planted her chin in her palm.

"I can forgive Kasey, for sure. I mean, she's in mourning, so she probably didn't understand the full impact of her actions."

I nearly spit Cheez-Its all over the steps. "Forgive her?"

Roxy cranked her head toward me. "You shouldn't eat after seven o'clock because it won't metabolize. For you, that means it's going to settle on your hips. And really, you shouldn't eat carbs like that anyway."

I plunged my hand into the cracker box and thrust a handful of orange squares into my mouth. While I chewed, I spoke to her, only a few crumbs shooting out. "That's pretty big of you to forgive someone who destroyed your marriage."

She lowered her hand. "It's what you did, and I know you're better off by not holding a grudge."

It was admirable the way Roxy lived in her own fiction, no matter the truth.

"Besides," she said. "It didn't ruin my marriage. Ted and I are stronger than any meaningless fling."

I'd been in the process of glugging my beer to wash down the mouthful of crackers and nearly choked. "You're going to forgive him too?"

Roxy sounded matter-of-fact. "Of course. But don't tell him that. He needs to suffer a little so he learns his lesson."

"Well, I admit I'm surprised you're so magnanimous."

She tapped my arm. "Ooooh. That's a word I don't know. You're so smart."

Ugh. "It means you're being pretty darned generous."

She flicked her hair, obviously pleased with my praise, not realizing I thought she was foolish. "Besides, it's not as if they did anything. The Universe saved him from a really stupid mistake by that accident."

Sure. The Universe or someone with more nefarious intentions. I could tell her this wasn't Kasey and Ted's first tryst, but that would be cruel. "You're sure they haven't done this before?"

"That's what Ted said, and I trust him."

Stupid.

She giggled. "But I made him prove it. He showed me the email that said she'd meet him and was looking forward to their first time together. It was dated last night. I checked." She gave me a sage nod. "Trust but verify."

I mulled that over. Kasey had been locked up last night. I wasn't sure when, but by her account, meeting him today wouldn't have been their first time. Roxy and Ted deserved each other, that was true. I didn't need to tiptoe through their relationship, even if I thought that email stank like a stagnant pond.

"What I don't understand, though, is why Kasey didn't warn me."

Did she think Kasey would confess to sleeping with Ted to give Roxy a heads-up?

"And that's why I'm so darned mad at Kasey. She welcomed Maureen here and acted like she was a good friend. When all along she must have known Maureen had designs on Ted."

Whoa. I set my empty bottle down on the step. Now it made sense to me. The email had been from Maureen, not Kasey. Roxy's beef with Kasey wasn't because Kasey slept with Ted, it was because Roxy thought Kasey should have protected her from Maureen. I needed to double-check my theory. "Maureen was meeting Ted at the Pullman?"

Roxy went on as if I hadn't spoken. "I feel so stupid. I mean, I should have known someone like Maureen couldn't be trusted."

I was too flummoxed by Maureen meeting Ted that I didn't answer Roxy.

Apparently, she didn't need me to participate. "I didn't put two and two together at first. Mo and Maureen. It just didn't occur to me. And she's had a lot of work done. New teeth and dyed her hair. And lost quite a bit of weight. I suppose personal trainers and liposuction helped."

This trail looped around on itself so many times, I was in the weeds. "What are you talking about?"

Roxy giggled. "Oh, I forget you're a bit younger than the rest of us."

Depended on your definition of "a bit."

"Maureen Steffen used to be Mo Green. From Montana. She hung around rodeos all the time, but no one ever paid any attention to her. She wasn't good-looking. It was like she didn't even try to fix herself up."

A terrible sin, as far as Roxy was concerned.

She sat up straighter and talked faster, obviously relishing the gossip. "But then she hooked up with this really cute bull rider, which shocked us all. But get this, his name was Dwayne Weber."

Well, now. That caught my attention. "How long ago was this?"

She tilted her head up to the stars and calculated. "It was when Ted and I had broken up and I was secretarying for the PRCA. So, maybe fifteen years ago? Before he married Helen Walsh, anyway."

"He and Maureen were a thing?"

"I know." She emphasized it like the idea was preposterous. "He was really hot, and she was so plain. But he'd had a super-bad broken leg from getting bucked off a bronc, and knowing Dwayne, I think he hooked up with her so he'd have a place to live and someone to look after him."

"But it didn't last long?"

Roxy faced toward the lake and sounded as if she reminisced. "If I remember right, Mo had raised a really good buckin' bull. It looked like she'd go into breeding and training, but then nothing much happened. Dwayne lived with her that winter, I think. Then next year he married Helen."

I guessed what happened was that Dwayne stole Mo's best breeding cow.

She twisted toward me. "And you know, I think he married Helen for the money. I don't like to speak ill of the dead, but Dwayne wasn't a great guy."

"Dwayne dumped Mo for money." Sounded about right.

Roxy waved her hand. "Can't feel too sorry for Mo. She did the very same thing. Married Fred Steffen, who had more money than an Arab sheik. She finally got someone to finance her bull habit. And it looks like she learned how to spend some of that on herself, because I'm telling you, she looks a whole lot better now than she did back then."

Roxy stood and brushed the back of her jeans. "So, anyways, I wanted to come by and thank you for taking such good care of Ted and getting him out of the Bronco. And for calling me. Now that I know I can't trust Kasey, you're my only real friend. I don't want to lose you."

The Cheez-Its in my stomach rolled into a hard ball. I stood, too, glad for the darkness so I wouldn't have to fake an earnest face. "Okay, then. Drive careful."

My hopes that she'd simply walk back to her pickup were crushed. She threw her arms around me and plastered her boobs into my face. I often wished I were taller, but never more so than when I struggled for air during her hugs.

While I savored the relief of watching her taillights retreat down my road, I dropped back to the porch steps.

I didn't sit there more than two seconds before knowing who killed Dwayne Weber and why.

# 32

Ten o'clock on a Friday night. The Long Branch should be hopping. Or at least the jukebox would be playing and a dozen people hanging around—what constituted hopping for Hodgekiss. I jumped from my porch steps, took a couple of seconds to change into my uniform while explaining to Poupon that I had to go, and dashed to the cruiser. It took ten minutes to pull up in front of the Long Branch.

Maureen's pickup wasn't anywhere in sight. Instead of wasting time looking for her, I gunned it down the highway and out to Kasey's, in case Maureen was there, maybe drinking the rest of the bourbon and commiserating about widowhood. If so, my theory would be wrong.

I seriously wanted to be wrong.

But it seemed obvious that Maureen had killed Dwayne. He was the man who broke her heart and took off with her best cow. He was behind Wild Fire. She must have known before she arrived here and lied about it to cover her tracks. She'd probably killed her husband. The chain scratches on her pickup might be evidence she'd dragged the Autogate away. Whether she'd intended to kill Ted or Michael, or if it mattered to her, she'd attempted murder.

The lights were on in Kasey's house, and loud music thrummed into the warm night. But Maureen's pickup wasn't there. This time, I shut the engine down and raced toward the house, jumping two stairs at a time up the front porch and banging on the door.

There was a bit of shuffling. Kasey yelled something that might have been "hold on." The music quieted, and footsteps pounded to the front door. She whipped it open and stood inside the screen, fully dressed in jeans, T-shirt, and cowboy boots. "What are you doing here?"

I didn't want to explain. "Where is Maureen?"

She cocked her hip. "How the hell should I know?"

I pushed closer to the screen to see her against the backlight from the house. "Has she been here?"

Kasey pushed through the door, and the screen scratched my nose and sent me stumbling backward to clatter on the deck. She slammed her door behind her. "I'm pretty sick of cops banging on my door and accusing me of killing Dwayne. He was a piece a shit."

Unexpectedly, she choked and slumped, and her brittle face seemed to shatter. I couldn't have predicted a breakdown and, frankly, hadn't been sure she was capable of it. I nearly sprang for the cruiser to call the ambulance.

With a sob, she said, "But I loved him. We were a team. Dwayne and me against the world. I don't know what I'll do without him."

In a state of shock, I reached out and laid a hand on her back. "I'm sorry." It wasn't as if I had a wagon full of useful and comforting words to say. When my sister Glenda died, there wasn't a word in the world that could ease my pain. And most of the words people chose to utter only made me mad.

Not the most sensitive thing to say, but I didn't have time to console her. "I really need to find Maureen."

She whipped her head up, watery eyes drilling into me. "You think she did it." She blinked as if putting it all together. "She killed Dwayne."

"I don't know." It was the truth, not that I wasn't fifty percent—okay, more like eighty percent—sure she had.

Kasey's tears evaporated. "It makes so much sense. How she miraculously showed up to help me out." She held her fingers up in air quotes on the last phrase. "She wanted Wild Fire. I'll bet she figured out Dwayne owned it, and she wanted in. She assumed she could buy in, and when

Dwayne wouldn't let her, she killed him. That's why she wanted me to go through the papers. To find out about Wild Fire so I would partner with her."

Okay. Maybe. None of that helped me right now. "Where do you suppose she went?"

A sly glint caught in Kasey's face. Maybe she and Maureen shared the same devious bent and she channeled it. "If she thinks you suspect her, she'll be long gone."

Goat tits and tar. I took a second to plan, then ran back to the cruiser. Instead of calling dispatch, I dialed Trey.

When I explained my suspicions and laid it out for him, it was a relief he didn't spend time railing at me about sticking my nose into the investigation. "Four highways out of town. One leads directly to the interstate in Ogallala. I'll send troopers on all four routes and head your way from here."

Dust flew in the red of my taillights. "I'm on my way south now."

I clicked on my light bar. I doubted Maureen would stop for me, but I didn't want to risk any traffic in the dark slowing me down. It was over eighty miles to Ogallala, and Trey racing my way would cut the distance in half. I hoped this was the route Maureen had taken and that stopping her wouldn't involve a high-speed chase or some dangerous endeavor. She was obviously a determined woman, fierce and smart.

I had second thoughts about finding her. If it were me on the run, I wouldn't take a well-trafficked route. Wouldn't go near an interstate. I'd hide out in the hills. Sure, Maureen didn't know the Sandhills, but she had a pickup and could travel back roads and cross-country a long way. Ranchers didn't always lock their fuel tanks. Food wouldn't be hard to find.

I worried this scenario for about ten miles, until the taillights of a pickup showed when I topped a hill. They disappeared around a rare curve in the highway. I'd have punched the gas, but I already had the pedal buried.

I lost sight of the taillights as I jetted down the dark road toward the curve. It would have been hard to miss my flashing lights, so she probably knew I was chasing her. She could turn off in any of the pastures, zoom over a hill, kill the lights, and I'd never find her. My speed stayed high as I took the curve, and the centrifugal force pulled me to the right.

My guardian angel, or whoever kept track of me, must have been on high alert because if not, I wouldn't have survived what happened next.

Directly around the corner, the pickup I'd chased had partially pulled off the road. I had to jerk the wheel to the left to avoid hitting it. Naturally, I wanted to slam on the brakes, but something stopped me. If I had, not even my trusty Charger would have resisted rolling. I straightened out and slowed, then U-turned and headed back to the pickup, surprised Maureen hadn't fled.

She stood outside the driver's door, hands in her jeans pockets, waiting for me.

I pulled off the road to the right. All the way off. Leaving my lightbar flaring, I jumped out and shouted at her. "Get that thing completely off the road before you kill someone!" The words came out before I considered them. If she could kill her husband and break Dwayne's neck with bare hands, what did she care if she caused an accident?

She started to yell something back, whipped her head to peer up and down the road as if considering what I'd said, and hiked herself back into her pickup.

I braced for her to take off, but the pickup momentarily roared to life, jerked ahead a few feet and off into the barrow pit, and the engine cut again. She popped out, hands upturned in annoyance. "What?"

I looked both ways and pounded across the highway toward her. Heat still rose from the pavement, and the night smells held none of that sweet dewy scent.

"Where are you going?" I felt for my cuffs, then let my hand glide over my gun. All ready in case I needed anything.

She took two steps toward me, irritation in her manner. "Why are you following me? Did something happen?"

I studied her pickup and scrutinized her annoyed face. "You're taking off pretty late at night, aren't you?"

With obvious effort, she pulled her authoritative persona on, like donning a jacket. "I've got no reason to stay in Nebraska. I know who Wild Fire is, and there's no need to worry about that anymore."

"Because you killed Dwayne Weber." I stated it with surety.

She drew her neck back as if I'd bitten her. "Are you nuts? I didn't kill Dwayne. I couldn't kill anyone. Not even a skunk in the grain bin."

We stood just off the road, illuminated slightly by the light cast from her headlights, the red and blue of my lightbar glowing on her face. I challenged her. "What about your husband?"

Her eyes flicked away from me and back. "Fred was quite a bit older than me. I always assumed I'd outlive him. But I wasn't ready for it when he died so unexpectedly. I know people thought I married him for his money. And that was part of it. But we had a relationship that worked. I'm sad he's gone."

"Was he the first person you killed? How many between him and Dwayne?"

Her eyebrows dipped low, and her face grew so hard her it could slice marble. "Let's get this straight. I didn't kill Fred *or* Dwayne."

"And you tried to kill someone when you dragged the Autogate from the road."

She shook her head and raised her hand. "Autogate?"

So frustrating. "Cattle guard. At the Pullman pasture. Who were you after? Ted or Michael?"

Her scowl lifted, and she grinned. "Oh, that was for Ted. You're welcome."

This was too much. I grabbed her arm and twisted her around, clamping the cuffs on her, despite her grunts of protest. "He could have died."

She spun back to me, looking far less murderous than I'd expected. "Oh, please. Men like that don't die. And even if he did, would it have been a big loss?"

"It would have to his wife and son."

Maureen sounded so reasonable, not like someone accused of murder. "He was going to sleep with me, with only a wink and nod from me to get his attention. We both know Roxy'd be fine without that loser. She only acts like an airhead to make him feel manly. If he was gone, she'd grow to her potential."

I might agree with her, but that didn't pardon attempted murder. "We're going to take you to Ogallala for that incident. And questioning about Dwayne's murder."

"I took you for smarter than that. I didn't kill Dwayne." She drilled her words directly into my face. "But we both know who did."

In the distance, red and blue whirled across the lonely hills. Trey on his way. I battered away at Maureen. "There's not any shadow cabal in the buckin' industry. You took your hatred of men and your drive for revenge too far."

The growl of Trey's engine grew until he pulled up, headlight to head-light, with Maureen's pickup. We waited while he climbed out and strode to us.

"Sheriff," he said to me and nodded. "This is Maureen Steffen?"

Maureen gazed at him as though he were covered in slag.

I stood back to let Trey take charge. "She confessed to removing the Autogate and causing Ted's accident. The investigation into Dwayne's murder is up to you."

Trey looked her up and down. "Well, let's get you loaded up, and we'll be on our way." He clamped his cuffs on her, used his key to unlock mine, and handed them to me.

It felt wrong to drop everything now. "I can fill you in on the details of the investigation."

Trey took her arm to direct her to his car. "Thanks for your help. I'll take it from here."

That seemed anticlimactic for solving a murder. "Do you want me to follow you? Help with the interrogation?"

He caught my eye and held steady. "Send me your report. If this all works out, I'll splash it everywhere, and you'll get full credit. But if it doesn't, I don't want it to damage you."

"I don't care about the recall. I want to see my case through to the end."

"It's not your case."

Maureen had been watching the exchange with a sardonic expression. "Listen to him, Kate. I can tell you arresting me is going nowhere. I have high-priced lawyers who will have me out of jail in an hour. And there is no proving I killed Dwayne Weber, because I didn't."

Trey urged her away.

She spoke over her shoulder. "You disappointment me."

Something struck me, and I said, "Wait."

Trey must have heard the urgency in my voice, because he looked back, swinging Maureen around to face me. He gave me a questioning look.

I caught up to them and looked up into Maureen's face as she gazed at me placidly. "You didn't kill Dwayne."

"That's right." She ended on an upturned note, as if urging me to say more.

"It was Kasey."

She gave me a smile like a proud teacher when a student answers correctly.

I worked it out. "Not because he slept with Gidget. Not because he lied to her about the new business or hid money from her."

Maureen nodded.

"But because he killed Pecos and Luke."

Trey glanced from me to Maureen and back. "Who're Pecos and Luke?"

A new thought pierced me with the sharp point of a poisoned arrow. "Did you tell her Dwayne had a partner?"

The sly grin slid from her face, and her eyes widened in alarm.

Grubs in gravy. "She knows Michael was part of Wild Fire, and she might think he had a hand in killing her bulls." I gulped the words as I spun toward my cruiser.

Trey might have hollered something at me, but I never heard it.

# 33

Stubborn. Blind. Just plain stupid. All of those recriminations spun through my head as I braced against the gas pedal and flew through the night. Because I'd wanted to be smarter than Trey or Ted or Michael or any other man on the planet. Because, even though I'd been butting up against stereotypes of women ever since I managed Frog Creek and especially as sheriff, I allowed Maureen to fire me up against men in general. Because I was too wrapped up in what I wanted and needed and my own pain. I'd ignored all the clues.

And now Kasey was on the loose and probably heading for Michael with vengeance on her mind.

It took twenty-five minutes but felt more like twenty-five years to make it to the turnoff to Michael's place. Thank the good green earth that Lauren and the girls weren't home. I couldn't imagine what Kasey might do to Michael, but she was smart and strong and had a mean streak wider than the Mississippi.

Before I reached the final curve into their place, Kasey's pickup loomed in the middle of the road. Lights off, engine dead. She'd obviously parked it here to sneak up on Michael. I considered bumping into the pasture and sailing around it but decided stealth might be the wisest choice.

As soon as I cut the engine and clicked my door shut, the silence of the night wrapped around me like a shroud. The quarter moon had hit the high point and was sliding down the western sky, giving just enough light to see the road ahead. It hadn't cooled much and smelled of dry prairie, a blank, sad whiff of nothingness, as if the world held its breath in the hope of rain. A 'yote howled somewhere so far away I strained to catch its lonely drift. A yip nearby let me know the 'yote wasn't as alone as I'd assumed. I couldn't even get that right.

My boots crunched on the gravel as I jogged a few yards and jumped off the road. I could cut over the hill and come down behind the new house and barn. I tried to keep my breath from chugging in the still night. It would defeat the purpose of sneaking up if I sounded like a freight train. But running up a hill was hard work.

When I reached the top, I rested my hands on my knees to catch my breath and get a feel for the scene. Michael and Lauren's place spread along the valley floor below me surrounded by hills. Their double-wide was tucked against the far hill facing me, and the barn stood across the yard from it. The new house sat off to the north of them, the apex of a triangle.

No lights shone from the house windows, but the front door was flung wide. That wasn't a good sign. Whatever it meant, it was clear I was late to the party.

The back barn door was slid open as well, and glow from a few bulbs dangling from the alley ceiling inside spilled out. The meager circle of light didn't reach the steel panels of a holding pen behind the barn. The gate that led from the back of the corral through sunflowers and tall grass into a narrow entrance to the back pasture gaped open. Something was happening here, but I couldn't guess what.

I inched down the slope, keeping my focus on the barn. The closer 'yote yipped again, raising the hairs on my neck. Other than that, my controlled breath, and the swish of boots through the grass, I heard nothing else.

The hill bottomed out with the corral fence a few feet away. I brushed aside sunflowers, their buds still in tight pods waiting to bloom. The peppery scent lifted on the night, and their sap left my fingers slightly sticky when I reached for the bottom rung of the fence and slipped through the opening into the corral.

A clank and grunt came from inside the barn. It sounded like Michael struggling with equipment. Glad I still wore my uniform and belt, complete with gun, cuffs, and my ever-present piggin' string, I unsnapped the safety strap on my holster to be ready for anything. Keeping low and wishing my feet didn't have to touch the ground, I hurried toward the barn as noiselessly as possible. I hugged the barn wall and eased my head around the door, peering inside.

I hadn't expected what I saw. With one glance around to make sure Kasey wasn't hiding and ready to lunge out at me, I stepped into the open doorway.

Michael jerked as if slapped, then his face radiated relief. "Thank God. Get me out of here."

I took a few steps into the barn, my boots swishing on the hay-strewn alleyway. Despite the seriousness of our situation, I had to fight back laughter. "Of course, but I want to know what and how."

Somehow Kasey had succeeded in wrangling Michael from his house and getting him into that worthless squeeze chute he'd anchored into the barn. Michael wasn't as big as Douglas, but he was scrappy. If Kasey was tough enough to capture him, I had little doubt she could dispatch Dwayne and drag him into the stock trailer.

Michael's neck was pinned in the headgate, similar to a Puritan sinner caught in a pillory. The panel on the left had been lowered, showing Michael's side and a collection of welts on his skin. Because his neck was caught too high for him to rest on his knees, his legs were in a kind of half squat with his bare feet pressed against the steel frame. I guessed he'd been in bed because all he had on were his baby-blue briefs. His hands clasped the gate, but his arms weren't long enough to use the lever to free himself.

He sounded exhausted but not defeated. "I told you she was crazy. Jumped me while I was asleep and had me out here before I knew it."

I gave him a few more seconds to suffer before I started for him. "Hang on. If this piece of crap isn't rusted, I'll release it."

He hung his head as if he needed to rest his neck. He flung an arm out to his left. "She used that on me."

I followed where he indicated and scanned the hay-strewn alleyway. There, not far from where the panel had been lowered, a flash of bright yellow caught my eye. I didn't need to get closer to know it was a Hot Shot.

A long-armed cattle prod, or a stun gun on an extension wand. A plastic-covered handle, similar to that of an electric carving knife, held the batteries and extended to an eighteen-inch wand. At the end, a U-shaped prong with metal tips could be stuck into an animal's side to complete the circuit so that when you pressed the button on the handle, an electric shock zapped into the critter.

I hated them, but people used them to urge cattle to go where they didn't naturally want to go, such as up a ramp into a trailer or into a squeeze chute.

Suddenly the humor scampered right out of the moment. Kasey had used the Hot Shot on my brother. That was torture. Maybe not on the scale of Guantanamo, more like sticking a fork into an outlet, but it darned sure hurt. Whatever sympathy I'd had for her—and not sure I'd had much—vanished, and now I wanted to tear that blond braid out of her head and let her brains dribble out.

I loped across the alley and grasped the steel handle to release the headgate. It stuck, as I'd expected of the ancient contraption. I braced myself to use all my body weight.

Michael issued a garbled yell.

I gave a little hop to get momentum to throw myself against the lever... and was hit by a Mack truck.

I lost my grip on the lever and was airborne for a few feet before slamming into the alley with a grunt and a shooting pain on my hip where I'd landed on the handle of the Hot Shot. Before I could register what hit me and if I could move or would be paralyzed for life, something fell on top of me.

Kasey had tackled me, and I fought back with all the wily skills of one of nine kids raised in a rambunctious family.

Slippery as I was, my moves weren't good enough to best six feet of pure muscle and malignance. With a deft move, she whipped the gun from my holster and shoved me away, jumping to her feet in one smooth motion.

She pointed the gun at me. "I thought you went after Maureen."

I assessed the layout of the barn. Me on the ground, facing the open doors in the back. Kasey, looking at me and Michael, with her back to the doors. She stood about six feet to the left of where Michael's head was caught in the chute.

Michael's head hung down, knees buckling, hands grasping the head-stall. His eyes were slits. If his legs gave out and his arms went limp, would his neck rest on the steel where the stall met and the weight of his head cut off his air supply? Michael was strong and as determined as any of us Foxes. He'd hold on for a while, but not forever.

I propped myself on my arms and leaned back, desperate for a plan and knowing brute force wouldn't win this fight. "But she didn't kill Dwayne, did she?"

Kasey smirked at me. "Just like everyone else, you underestimated me. No one thought I'd make anything of myself. Mom and Dad sure didn't. Even Dwayne didn't believe in me. It's no wonder you didn't think I could pull off murder."

"I've been defending you for days. Telling everyone you wouldn't kill Dwayne because you had no incentive. I know you were the one running the business. You trained the bulls. You took care of them. I believed you were too strong to let Dwayne's affairs drag you down. And you were too smart to kill someone."

She snorted. "As if you have the least bit of respect for me and what I've accomplished. I'm not fooled by your sudden bond with the 'sisterhood.'"

She swung her chin up to indicate Michael in the headstall. "You probably knew he was in business with Dwayne. But did you tell me? No. Because you're all about them."

"Them?"

She swayed from foot to foot as if building up energy on her way to exploding. Her lips glistened like venom squirting from a snake. "Men. They're all bad."

"It's not them. You killed—"

"Shut up!" Her shriek spiked like tiny razors down my spine and echoed in the barn.

I didn't want to shut up. As long as I kept her talking, I might come up with some way to get us out of here. She not only had my gun but also the weight and height advantage over me. She wrangled bulls daily, so she outmuscled me. But I'd worked at Frog Creek for eight years. Mostly on my own. There were plenty of times I needed to do a job I wasn't man enough for. There were workarounds. If you used your head. And I needed more time to figure this one out.

Something moved behind her into the open doorway. Had Trey followed me here? Left Maureen in the back of his car as I'd done with Tony? Thank...

The shadow let out a long, low groan. Only for the bull, it was more like a love song. He was the size of Mom's old Vanagon. And like the old hippie love-mobile, he might be full of benevolence and amorous vibes, but all the hearts and rose petals in the world wouldn't save you if he ran over you. Big and black, drawing breaths like a locomotive, he had a snout full of snot and a tongue long enough to lick it clean.

Kasey nodded in his direction but didn't take her eyes, or the gun, off of me. "He's a beauty, isn't he? I raised him from the day he was born. He loves me. And Dwayne told me he was dead."

I recalled one of Michael's daughters talking about turning Luke out. "Is that Lucky Luke?"

"I'd have never known he was alive if your brother here hadn't confessed just now because he got scared."

Michael didn't react to her goading.

She tilted her chin at Lucky Luke. "Dwayne stole him. Put him out here where he doesn't know anyone. He's used to being bathed and brushed and hand-fed. But they turned him out to a pasture all alone. He had to be so scared and lonely." Her eyes misted.

I had to look up to see directly into his eyes. Like dark chocolate, warm and calm, not at all like the white-rimmed eyes of Slim in the arena. I figured it wouldn't take much to spook him, and in the alley of the barn, his bucking and spinning would be deadly. I kept my voice low.


It sounded loopy, but I was raised by a mother who talked to flowers and believed a bee landing in her kitchen was a sign of good fortune. Even killers could have love in their hearts. "Dwayne didn't do right by you."

She stiffened and glared at Michael. "*Him.*" She spit it out like poison. "He was in on it, too. They told me Luke was dead. Dwayne said he took the body away so I wouldn't have to see him. All the while I was grieving."

She kicked straw at Michael, but his eyes were closed and he didn't seem to notice. She aimed words at me. "Do you know how many times I had to hit your brother with the Hot Shot before he told me Luke was here? Just around that hill. If they'd have told me he was alive…" She thought about it a moment. "And if they hadn't murdered Pecos."

Michael stirred and answered in a weak voice. "I didn't kill him."

Kasey didn't seem to care. "It's called accessory, right, Kate? Anyway, Dwayne signed his own death warrant. You don't get to kill anyone I love and live to tell about it."

Lucky Luke lifted his nose in the air and wrinkled it back as if sniffing the most fragrant flowers in the field. His bulk filled the doorway as he soaked up the light, his horns spanning a terrifying length. He let out a low bellow again and took a lumbering step into the barn.

Michael's eyes opened, and he strained to look at me. With a flick of his focus, he let me know what he was thinking. Michael was tough, smart, quick, and strong. But none of that would help him if he didn't judge this right. His plan held out the tiniest sliver of hope to escape this situation where Kasey had the gun and every other advantage.

Luke moved closer, head down, rolling his neck a bit from side to side. Each breath pulled in and huffed out, each lumbering footfall pounded on the cement under the thin layer of straw. If he came close enough to stand by me, the tip of my head would reach Luke's shoulder. Simply backing me into a stall wall would break all of my bones.

I fought the urge to watch him and force his steps closer, all the while wanting to get clear of him. But I made myself give Kasey my full attention. "Too bad you didn't reach out to Maureen before you killed Dwayne. You would have made a great team. Wouldn't it have been satisfying to outdo Dwayne at his own game? And you could have. You're both smarter and work harder than any man I ever knew." I wanted to lay it on juicy and thick, get her imagination charged up. Stop her from noticing that hulking bovine heading toward her with love in his eyes.

It didn't work. She swiveled her head enough to catch his movement in her peripheral vision. "Woulda, coulda. None of that matters now."

Luke released a low moan and shambled another step closer, not exactly focused on Kasey as a dog might run to an owner who'd been gone for an hour to the grocery store. More like Frankenstein's monster being drawn in by something he can't quite understand.

Frustrated, I spat at her. "So what? You're going to kill me and Michael and escape into the hills? Who's going to take care of Luke then?"

Luke lifted his head and sniffed again. His tongue snaked from between his teeth and curled up to tip into a nostril. Pointed up to the sky, his nose wrinkled and pulled back, clearly loving the barn's odor. He wasn't far behind Kasey.

She sneered at me. "Who's going to take care of him if I go to jail?"

"There's parole and early release for good behavior. At least you'd have more chances than if you add two more murders to your list, especially if one is a sheriff. They'll never let you out then."

Finally, my words seemed to get her dander up, at least enough to lose a smidgeon of focus. "If they catch me."

None of my efforts would have worked if Luke hadn't taken the bull by the horns, so to speak. He was now close enough to Kasey to give an affectionate head bump to her shooting arm. His head was as big as a bushel basket full of lead bowling balls. I'd been praying for this opportunity and blessed Luke for disrupting her aim.

Thinking of Michael's plan, I made a strategic kick under the straw, not pausing to see if I'd been successful before lunging at Kasey.

She recovered from Luke's love nudge quickly and swung the gun my way, firing off a shot that whizzed past my ear.

Luke startled and swung his train engine of a head into Kasey again, this time pushing her a few feet closer to Michael.

Despite being jiggled by a two-thousand-pound mass of muscle with the brain of a bumblebee, Kasey shook it off and regained her balance. She narrowed her eyes at me and pulled up the gun, aiming for center mass of my speeding body.

I was only a step away from shoving her arm and wrecking her shot, but that step would take longer than a twitch of her finger. So close to stopping her. And she'd send a bullet ripping through me instead.

She'd turn the gun on Michael next.

It felt like slow motion as I launched myself toward her, my arm outstretched. My vision focused on her hand and that trigger finger shuddering, releasing my death.

And she shrieked.

Thank all the stars and planets that aligned to make Michael's last-ditch plan work out. He'd shown me the Hot Shot, and I'd had scant opportunity to kick it toward him. Improbably, he'd reached it, and Kasey had stepped close enough for him to zap her.

Startled by the shock, Kasey's arm flew up as she pulled the trigger. The bullet hit a light bulb, and it shattered with a pop like fireworks on the Fourth. The barn was plunged into darkness.

The *zzzz-zzzap* of the Hot Shot filled a beat of silence, and Kasey screamed again when Michael poked her for a second time. She fell to the ground.

He might have been an oversized Pepé Le Pew with love on his mind, but the hullabaloo was too much for Lucky Luke. Scared, he did exactly what he was bred to do, despite all of Kasey's coddling and cooing. He lunged onto his front legs and kicked out with his back legs. Stretched out in the barn alley, snorting and wild, Luke was like a tornado in a box. Like lightning, he could strike anywhere in a split second with no warning. When his hooves crashed into the barn door, almost as loud as the gunshot, he wrenched and twisted and kicked out again.

Kasey was underneath all that bulk and those razor-sharp hooves as she crab-walked in a mad scramble toward a stall door, but there was really no place to hide. The best we could hope for was that Luke's panicked kicks and spins would miss us.

I shoved myself backward from where I'd fallen, pressing my arms around my head. I managed to survive with only a swipe of his tail and a brush of his back legs.

Kasey wasn't so lucky. She screeched when he landed on her calf, and I heard a crunch of bone.

I sprang to my feet and waved my arms at Luke. "Heyaw. Get, get." I made myself as big and menacing as possible, windmilling my arms and yelling at him, swatting and advancing. I'd wrangled plenty of critters bigger and tougher than me, and this guy wasn't as bad as some others I'd dealt with.

Luke seemed glad someone was taking charge and reminding him about rear doors and the wide-open prairie beyond them. He whirled around and bounded from the barn.

Filling my lungs with night air and sweet relief, I turned around to assess the damages. I'd thought to release Michael first, then tend to Kasey's broken leg while Michael called Trey.

But seeing Kasey standing in the darkened barn, favoring her good leg, with my gun in her hand leveled at Michael stopped me cold.

Nope.

This was too much.

I'd had enough of her and that gun. My own damned gun! Too much adrenaline, too much death. I let loose with a yell that came from the center of my gut and burst with such force Kasey flinched.

My bellow fueled what felt like flight since I honestly didn't know how I got across the barn and bulleted into Kasey's chest. If Luke hadn't shattered her leg, I might not have been able to topple her, but he had, and I did. We crashed in a heap with me on top. I pulled back my arm and shot my fist into her nose.

Police brutality? Only if I'd kept hitting her. Which I wanted to do but restrained myself. Instead, I whipped the piggin' string from my back pocket and, quicker than I'd ever done it in the rodeo arena, had her wrists bound in less than two seconds.

She dropped her head back on the ground in defeat. Her thick braid was laced with dusty straw. Dirt and blood streaked her face, which was tinged with gray from the pain that must have been throbbing through her leg. She hitched as if stanching a sob, and her voice fell from her with the weight of defeat. "Why couldn't I win? Just this once."

I scrabbled in the straw for my gun and handed it to Michael. He managed to keep a wobbly bead on Kasey, though she sprawled on her back, her face slack as she stared at the ceiling.

With every ounce of strength I had left, I threw myself against the lever to release the piece-of-crap gate.

It screeched open, and Michael crawled through. He plopped against the headgate. He swallowed a few times and rubbed his neck. In a creaking voice, he said, "I suppose you want a thank-you."

I dabbed at my cheekbone, feeling a nasty bruise beginning. Pain hammered me, from dull to attention-grabbing, and radiated from my hips, knees, back, and right elbow. Fighting an Amazon with a blond braid took a toll. "Why start now?"

A few choppy breaths substituted for a laugh. "Guess I'm lucky you're my sister."

Sister, sure. What about sheriff?

## 34

It'd been a short night of sleep. Truthfully, mostly a nonexistent one. Trey had handed off Maureen to a trooper he'd called and turned around. He made it to Hodgekiss about the time Eunice Fleenor and Harold Graham passed through with Kasey strapped down and sedated. I gave him the details, and he sped after them. Since it was his case, he'd do all the arresting and follow-up. Something to be grateful for.

I'd made it home just before sunrise. Poupon didn't seem concerned I'd been out all night. He shook and stretched when I tugged him off the couch, then he wandered out to the front yard. I plopped onto a Morris chair on the porch and waited for the first robin to herald the day.

Thirty-six years old. No family of my own. No special person in my life, unless I wanted to make amends with Garrett Haney and see where that might lead. Even if I wanted to, Garrett probably wanted nothing to do with me. A job that had no growth potential and one I'd need to fight for every four years. I owned a tiny bungalow on a shallow lake and a 1973 Ranchero.

Poupon padded up the stairs and sat next to my chair, keeping an eye on his kingdom. I rifled my fingers through the silky curls on the top of his head. "I'm tired."

I was sure he didn't understand I wasn't talking only about missing sleep. I didn't want to feel this alone anymore. I needed someone besides an arrogant hound to love me. Maybe my family was right. Being sheriff wasn't for me.

I would find another way to earn a living. Go back to being a better sister, aunt, daughter, friend. No more digging into the sordid affairs of the good citizens (and bad) of Grand County.

Resigning the office wasn't really quitting. It signaled a step forward. A chance to go back to what I loved. I'd take Carly up on her offer to manage the Bar J. Life would settle down to the rhythms of the land and animals.

It would be fine. I would be fine. Fine.

At least I'd have my family.

Showering and dressing in my uniform became a journey of discovery as I found new bruises and sore muscles. With no one to hear me except Poupon, I didn't mind letting out an "ow" or a grunt during the process.

At eight o'clock, I loaded Poupon into the back seat of the cruiser and headed to town. It was Saturday, so I'd leave a note on Ethel's desk to give her a happy Monday by calling off the recall election. But first I owed Louise the news.

Maybe my subconscious wanted to save me the humiliation, or maybe my body signaled the reality, but before I made it to the highway, my stomach opened up and started to growl like a threatened grizzly bear. I hadn't eaten since, well, maybe lunch yesterday? No, not even then. Except for that half a box of Cheez-Its.

Louise would be as happy to hear from me after breakfast as she would be before, so I detoured to the Long Branch.

I drove around the block, scouting for Carly's pickup. Maybe she'd gone back to Lincoln, but what if she hadn't? I didn't need another Baxter encounter to scramble all my cells and leave me a quivering puddle of goo. Since the coast was clear, I pulled into an angled spot on the lower part of Main Street and climbed out. I leaned into the door of the cruiser and spoke to Poupon. "I'll bring you a sausage patty, don't worry."

If he was worried, he hid it well.

Before I'd taken more than two steps toward the restaurant, a gray pickup careened into the spot next to me and cut the engine.

I didn't know whether I was relieved or upset, but I was definitely nervous as Garrett slid from behind the wheel. I stopped and tried for a welcoming smile, but it probably showed all my angst.

He hurried toward me, his face an implacable, professional handsome. "Glad I caught you. Got a minute?"

Forgiving? Interested? Angry? Insulted? He wore his court face that hid all emotion. But I'd stood him up. Run away from him in plain sight. "Sure. Want to grab a bite?"

Then he cracked. An incredulous look tipped the corner of his mouth in such a Sarah way, I could predict what he'd say. "Not likely. I don't know what game you and Sarah are playing, but it's nasty and even cruel."

No ambiguity there. I crumpled inside. "I'm not playing. Something came up. I-I had to leave."

Even if his face remained smooth and professional, barbs flew from his brown eyes. "You can parade out any excuse you want. I know you had a sheriff thing last night about Dwayne Weber's murder."

Sheriff thing. Yup. In which my brother and I were nearly killed. But, whatever.

He didn't pause. "I also know it didn't happen until much later. I saw you run away from the Long Branch. And there I sat like a schmuck in front of half the county."

I interjected as if it mattered. "There weren't that many people there."

He spat at me. "Multiplied by the gossip factor and it was the whole county. I don't appreciate being played for a fool. I can't figure out what you and Sarah hope to gain by humiliating me, but it's not going to work. I'm cleaning the Blume, and Tony and I will move in there as soon as it's done. I'm here to stay."

Making him feel embarrassed and duped made me feel greasy. But Garrett being so sensitive and jumping to conclusions without talking to me first rankled. The ruffled feathers trumped guilt. "You're paranoid. I was looking forward to dinner and getting to know you better. You don't seem interested in why I had to leave. So, let's forget it."

He glared at me. "Forgotten."

I bounced it right back at him. "Sarah's right about you." I spun around and sashayed back to the car with all the dignity I could muster. Good play, because Aileen and Jack Carson stared at us from the front door of the bank.

Garrett beat me to his pickup, and I had to wait while he backed up and gunned it down Main Street, all but squealing his tires when he turned onto the highway.

I continued down the hill. I lied to Poupon while we drove toward my next uncomfortable encounter. "I wasn't hungry, anyway."

Louise held a garden hose spraying on a row of snapdragons and petunias below her front porch, the same kind of flowers Grandma Ardith had planted there. The familiar blooms nodding in the heat should have brought me comfort. But my empty stomach roiled. Maybe after I talked to her, I'd let her feed me—a double victory for her.

She ignored me as I approached, her mouth set in a straight line.

I tried for friendly. "Got a minute?" Repeating the same line Garrett had used made me cringe.

She kept her eyes on the spray. "No."

"Uncle."

Her head snapped to me. "What?"

I held up my hands. "I give up. I'll resign."

She lowered the hose, and her mouth dropped open, folding her chins into an accordion. "Are you serious?"

I glanced away, the mix of defeat and something like shame running through me. Then forced myself to look at her. "You win."

She smacked her lips together and drew herself up to her wise-elder stance. "It's not about winning. It's about what's best for you."

"You're holding my family hostage, so there's really no choice. Because my family means more to me than this job."

Water continued to spray. "Of course it does. And you're making the right decision. You don't need to run around like a knight on a white horse and rescue the whole county."

She made it sound trivial, as if I were playing a game. "What I do is serious. I help people. I'm sure you heard about what happened last night."

Puddles formed under the snapdragons as Louise huffed. "Of course. Thank the Lord you were there to help Michael or who knows what that lunatic would have done. But you don't need a badge to help out family. You've always done that."

Hadn't I told Diane I was done helping out our brothers and sisters? Dad had even hinted it was time for me to let go of that role.

She got all Louise-teary. "You're so good at that. We all love you for it."

Suddenly I felt as if I'd landed in a Jane Austen novel, and I was the spinster aunt destined to take care of everyone and embroider baby bonnets for other people's children.

Louise wasn't done, though I thought maybe the snapdragons might be. She'd forgotten she still held the hose, and the river she'd created now rushed to the hollyhocks. "Your priorities are..." She raised her hand to count them off, then realized she still had the hose and dropped it to run harmlessly on the lawn. Up went her hand and one finger. "Your priorities are your family." Another finger raised. "Supporting yourself. But there's only one of you, so that won't take much."

A few days ago, I'd considered that Poupon and I didn't need much, but it scraped a raw spot to have Louise decide for me.

Another finger came up. "And. Well, I don't know what else. That's for you to figure out."

Generous of her.

"If you're always running around taking sheriff calls, how can you do what you really need to? Look at the last few years. You've missed most of David's basketball games, and you had to rush out on Christmas Eve to pull Evelyn Dornbush out of ditch."

I hadn't really needed to help Evelyn. Stormy was already on his way with a tow truck. But I'd had enough of the ruckus of the whole Fox clan and kids hyped up on Santa and sugar. Most of them had so many presents, they hadn't given me more than a rapid thanks before tearing into the next one.

Evelyn had been overjoyed to see me and even happier with the hot chocolate I'd brought in a thermos.

Louise threw her arms around me, burying me. Smothered, sure, but by maybe something more than her flesh.

My phone blared and vibrated in my back pocket, and I struggled free of Louise's ambush. "Sheriff." One of the last times I'd answer with that title, and I clung to it a little.

Ralph Stumpf's wavy voice staggered out to me. "He's back, Katie. This time he took my mail. I had it on the kitchen table. My social security check was in there. Maybe you could come get fingerprints and put him away this time."

"Stay inside, Ralph. I'll be right there." I figured I'd find the mail next to the peanut butter or in his sock drawer.

He sounded relieved. "Thank you, Sheriff. I can always count on you."

I slipped the phone back in my pocket, thinking maybe breakfast would be a couple of Werther's candies.

Louise beamed at me. Maybe the face of a benevolent conqueror ready to forgive and welcome the traitor home. Maybe more like a gloating bully clutching all the lunch money.

It took only two seconds for a seed of righteous anger to sprout and bloom. "You know what? I'm sticking with it."

She seemed puzzled. "What do you mean?"

Maybe I didn't quite fit right now, but I was going to elbow my way into this life. "I'm not going to resign."

That emoji of an exploding head was close to what she looked like. "That's not fair! You said you'd quit. No take-backs."

I shrugged.

All her features hardened into the same expression I'd seen when Diane challenged her for the good bed twenty-five years ago. "I'm warning you. I'll make sure you're recalled if it's the last thing I do."

I was already striding toward my car and hollered over my shoulder, "Knock yourself out."

I'd probably live to regret those words.

## CLOSE RANGE
### Kate Fox #9

**Danger hides behind the faces you know.**

In a small town shaken by tragedy, Kate Fox finds herself at the center of a deadly mystery that threatens those she loves. When attorney Garrett Haney is found electrocuted, it's quickly deemed an accident. But as Kate assists young Sheriff Zoe in the investigation, they uncover a tangled web of lies involving the Haney family and Garrett's powerful clients.

As shocking secrets come to light, Kate discovers the person behind the murders is closer to home than she ever imagined. With the help of her niece Carly and Sheriff Zoe, Kate races against the clock to protect those dear to her in a pulse-pounding showdown that will change everything.

In *Close Range*, loyalties are tested, and the hidden darkness within a family threatens to destroy lives.

Get your copy today at
severnriverbooks.com

# ACKNOWLEDGMENTS

A giant thank you to the usual suspects who have tromped through the Sandhills with me through all eight of the books so far. Especially my agent, Jill Marsal, my publisher, Severn River Publishing, and Amber Hudock, Julia Hastings, and Mo Metlen. Gratitude to editors Jessica Morrell and Kate Schomaker.

A hug and thanks to those Sandhillers who answer questions and keep me laughing: Shawn Hebbert, Sharon Connealy, Mickie Hebbert, and Terry Rothwell. No words would be written without my compatriots, Wendy Barnhart, Jessica Lourey, Susanna Calkins, Erica Ruth Neubauer.

My daughters, Erin and Joslyn always inspire me but more than that, they make me laugh so hard I cry. Deep gratitude for Dave whose eyes may cloud over from time to time while I hash through plots, but who seems to love me anyway.

My heart is broken as I write this acknowledgment. There aren't words important enough to describe my friend Janet Fogg. For thirty years, she read all my words, and advised me on everything from writing, to love, to child care. Though I am undeservedly fortunate to have been her friend, there is a crater in my life now that she's gone. Write on, Janet.

# ABOUT THE AUTHOR

Shannon Baker is the award-winning author of *The Desert Behind Me* and the Kate Fox series, along with the Nora Abbott mysteries and the Michaela Sanchez Southwest Crime Thrillers. She is the proud recipient of the Rocky Mountain Fiction Writers 2014 and 2017-18 Writer of the Year Award.

Baker spent 20 years in the Nebraska Sandhills, where cattle outnumber people by more than 50:1. She now lives on the edge of the desert in Tucson with her crazy Weimaraner and her favorite human. A lover of the great outdoors, she can be found backpacking, traipsing to the bottom of the Grand Canyon, skiing mountains and plains, kayaking lakes, river running, hiking, cycling, and scuba diving whenever she gets a chance. Arizona sunsets notwithstanding, Baker is, and always will be a Nebraska Husker. Go Big Red.

Sign up for Shannon Baker's reader list at
severnriverbooks.com